Haven of Dante

Leonardo Ramirez

Haven of Dante

Written by Leonardo Ramirez

Cover Art: Davy Fisher
Editor: Ileana L. Kinnie

Published by Beyond Books, Nashville, TN

Copyright © 2021 Leonardo Ramirez
leonardoverse.com

All rights reserved. No part of this book may be reproduced or transmitted in any form or by any means without expressed written permission of the author.

Printed in the United States of America

ISBN: 978-1-7364573-0-6 (Paperback)
ISBN:978-1-7364573-1-3 (eBook)

Dedication

For anyone who has ever suffered a horrific assault of mind, soul or body.

You are the hero of this story.

Special Thanks

The Giver of all gifts who is faithful and good. Some call Him God. I call Him Papa.

My beloved wife, Kristen, and my brown-eyed-girl, Mackenzy. You are the joys of my soul. I love you more than pie.

Ileana L. Kinnie, future ruler of the edit kingdom.

Davy Fisher, faithful friend and traveling companion to Mordor and back.

Karen Covell (Founder), Staff (Kaelyn Timmons, Kim Roberts, Danae Samms and Virginia Tucker), Board Member- Dr. Naima Lett and the Army of Prayer of the Hollywood Prayer Network with Ron Planting.

Prayer works and you can't break a stick in a bundle.

…the person who follows me in faith, believing in me, will do the same mighty miracles that I do - even GREATER miracles than these…

~John 14:12

Contents

A History of the Dante Family Line................1
The Aristocracy 5

Ascensione (The Ascent).........................7
Perdito (Apart)................................21
Decadere (Descent) 53
Desolare (Shattered)...........................65
Procedimento..................................69
Sussurare (Whispers) 79
Mostro (Monster)..............................93
Prova (Evidence) 113
Missione (The Mission) 125
Verdetto (The Verdict): The First Terrace..........145
Fierrezza (The Proud): The Second Terrace.........157
Furia (The Wrathful): The Third Terrace 171
Misericordia (Mercy): The Fourth Terrace 181
Gentilezza (Kindness): The Fifth Terrace 193
The Wedding Feast 201

Mount Judgement	221
Ascent	233
Phantasms	247
Abandon All Hope	265
Masks	277
The Pot is Stirred	295
One Girl Army	309
A Peg or Two	323
The Letter	339
Epilogue: Fun in the Sun	341
About the Author	343
Other Books by the Author	345

A History of the Dante Family Line

1265-1321
Dante Alighieri travels through the Nine Circles of Hell and leaves unscathed.

1321-1346
UNCIVIL WAR! - Members of the Nine Circles of Hell fight for leadership and form the Aristocracy.

1347
The Witness initiates contact with the family line to combat the Aristocracy. Clues of periodic contact are left throughout history. Members of the Line are given varying degrees of power.

1760-1790
Benjamin Esteban Dante seeks amnesty in the New World from England and after changing his name he fights bravely on the side of the United States.

Father Thomas Alberto Carlino de Maro, a descendent of Publius Virgilius Maro and close friend of Benjamin Dante, shared quarters with Benjamin during his voyage to the New World on *HMS Ulysses* in 1780.

During the War of Independence, Father Carlino established the Virgilian Order to render medical aid for the soldiers of the Continental Army.

1922-1945
Kristen Amorosa Dante worked as an archivist for the German military during World War II. Dante used underground tunnels to free prisoners from the Nazis with the help of her friend David whom she married. Together they returned to the United States.

1943-1994
Amado Ayende Dante worked as a liaison officer in the United States Embassy in what was once the Soviet Union. After living there for 10 years he returned to the United States once the Berlin Wall fell.

1977
Roberto's heart was not right for the mantle. Because he was not chosen, resentment grew in his soul. Without the blessing of the "Witness", he sought to become a hero in his own power. By imagining and creating new technologies that would aid mankind, he formed, "Dante Technologies".

1980
Roberto and Beatrice Dante were wed.

1984-2001
Rebecca Mariana Dante (Roberto's younger sister) was 17 and full of life. She was lost in the terrorist attacks on the World Trade Center.

1985
Haven Irena Dante is born.

2002-2004
Haven goes missing for two years.

2004
HAVEN ASSUMES THE MANTLE.

The Aristocracy

After Dante Alighieri's exit from the nine circles of hell, the inhabitants were incensed that man had the guile to leave their realm unscathed. In their rage, they vowed to replace them on the surface. To that effort, they formed an alliance between the circles and called it, The Aristocracy.

Members of the Aristocracy may overcome and occupy a weak or crushed soul or operate as its own entity. Once a willing host and demon merge, a new personality is created and referred to as a "hybrid". Some take on a new identity to reflect the nature of the hybrid. One such hybrid is Prince Luminos, the leader of the Aristocracy who embodies the host of an eight-year-old boy.

Each circle's nature consists of and operates within the milieu of the following:

Circle One - Those in limbo led by Lord Limbus. This demon transports humans into the Nine Circles. According to the code of the Aristocracy, no human can be transported out of the realm of the Nine Circles except of their own volition.

Circle Two - The lustful led by Lord Hedonis.

Circle Three – The gluttonous led by Lord Voratum.

Circle Four – The hoarders led by Lord Hordran. This demon is a hoarder of minds.

Circle Five – The wrathful led by Lord Vengus.

Circle Six – The heretics led by Lord Retic.

Circle Seven – The violent led by Lord Ravage. This demon is a mindless savage beast bent on the destruction of the Dante family line and all human life. The more he kills the stronger he gets.

Circle Eight – The sorcerers led by Lord Lock

Circle Nine – The traitors led by Lord Traiton. This treacherous demon infiltrates any circle of influence in an effort to take it over.

Ascensrone (The Ascent)

It was the year of our Lord Thirteen Hundred and Six. From the dark pit, amid the hues of dimming red and rising vapor came the foul stench of things wicked and vile. A robed man climbed a steep rock face that would bring him to freedom, but not soon enough. His marred and swollen knuckles hurt as he clung to the steaming, jagged rocks. His brow dripped with sweat and muck. The blades of rock cut across his fingers and kind face like paper and the dripping blood made his grip unsure. Gusts of ash and cinder replaced the air in his lungs and his chest heaved deeper and deeper on each exhale. When the waters of Coctycus met the scorching rock, steam rose to envelope the walls of this realm. Robed in red, the traveler carried his trusty guisarme sword on his back and a worn, tattered satchel over his shoulder. Between quick bursts of panicked breaths, his eyes fluttered in quiet desperation to reach the top. In one burst of frantic strength, he pulled himself up the steep, rocky terrain knowing that his very soul depended on it. Not because of the bottomless pit beneath him but because of the beasts that place of torment housed. No human being had ever escaped from Hades. The Lords of the Nine Circles who resided there would not have their reputation tarnished by what they had come to revile in centuries past: the despicable and arrogant abomination known as man.

Despite the absence of light, he could sense the presence of the creatures below enough that his visions of them hastened his pace, his sword rocking back and forth on his back as he climbed. Angst added to his dread as his thoughts filled with a longing for the love he had lost so long ago . . . his beauty . . . his beloved. As it is with all good men, his strength was fueled by the memories of his true love. He had first laid eyes on her at the age of nine but did not speak to her until nine years later. As a man who loved deeply, he felt robbed because he had been betrothed to another as per tradition, and he would never belong to his crimson-haired angel, except in his dreams. This fate was sealed upon her death. The sting of that grave loss moved him to take this journey; a journey to soften a hardened heart by looking into the eyes of God. If he could only arrive at this place of solace, he would find rest for his aching soul. Even his morals would he forsake to achieve his goal, as proven by the act of thievery from the Lord of Hades himself.

As the robed man advanced upward he lost his footing; his scabbard slammed against his back. In a frantic rush to his friend, the robed man's companion and master, Virgil, swiftly reached out his hand. Virgil, a poet himself, had accompanied him to this dreadful place as his master and guide through each trial and each victory along every step of the way as a good friend would. Now, Virgil could barely keep his own footing on the crumbled rock beneath his feet. "Cling fast!" Virgil cried.

A voice from the wall of the pit rumbled, and then worked up to a high pitch.

"Nnnoooo! Youuu will never leeeeaaaave thisssss placcce!" the voice screeched. A deeper growl emanating from the darkness followed in suit, "You have desecrated our realm with your impudent arrogance."

Worried, the man gazed up into the waiting eyes of his faithful friend.

Virgil reached out with his other hand for a sturdy boulder just beyond his reach.

"Cling fast . . . hold," said his master, panting wearily. "For by such stairs it behooves us to depart from this evil!" Virgil's footing shifted on the fragile rubble that gave way beneath him.

The robed man looked down into the abyss and then up again in resignation at Virgil.

"Should the evil consume me my master, the pain of loss may be no more!" he cried.

"Think not on this path, my brother. For should this evil be thine, it shall surely be thy master and replace your pain with a greater torment!"

Virgil hastened and managed to grab his hand.

"Aaaaahh!!" cried the robed man, almost losing his grip. Virgil strengthened his hold on his friend's hand and pulled, the weight of his friend taxing him. He secured his feet behind sturdy rock and used his legs to pull harder. Virgil stretched his freed arm toward a surer hold and pulled.

"Come nigh unto me," Virgil prayed.

Virgil quickly decided that the rock was indeed too far and instead focused his attention on his grip joining one hand to the other.

"Strength, I pray thee bestow upon my unsteady hands!" cried Virgil.

He pulled harder still.

The robed man managed to grab hold of the ledge just above him. Virgil scurried onto his feet and pulled his robe off. Ripping it and his sash into a long cloth, he tied it around the boulder and went back to his friend. "Take hold!" He threw his end down. As he did, his eyes wandered into the abyss. Two glowing eyes on the inside wall of the abyss stared with great contempt at the ones who dared to taint their domain. Two more eyes appeared in the darkness . . . then four eyes became looming shadows moving towards the trespassers.

"Oh, heavens above and angels beware," whispered Virgil.

"What is it?" asked his panting friend.

"A beast has departed the ice lake of Coctycus and demands a feast! Haste! Pull!!"

The robed man pulled with all of his might as the crusts of rock fell into the darkness. In a short burst of energy, he was able to stand to his feet on solid ground.

Still panting, they both turned away from the abyss below and proceeded towards their goal; a shimmering beam of light a few steps beyond that held in its grasp the splendor of ages known simply as The White Rose.

No human had ever descended into The Nine Circles of Hell or laid eyes on the beauty of The White Rose. A doorway led into the next realm and away from the dread and hatred that permeated The Nine Circles, The White Rose floated humbly and stalwart in a shower of glimmering light, waiting for one who would be worthy to gaze upon it and smell its freeing fragrance.

"Approach the White Rose, my friend," ordered Virgil. "Let peace be your guide." While the screeches and squeals of the monsters below quickly approached, the pupil humbly fearfully stepped forward.

"Hold the rose," ordered Virgil. "For death shall be a pleasure should you not unlock the passage from this realm."

The robed man held out his hand in trepidation knowing that there was no turning back.

As he drew cautiously near, drops of light bounced off of his hand as they went into the light. He paused just short of the rose, which responded by floating towards his hand. He gasped.

The White Rose found its home in the hands of the robed man.

The robed man drew it closer to him. As it left the light, the petals began to slowly fall, but not to the ground.

The petals floated gently and surrounded the master and his friend, bathing them in light as if caressing a long-lost friend who had just come home. Swiftly, the petals left them and began to create a circle directly in front of the travelers. Faster and faster, the petals rotated and expanded outward forming a spiral and, in a sudden burst of radiance, each petal transformed into a magnificent being of radiant light. They took shape and finally rested into what the travelers thought would be their final form. In a burst of radiance, a staircase made of glass and pure light formed. Each angel stood on a step of the brilliant staircase whose light engulfed Virgil and his friend. The beauty of this passageway was kept beyond the reach of the travelers by a gate of shimming colors that shined like a glimmering aurora just beyond the vortex of petals.

The screeches heard throughout the cavern were piercing to the soul.

Barred from approaching the travelers by the torment of the light, the three-headed, dog-beast Cerberus howled in agony from the painful light as the harpies screeched in despair. The Malebranche demons, with their hooks and claws, scratched the walls in anger against the defilement of their domain. In a feeble attempt to ease its pain, Geryon the three-bodied shade, with reptilian scales and a scorpion's tail, buried its face in rock and mire in desperation. The very walls of the cavern boiled in the light.

The robed man stood motionless as the sparkling light of the gate glossed his face.

"Open it," Virgil commanded. "For by its unlock shall we find our freedom!"

The robed man lifted his hand as if hypnotized by the light. He began to reach through the vortex and towards the gate so they could escape this dreadful place. As he leaned towards in . . .

. . . nothing happened. The energy of the vortex blocked his reach. They were trapped.

"What manner of trickery is this?" cried the robed man.

Virgil paused and thought for a moment. "Of course! We need the Rod of Moshe! Make haste! Pull the rod from your satchel and hold it high that we may be delivered!"

The robed man reached into his satchel and pulled out what they had stolen from the Lake of Coctycus - the Rod of Moshe, the staff of Moses. While in this dreadful place of hopelessness and torment, the rod had become covered in ash and shriveled to an arm's length. The inscriptions could barely be seen through the soot which covered it. But as the robed man pulled the rod out, it began to grow as if the rod sensed a kinship between itself and its wielder. Since they did not come to find the rod, it seemed that the rod did indeed find them, and in finding them, found its freedom.

Suddenly, the robed man felt a cold, strong hand grab his shoulder.

"No," said a deep, sonorous voice from behind, as its owner pulled the robed man's shoulder towards him.

The robed man tried to pull away and proceed towards the glass stairs.

"I said, no!" The imposing and cogent hand reached over the robed man's shoulder and in one swift move knocked the rod from his hand and lifted him from his feet. The assailant threw him clear across the cavern, slamming him against the jagged walls, his head taking the brunt of the blow. The handle of his own sword then delivered another blow to his head. Once removed from his hand, the rod ceased its growth.

After falling to the ground, he quickly tried to shake it off and get up on his feet, but the sounds of hoofs running towards him distracted him. The hoofed beast cast its shadow over the fallen poet, who slowly gazed up at his attacker. The towering satyr stood before the robed man with arms opened wide and grunted and snorted. His bright yellow eyes pierced the darkness with the deepest of evils. The robed man reached behind him to draw his sword.

"You stand no chance, human filth," the satyr said as he reached for him. The Malebranche, Cerberus and the harpies squealed and howled in agreement.

"Silence!" ordered the satyr. "Take no action! His sword shall be mine as well, and I will deliver his soul to my master as a gift."

Pulling the human to his feet, the satyr picked him up again and threw him over his shoulder and, to his surprise, the robed man, this poet, landed on his feet with his Guisarme sword drawn. The satyr stopped in puzzlement. "You have done battle before."

The robed man stood defiantly. "Many of the enemies of the Guelph have fallen to this sword and, as you are no ally, you shall fall as well."

"Not likely," said the mighty beast.

The robed man had read the myth and lore and had come to think of the satyr as a creature smaller in stature. This beast was an abomination. The monstrous satyr stood tall and mighty with outstretched arms and reached behind his back. Taking two steps back the beast pulled a sword with three blades on it from behind and brought it to a defensive stance. He held it in poor fashion much as a child holds a hammer too heavy for his strength.

"Clearly you are not the master of your weapon, beast," declared the robed man.

From across the cavern, Virgil could see the markings on the staff begin to glow and recognizing them, shouted, "These are the markings of the ineffable name on the rod of the deliverer! This is the very rod carried by the one who lead his people out of bondage. See how it glows with proximity to The White Rose in the presence of holiness! Tell me, beast, how your master lost the battle over the body of Moses to the archangel and travelled to Mount Nebo in the land of Moab only to meet humiliation."

The satyr turned to face Virgil. "My master may have lost the battle for the body of Moses against the archangel, but his staff remains with us as a consolation prize. The raid on the temple of Judea by the Babylonians proved a worthwhile one as was this find. You've stolen it from my master and to him it shall return!"

"The only prize your master claims is the title of the forever thief!" yelled the robed man from behind. "He has stolen the staff and much more! My life . . . my love, stolen from me by traditions that your kind may have indeed planted as seeds in humankind, which have no merit! Your kind comes in whatever form necessary to achieve its gain but there shall be no more gain upon my wounded soul this very night." With those words the robed man lifted his sword to strike the satyr. "And while your master is known by all of mankind, it is you I do not know! Who are you? What is your name, ugly beast?"

The satyr stepped closer to the robed man and glared at him with his bright yellow eyes. "I am Hedonis of the Second of The Nine Circles and soon to be your slayer! Tell me, I command you, under whose name do you make war with The Nine Circles?"

The robed man ignored the question and instead struck the satyr with his sword and was met with the might of the beastly sword. Each blow was met with a harder consequence for the robed man. The otherworldly strength of the satyr was beyond the match of mere mankind.

Virgil quickly ran to the fallen scepter and held it firm. "Deliver us, mighty rod of Moshe," he whispered. No effect. "Can it be that the wielder of the staff must be one who is chosen?" he mumbled to himself. "Forgive us our trespasses. . ." Still nothing. Virgil closed his eyes and whispered, "You have spoken in a subtle voice of the spirit and this humble master will obey."

He put the staff down and reached into satchel of his own and he pulled out a vial and a rod with a holy water sprinkler tethered to it. After filling the sprinkler from the vial, he tapped on its outer shell, testing the thickness to make sure it would shatter at the appointed time and not before. As the warriors' clash raged on, Virgil rose to his feet and began to swing the rod around his head. As the speed of the glass sprinkler increased, the wise master took a defensive posture. Just before he released the rod, he screamed, "Take heed, my friend!"

The robed man took his last swing at the beast, but instead of clashing with the monster's sword, he ducked and rolled into a position behind the abomination. The sprinkler shattered upon the shoulder of the beast, the holy water burning it and causing him to drop his sword. While the monster seethed in agony, the robed man sprang towards the staff and lifted it high above his head. The staff began to grow back to its original form. The angelic writing of the ineffable name began to burn away the ash and cinder that had accumulated over the centuries.

As he stood tall, yet humble, the robed man turned towards the satyr, still writhing in pain. "Witness now our deliverance from this place of torment and forever remember that it was a mere human named Dante Alighieri who escaped the chains of hell unscathed!"

As Dante turned towards the circling petals of The White Rose, the vortex aperture grew wider and opened the gate to the stairwell ahead. Hedonis lay on the ground holding his charred shoulder, drowning in a sea of rage.

Virgil placed his hands on the shoulders of his friend and staring at him with determination, said, "Though tossed and scorned you have mastered more than your blade. You have taken the first step to master your humanity. May I serve your purpose forever as master and friend."

Dante Alighieri and his faithful companion, Virgil, walked through the gate and up the stairs where a crimson-haired angel awaited their arrival with open arms.

This was the day that all had changed for The Nine Circles of Hell. This was the day that in the bedlam that is Hades, the first agreement between the circles was reached. The Nine Circles would band together to combat the infestation that is man and bring about every imaginable evil upon the surface world until the humans would be no more. As with all goals, the leaders of each circle would delegate their plans to their underlings and the inevitable power struggle and internal strife would follow. This Uncivil War lasted 40 years and culminated in the appointments of lords for each of The Nine Circles of Hades.

The leaders came to be known as: Lord Limbus of the First Circle (lord of those in limbo), who transports human captives to the abyss); Lord Hedonis of the Second Circle (lord of those led by lust), whose very name wreaks of all things depraved; Lord Voratum of the Third Circle (lord of the gluttonous, whose insatiable hunger can only be quenched by the fears and dread of souls); Lord Hordran of the Fourth Circle (leading the hoarders and whose hunger for the torment of minds knows no bounds); Lord Vengus of the Fifth Circle (lord of the wrathful, who thrives on the defeat of all things good); Lord Retic of the Sixth Circle (who leads the heretics and whose aim is the distortion of the truth and the and the corruption of the hearts of good men); Lord Ravage of the Seventh Circle (who leads the violent), Lord Lock of the Eighth Circle, (leader of the sorcerers) and Lord Traiton of the Ninth Circle, (whom traitors follow).

Upon consensus, The Nine Circles named themselves as they are seen in their own nefarious eyes.

The Aristocracy.

They were to blame for every evil known since the time that a man walked through their realm and left with his pure soul unmarred. Through the years, evil increased upon the surface world and it became necessary for all that is good to intervene. At the appointed time, a stranger among men only known as "The Witness" made direct contact with the family line that had stood bold and strong in the face of pure evil, the Dantes.

In this encounter, The Witness charged the first of the line to stand against the Aristocracy's plans for the surface world, but upon his failure, and the passage of many years, another rose in his place. His name was Benjamin Esteban Dante, who sought amnesty in the New World from England and fought bravely on the side of what was to become the nation of freedom known as the United States of America. He would later be succeeded by Kristen Cameron Dante who, being fluent in German, was sent to Germany as an intelligence officer. Kristen worked as an archivist for the Nazi Party during World War II. Under this guise, she used underground tunnels to free prisoners of the Nazis; with the help of her friend David, whom she later married. Together they returned to the United States.

Amado Ayende Dante worked as a liaison officer in the United States Embassy in what was once the Soviet

Union. After living there for 10 years, he returned to the United States once the Berlin Wall crumbled. Rebecca Mariana Dante was seventeen and full of life. Regrettably, she was lost in the terrorist attacks on the World Trade Center. Each was chosen for their time in accordance to the goals of the Aristocracy in that era and given tools in accordance to their needs and strengths, be it enhanced cunning, superior intelligence, or super-human strength.

Only one was given the task according to her weaknesses.

Perdito (Apart)

Haven Irena Dante frantically searched through her drawers in her bedroom in the three-story home in the hills, just outside the city limits of Charity Vane. The house had the very first of its kind integrated fluidic computer system that flowed throughout like a nervous system. Liquid interfaces adorned the walls in each room which managed in-home systems including appliances and security. Haven's father, Rob Dante, built Dante Technologies, the company responsible for the tech also had developed holographic interfacing technology which was used throughout the house. Dante Tech had applications not only for in-home systems but also the medical and energy sectors. With their new Holographic Super Radiometric Imaging System, the company was able to construct a holographic imaging system of oil deposits, no matter the depth. For years, scientists and engineers had attempted to construct a mapping system that was more sensitive to the environment than traditional geophysical instruments. Rob Dante developed a revolutionary gyroscopic system to produce a holographic image that significantly improved earthquake predictions and petroleum deposit mapping.

No other company on the planet had as much of an impact on society as Dante Tech. This made the Dante family richer than the Walton, Koch or Rockefeller families. But because of Rob's zealous devotion, it also made it a one-parent family--mother and a daughter who were best friends. Haven looked very much like her mom. Big brown eyes, olive skin, and brown hair. The one thing Haven did not share with her mom was Beatrice's tall stature. She didn't mind. In fact, Haven's diminutive size never occurred to her. She was never aware that her parents towered over her. Beatrice liked to keep her hair short and manageable as most busy moms did, while her daughter preferred hers long and kept in a pony-tail.

Exasperated, Haven moved everything around in her drawer and still could not find her karate uniform. "Momma, where is my gi?" she shouted. Running into her closet, she continued her search as she overheard her mother's response from downstairs.

"If you'd keep your closet clean, your stuff would be easier to find, honey."

"Yes, yes, blah, blah, blah," Haven muttered. And then she turned. Beatrice Rose Dante was standing right behind her with a stern look on her face.

"Well? I can't find it!" Haven had gotten used to her mom sneaking up on her. It was a gift her mom had learned a long time ago. Beatrice reached deep into Haven's closet and pulled out her gi. "Here you go, little star." Beatrice smirked and raised one eyebrow.

"Oh Momma," Haven said with an exhausted sigh.

Beatrice moved closer to Haven and pushed back her long brown bangs to reveal her big, anxious eyes.

"Are you nervous?" Beatrice asked.

"No, not really." Haven looked over to the picture on the dresser.

"Then what is it?" Besides having the usual "mom-sense", Beatrice had a knack for knowing what the answer to the question was going to be before she asked it, and had a solution to every problem before it even happened . . . at least, most problems.

"Is Dad coming to see this time?" Haven asked.

Beatrice sighed. "He's about to leave so you better go ask him." Haven turned and ran to the front entrance where she found Rob fumbling for his keys.

"Dad, you're coming, right? To the tournament?" Still searching through his pockets, Rob answered, "Yes, little star. I promise. I'll be there." Haven shoved both pinkies in front of Rob's face which startled him.

"Double-pinky promise?" Haven asked.

Rob paused. "Don't worry. Thirty minutes tops," he said.

Haven wasn't convinced. "Dad," she added.

As if offended by the notion that he wasn't trustworthy, Rob sighed. "Hey, it's me. Come on," he added. He let his shoulders drop and reached out to her. Haven still wasn't buying it, so she kept him at arm's length.

"Listen," Rob began.

Haven interrupted. "Dad, I'm serious. This is the last one…ever."

"The last tournament?" Rob asked. "Ever?"

"Dad! We talked about this!" Haven answered. Her voice was getting louder.

"But I thought you loved karate," Rob said.

"Dad!" Haven shouted.

"Thirty minutes tops. Promise!" Rob added.

"You better," Haven answered. Rob started to turn but stopped himself when he remembered. "Oh wait. Almost forgot." He reached down into his briefcase and pulled out a book. It was unwrapped. "I got something for you," he said. "Kind of a good luck present." Rob handed the book to Haven face down. Then he turned, grabbed his briefcase and walked out. "Love you, little star," he said as he exited.

"Love you too, Dad," Haven said unexcitedly. She turned the book over. The Divine Comedy by Dante Alighieri. Haven squinted.

"Ok," she said dryly.

Haven walked back into her bedroom to collect her things. As she walked past her dresser, she caught a glimpse of the only picture in existence of her brother, Cameron. It was an image of Beatrice holding a newborn baby swaddled tightly in blankets and a cap on his head with Haven, who was about seven at the time, reaching over her shoulder to hold his head. Haven sighed deeply.

Just as she paused, Beatrice walked in.

"You ok, honey?" Beatrice asked.

"Mom, do you think Cameron would have liked karate?" Haven asked.

"I think he would have loved anything you did," Beatrice lovingly responded.

Cameron Neriah Dante had been born with a tiny hole in his heart. During the delivery, which lasted forty hours, Cameron became lodged inside of his mother, and it took some effort to get him out. Beatrice had to be sedated completely while the doctors worked on dislodging him. The delivery was exhausting to everyone involved, especially Cameron. Despite this, the doctors said that he would make a complete recovery - that the hole in his heart would heal in time with no permanent damage. They were wrong. He was only here long enough for Beatrice to hold him close to her heart. Suddenly, his heart stopped and he was rushed to emergency surgery. Utter devastation followed the news that he had not made it through the surgery. The doctors never had a solid explanation. Rob retreated into his job, and Beatrice and Haven clung to each other. "You have a tournament to compete in today. It's ok to focus on that. And you should. By the way, did you call Sol about your girls' night out tonight?"

"Yes, I did," Haven answered.

"Let's get going," Beatrice said.

Beatrice was about to step away, but instead stepped closer to Haven. "Honey, I'm proud of you. I'm sure you'll do fine at the tournament but whatever happens, I'm proud of you and I love you very much. Always remember that, my "little star". Beatrice brushed Haven's nose with her finger.

"I love you too, Mom," Haven whispered. Beatrice held Haven close to her for a moment. Her short black hair met with Haven's as she kissed her on the forehead. "We've got another hour before we have to be at the tournament. Your dad forgot his lunch, so we need to go drop it off before we head over to the tournament."

"You're just going to make sure he remembers today," retorted Haven.

Beatrice turned. "Let's go," she said. "Dad forgot his lunch again, so we need to drop it off on the way. You know how he is when he doesn't eat."

"Forgetful?" Haven said. Beatrice sighed.

Beatrice Rose Dante was born Beatrice Rosario Cohen to her parents, David and Anna. David had fled Germany with his parents during World War II, while he was a child. He met Anna in high school and fell in love at first sight. Sadly, David died before Beatrice was seventeen from complications of heart surgery. He loved his daughter deeply. From her parents, Beatrice learned that there was no better mission, no greater calling than to love your children and that this was the greatest joy of all. Beatrice's parents were not able to bestow a great financial inheritance upon their only daughter, but they left her with a legacy of wisdom that would surpass any riches. They were content with very little and joyous in the simplicities of life.

Beatrice's parents instilled in her a strong sense of right and wrong. She wanted to see the wrongs of the world corrected so she enlisted in the CIA. Being an information analyst was not enough for her, so she took to the field.

There she saw plenty of action. And after five years of hacking systems, gathering intelligence on enemies foreign and domestic or toppling drug rings and trafficking cabals, she met and married Rob. After Haven was born she felt strongly that, with Rob's business growing, she could devote her time to her family, leaving one mission for another. In Rob's absence, she and Haven spent many nights in deep conversations about matters of life, and she tried to instill in Haven the same sense of right and wrong that was instilled in her. Things like what matters most and what does not, seemed to be the prevailing topic.

As the bright morning sun shined its light on Charity Vane, Haven and Beatrice were greeted at the front door by their driver, Shepherd Guildford. A balding brit with a goatee, Mr. Guildford opened the door for Haven and Beatrice and sat back down into the driver's seat. Haven patted him on the shoulder. "On, Jeeves," she said.

"It's Mr. Guildford," he answered.

"Sorry," Haven answered. Beatrice gave Haven a stern look.

"I've always wanted to say that," Haven added. Mr. Guildford rolled his eyes and pulled out of the driveway.

Haven and Beatrice pulled up to Dante Tech. Beatrice turned to Haven who was engrossed in her phone. "You coming? She asked.

"I just got a text from Sol. Just tell him to be there," Haven answered.

"Copy that," Beatrice said.

Beatrice walked across the marble floor of the grand lobby of the Dante Tech Tower towards the two security guards standing just before the elevators. Etched into the marble walls of the lobby were the heroes and villains of Dante Alighieri's epic journey through the three realms. From satyrs to the three-headed dog Cerberus, to Dante and Virgil himself, the markings tell the history of the Dante family through the centuries. Protruding from the walls above, were sculptures of the terraces of purgatory with the celestial doorway in the center of the ceiling above. Between the terraces and the center were the celestials. Constellations adorned the space between with hints of sapphire. A statue of Dante Alighieri stood in the middle of the lobby.

Beatrice had been through these halls many times. And each time she found the gleaming tower of modern technology more pretentious than the last. She sighed and shook her head from side to side. With lunch in hand and her wallet in the other she walked up to the two guards.

"Good Afternoon, Mrs. Dante," greeted one of the guards.

"Hi, Eddie . . . Frank," answered Beatrice.

The guards initiated the scanning process. As the scanning beam shone through her, one of the guards walked over to a liquid control panel and moved his glove around in the water as he noticed something. "Mrs. Dante, what's in the bag?" he asked.

"It's just lunch for my husband, Eddie."

"Yes, ma'am but I still need to see it."

Beatrice opened her bag and the guard came over. Two sandwiches, chips, two chocolate pudding cups and one soup thermos were in the pale.

"What . . . no pat down?" Beatrice asked sarcastically.

"Not this time," Frank replied.

"Roast beef and Swiss on rye?" Eddie asked.

"Next time, I'll bring you one, Eddie," answered Beatrice.

"Nice. Come on through, Mrs. Dante."

Beatrice walked through the scanner and into the brightly lit elevator. Lights zoomed downwards indicating a rapid ascent. She looked up at the floor indicator . . . *205 . . . 206 . . . 207 . . . 210.*

Finally, the doors opened to the lobby of the office of the CEO, Roberto Bonifacio Dante. Two pillars emitting the last of the scanning beams stood on either side of the elevator exit. As Beatrice walked through them, the light sprinkled outward, permitting her to pass. The five receptionists stood off to the side of the entrance to Rob's office, manipulating more liquid panels.

"Good afternoon, ladies," Beatrice greeted.

"Good afternoon, Mrs. Dante," one of them replied. "Please go right ahead."

"Thank you," responded Beatrice sharply.

The massive doors opened up and allowed their guest in. On the walls of the round office were liquid screens that reflected all sorts of data pertinent to Rob's current research. Beatrice ignored these and walked straight to her husband, who had his back turned and was intensely focused on the matter at hand - a massive machine that stood above the rest of the tech in the room. An ominous beast, the device had spider-like legs that protruded out of the center as if it would rise any second and slay anything standing in its way. After all, he was trying to keep the world safe.

"Nice toy," Beatrice said. Rob kept working.

"How's our little star?" Rob asked.

"You know she has a tournament today."

"Yes, we talked about this," answered Rob. Beatrice looked all around the lab. She gazed back at Rob; hoping things would be different this time. "I brought you some lunch. You know how you get when you don't eat." Beatrice paused for a moment, waiting for some kind of response. Beatrice sighed, knowing that there would be no way to pry Rob's attention from what he was doing at the moment. "I'll just leave it here." Beatrice dropped the bag on the desk.

Rob did not turn around. "I'll be there." The chill from Beatrice's cold stare was more than he could ignore. He finally turned to face her.

"B, do you think I want to do this forever?" he asked.

"Actually, yes," Beatrice answered.

"Uh, no," Rob retorted. "Every Dante before me who has stood to fight against the evil of this world was given an edge. Not me." He pointed towards his mind. "All I have is this,"

"And us," Beatrice said.

"There won't be an us if they're left unchecked," Rob said. "Fight the dark, as they say. No more than an hour, B. I promise."

A shadow emerged from behind one of the screens. It was Harry Reeve, Rob's right-hand man and chief negotiator.

"Hello Mrs. Dante. Hope you are well." Harry looked down at the desk where the lunches were.

Harry Reeve was about to celebrate his 10th anniversary at Dante Technologies. While Rob's forté was the actual technology, it was Harry who not only saw to the day-to-day operations of the company but was also the point of contact for the business deals that Dante Tech engaged in. He had graduated from the Harvard Business School at the top of his class and, although he had little experience in the business sector, he did have a great deal of talent. He sought out Dante Tech soon after graduation through a government contact Rob had just made his first deal with. Harry was a short, stout, bald man who had never been married except to his work. He had no family that he spoke of or relatives that he visited. He was very well-spoken albeit gruff, which gave him an edge in all business deals concerning Dante Tech.

"I'm sorry," Harry stated.

"No, it's me who should be leaving, Harry. I don't want to keep my husband from his work."

Beatrice picked up her purse. "It's fine. I need to get back to Haven anyway. She has a tournament this afternoon that I don't want to be late for." She glared at Rob. "It means a lot to children when their parents support them in what they do."

Rob finally turned half-way around. Beatrice glared at her husband.

Harry interjected, "Forgive me, Mrs. Dante. If I may be so bold. We are on the brink of creating an alliance with a nation that our own government could not. Together, we're poised to create a mapping system that will generate unlimited sources of geothermal energy for the entire world."

Beatrice turned to Harry. "I may have left the CIA, but the CIA never left me. How ridiculous is it to think that the Chinese have the best interests of others at heart? It's a front, Harry! They want to pirate the tech like they do everything else."

Rob and Harry looked at each other in astonishment.

Beatrice stood, indignant. "You know, Harry, I think I will have that moment alone with my husband." "I understand, ma'am," answered Harry. He turned and walked out of the office.

Beatrice slammed her hands on the desk. "Rob Dante, the only dark that has to be fought is the one that exists in this office! Your family name may carry a burden with it to fight evil and make a difference, but you totally ignore the here and now and what is right under your very nose. Neither you nor anyone else for that matter, have any right to try and save the world when you can't even tend to your own family! I tried it once, remember? It's why I resigned from the CIA. There are more important things at stake here, Rob."

Rob moved his hands away from the console he was working on. "B, you've seen what's happened in the past. I take a vacation; they kill innocent civilians by blowing up a building. The Aristocracy targeted me, and they did so for a reason. I am certain that it's because of the good we're doing here. B, evil doesn't go after the lazy people who do nothing to stop it. They go after people like us. It's why what happened to Cameron happened. The combination of this technology along with international cooperation will alert us to anything going on below the surface."

Beatrice turned and looked out the window. "This mapping system of yours can only be used on the border of tectonic plates. The technology you're creating can also be used in other ways by your 'friends', or anyone else who wants to get their hands on it." Beatrice added.

"Think about what you're doing, Rob. You could be making things worse." Unbeknownst to Rob, Beatrice removed a small device from her jacket and placed it on the backside of a beam by the window where it attached itself magnetically. Slowly, she walked away.

Rob shot back, "You've never understood what my work means to me, B. I don't know if you simply can't or won't."

"Rob . . . be nice. Don't go there."

Rob got quiet and wouldn't respond.

Beatrice turned and proceeded to leave the room. As she half-turned, she mumbled, "I'll leave you to fight the dark."

Harry glared at Beatrice from the other side of the glass as she left the room. Rob simply turned around and focused on his screen.

As Beatrice descended in the elevator, she tapped on a communication device in her ear. "The device is in place." A voice of an older woman on the other side of the com responded. "Good work, love. You're doing the right thing." Beatrice rolled her eyes. "Not helping," she responded. Beatrice failed to notice the wall behind liquefying and turning into the shape of a claw. She looked down at her wristwatch. The lights in the elevator flickered.

The emergency speaker on the elevator came on with blaring static. Beatrice gasped loudly. The speaker static dulled to a subtle sound and it was then she could make out a voice emerging. "Beatrice," came through the speaker. Just as the claw had protruded enough out of the elevator wall to reach her, the door opened. Beatrice ran out of the elevator and turned around as if there might be someone behind her playing a joke on her. Nothing. "Switching to decaf," she mumbled.

Beatrice walked past the grand statues of legends past; not noticing the eyes of the satyr embedded in the wall following her every step.

The stands were overflowing at the massive Charity Vane arena where the contestants of the annual Yenga Kyanshi Karate Tournament took place. Fluidic interfaces lined the walls of the arena with walls of water that came down from the ceiling with images of the contestants. In the center of the arena in front of the crowd, Haven bowed to her opponent, Arlin Kryll who stood a full head over Haven. The muscular behemoth returned

Haven's bow in the center of the ring. There were three judges -- one on each corner of the mat and one center judge who stood between the two contestants. The center judge approached the opponents.

"Ready?" shouted the judge. "Hajime!"

But just as he ordered them ready, Haven looked over at Beatrice who sat on the edge of her seat. Next to her was an empty chair. Just as Haven turned back to face Arlin, she received a hard-spinning round kick to the face.

"Uhh!" she grumbled as she hit the mat. The center judge popped back in.

"Judges call?" he shouted. All three judges pointed to Arlin. "Point, Kryll!" declared the center judge. "Again!" The opponents bowed towards each other once again. The center judge came between them.

"Ready? Hajime!"

In a flash, Haven landed a double spinning round kick to Arlin's head. "That's right," she mumbled. The crowd cheered. "Stop!" yelled the center judge. "Judges call?" All three judges pointed to Haven. "Point, Dante!" The crowd cheered even louder. Arlin wiped his brow and returned to the center along with the center judge. "Ready?" asked the judge. "Hajime!" Haven took two steps and jumped. Arlin threw a spinning side kick and missed. Haven spun around and landed a backfist on Arlin's face, spun around again and landed a straight punch into Arlin's gut. Arlin dropped to the ground and rolled backwards, landing back on his feet. With gritted teeth he took two steps forwards towards Haven.

"Stop!" shouted the center judge as he came between them. Arlin threw his arms up and backed up a step. "Judges call?" shouted the center judge. All three judges pointed to Haven.

"Point, Dante! And winner!" The crowd went wild. Haven smiled as she bowed to her disappointed opponent. She turned to notice Beatrice clapping and screaming at the top of her lungs as the proud mom that she is. But Haven's joy was cut short when she noticed Beatrice's chair was still empty. Beatrice's clapping slowed to a stop and instead, she blew Haven a kiss.

As the lights were dim in the meeting auditorium of Dante Tech, a short, stout Harry Reeve quickly put the cap back on to a small liquor bottle and tucked it into his shirt. He wrapped his jacket around his belly as far as it would go and then approached the lectern to address the employees of the tech giant. As always, Harry looked disheveled and worn. He pushed aside his stringy, gray hair and adjusted his steel frame glasses over his bloodshot eyes. It was painfully obvious that Harry did not like to speak in front of a crowd. As he placed his pad on the lectern, his hands shook, and his red cheeks rippled. He adjusted his glasses once again. And again.

"Good Morning," Harry began. "You've all seen the results of catastrophic earthquakes and their effects on the local population that include economic as well as environmental. Countries around the world including

China, Indonesia, Japan and the United States have all suffered in devastating fashion. The Haiti earthquake alone killed 250,000 people. At Dante Tech, we've come up with a solution. The Tectonic Resonating Stabilizer will change all of that. To explain, here is the brain behind the feat of engineering, Mr. Rob Dante." The crowd stood up in applause as Rob walked up to the lectern.

"Thank you, Harry. As science shows, earthquakes are associated with displacements at fault lines. Erosion over time among other factors, can naturally cause destabilization along these fault lines resulting in devastating earthquakes. The Tectonic Resonating Stabilizer or TaRS can send a magnetic resonance pulse that can instantly convert loose material along the fault lines into condensed matter. Much like a cold fusion device uses fusion, our device uses safe levels of electromagnetic energy that results in a permanent solid state." A department head raised his hand. "Mr. Dante, respectfully, what would happen if the waves of the burst were configured to loosen the material?"

Rob smiled. "The effect would be the same except in the opposite direction. A wider and deeper opening would become permanent. But we're not about creating a super-highway to hell, so no worries." The crowd laughed.

Another employee stood up. "Fault lines run hundreds of miles. Can the pulse reach that far?"

"No," Rob answered. "Its range is limited. TaRS sends out a low level EMP that is detectable by a network of devices along the fault line. With each pulse, the next device triggers. This one is the prototype." The curtain then opened to reveal the device in all its splendor and was met with thunderous applause. Just then, Harry walked up to Rob and whispered something into his ear.

"Thank you all. Thank you for coming," Rob added. After the crowd began to disperse, Rob turned to Harry. "Let's check out that fluctuation."

Back at the arena, Haven stood among four other contestants on a large mat. From the announcer's box, the introduction to the final event began. "Ladies and gentleman, the last event of the day, 'Circle of Death' will now begin. In the center ring, winners from today's single matches will face off against each other for the championship title." Haven looked over at Beatrice who nervously looked on. Next to her, an empty seat. Haven turned and shook her head. All five contestants stood in a circle. From a lectern standing outside of the circle, the center judge was ready.

"Ready?" he asked. "Hajime!"

Attacker one threw a flying sidekick. Haven rolled under it, came up and threw a spinning hook kick but missed. Attacker two rolled on the ground, jumped up and threw a flying punch. Haven dodged it, grabbed the attacker from behind and threw him off the mat. As a result, he was out of the game. Attacker three threw a barrage of alternating strikes - back fist, spear hand, ridge hand. Haven blocked them all. This attacker lifted her knee to strike but Haven blocked it. Attacker four flipped into an axe kick. Haven dodged it and kneed him in the chin. He was out. In the background, Arlin waited for Haven to tire. Attacker three spun a hook kick. Haven dodged it and landed a spinning back fist into her face and she was out. At this point, Haven began to breathe heavily. Arlin jumped and grabbed Haven by the shoulder and head butted her on the nose. Haven began to bleed out of her nostrils. Attacker one jumped and came crashing down on Haven with his elbow. Haven tucked, grabbed his arm and threw him off the mat. Out.

Arlin then jumped in with a barrage of kicks - side kick, spinning side kick, spinning hook kick. Haven dodged them all but the last. She landed on the edge of the mat. Arlin jumped high into the air and landed where Haven's head once was. Haven rolled over, jumped into the air and did a flying tornado kick hitting Arlin twice in the face. He flew off the mat.

"Stop!" cried the judge. "Judges call?" All the judges pointed towards Haven. The crowd stood to their feet in thunderous applause. As Haven wiped the blood from her brow, Beatrice jumped for joy. Haven glanced at the empty seat next to Beatrice one last time. Her shoulders dropped and she covered her face with her hands to cover her watery eyes. Victory came at the price of a gutted soul.

Back at the lab, Rob had turned a lever inside the device with a handheld tool. Harry and the other techs stood at a distance. "Ok, turn to one-quarter power. Keep it there. We just want to see where the issue is," Rob ordered. One of the techs walked over to a fluidic console and manipulated the liquid interface within. The device began to hum.

"Ok, good," Rob began. "Now let's take a look at the…"

The entire building shook. Glass shattered and walls began to crack. The tech scattered to hold on to something. "Shut it down!" Rob shouted. "Shut it down, now!"

"Do it!" Harry added. A tech made his way to the interface and ran his hand through the fluid until the device shut down. "Everybody OK?" Rob asked as the shaking stopped. "Yes, we're good," Harry answered. Rob took a look inside. "OK, I think I see what the problem is. No worries. Just…let me…take this..one thing…" Rob began to take parts off the device. "I see it!"

"How's it look?" Harry asked. "It's fine," Rob said. "One hour…tops."

Beatrice and Haven sat on the floor of Haven's bedroom and studied the pieces of a jigsaw puzzle they had laid out before them. Putting jigsaw puzzles together was their solace. The place where they could release the day to the wind behind them and embrace the moment and find healing within. Beatrice liked to hum to herself as she looked for the pieces that fit.

Then you show your little light,
Twinkle, twinkle, all the night.

Haven looked up at Beatrice's hand. "Is that my piece you have in your hand?" Beatrice moved her hands away from Haven as if they were playing cards and she didn't want her to see her hand. "I have five pieces that I'm holding in my hand. To which do you refer?" Beatrice asked. Haven pointed to one. "This one. Gimme," Haven demanded. Beatrice pulled even farther away. "You have a whole stash right under your knee. Pick up your right knee. See? Right there." Haven wasn't buying it. "It's not in there," she replied. "Did you even look?" Beatrice asked. "Momma," Haven began. It's not in there. Let me see the one in your hand. Come on, come on."

"No, see you didn't even look," Beatrice answered. Haven lifted her knee. "Ok, I'm looking. See? I'm looking." Stealthily, Beatrice placed the one-piece Haven was looking for into the puzzle. Haven's jaw dropped. "Momma! Why?"

"Peace be still," Beatrice answered. "Momma, stop," Haven replied.

"Do you forgive me?" Beatrice asked as she chuckled.

"No!" Haven answered. "I had a rhythm going and you messed it up. You and your secret agent sleight of hand thing."

"I love you, little star," Beatrice said.

"Yeah, yeah. I might forgive you then. Maybe," Haven said.

"That's my girl," Beatrice said lovingly.

"I said maybe," Haven added.

"By the way," Beatrice began. "Was that a book dad gave you?"

"You mean the present he gave me right before the tournament he missed?"

"Well, so much for surprises," Beatrice said.

"It wasn't wrapped so there's that," Haven said. "So I wasn't surprised."

"Are we still talking about the book?" Beatrice asked.

"What do you think?" Haven asked wryly.

Beatrice sighed. "He's trying. He's just…"

"Obsessed?"

"It's a good book," Beatrice said.

"Momma, do you miss the CIA?"

"Don't change the subject. And no, I don't. Now about that book…"

"What's so good about it? Oh wait, let's ask him. Dad? DAD? I can't hear him from seven freakin' miles away!"

"Haven, be nice."

"Uh huh. Ok, so this book…demons and angels?" Haven asked.

"Demons. Angels. God. Where we fit in with all of it," Beatrice answered.

"Or a weak argument people use just to make themselves feel better."

"Better about what?" Beatrice asked.

"Ignoring their family maybe? Fear of dying? I don't know."

"That's enough of that. Besides, it's time to go pick your buddy Sol up."

"Girls night in," Haven added.

"Girls night in," Beatrice said. She reached out and hugged her daughter, her joy, tight. Then they both left the puzzle unfinished and walked out.

As they drove up to Sol's house, Beatrice's concern grew, with good reason. Soledad Alden lived in a frayed and decayed part of town. The 20-story buildings, whose utilities and maintenance were subsidized by the government, abutted each other. Dante Tech had fought against the city government who had tried to stop him from building state-of-the-art living quarters for the less fortunate. When the government finally won their war for control, they took over the area and changed the plans for the community installing only the cheapest, simple basics for the residents. The company had to leave the newly built dwellings in control of the greedy, corrupt politicians who made deals in the dead of night at the expense of the residents, while touting their good intentions. The original plan had called for including commercial spaces so that the residents could freely use their talents to make life better. Now, with no hope of bettering themselves, the residents became complacent with who they were and content with getting a handout from the government. Innovation died a slow death. This was the place where dreams died and any hope for the future lay rotting in waste.

They walked up the splintered stairs to the apartment and noticed the door had been left open.

Beatrice knocked. "Sol? Hello?"

A low grumbling noise emanated from within. Beatrice carefully pushed the door open, but before it opened all the way, Haven gave it a swift front kick, slamming the door on the wall. "Haven, wait!" The room reeked of alcohol. A burnt frozen dinner laid smoking on the dining room table. Beatrice quickly threw it on the fire escape through an opened window. The rug had been ripped up and a fist had made its way through the dividing wall between the kitchen and living room.

Haven cried out, "Sol! Are you in here?"

"Haven?" mumbled a male voice from the kitchen. Both Haven and Beatrice cautiously turned the corner into the kitchen. Sol's father was lying drunk on the kitchen floor with the oven open, trying to shuffle his way onto his feet. Beatrice immediately placed her hand on Haven's chest to hold her back and keep her safe from whatever unknown could surface next. She motioned Haven to step back and then she stepped forward. "Mr. Alden? Mr. Alden it's me, Beatrice Dante. Haven's mother?"

"Oooh, Beatrice. I'm so sorry I was (hic) cooking something for Sol and I . . . I . . ."

"Mr. Alden, come over and sit down on the couch." Beatrice motioned him in that direction.

"Yeah . . . yeah, I . . . I, uh . . ." Haven appeared in his line of sight. "Hi, Haven. How are ya?"

Beatrice grabbed Trevor Alden's arm and moved him towards the couch. As they walked by Haven, he tried to give her a hug. Haven was repulsed and stepped back.

"Oh, the stench is nauseating." Haven whispered.

Trevor lost his footing but safely landed on the couch.

Beatrice turned towards Haven, "Honey, see if you can find Sol."

Haven snapped her head towards the open window leading out to the fire escape. "Oh great. I get to climb stairs outside of a twenty-story building." Haven hesitantly stuck her head out of the window and then back in again. She turned and looked anxiously at her mother.

Beatrice didn't notice as she was busy caring for Trevor. Haven picked one foot up and stepped out onto the fire escape. She looked around. The other foot followed as she held onto the window frame. She breathed in deeply and proceeded to the stairs. Her heart pounded in her chest with the weight of twenty men; each heartbeat deeper and heavier than the last. With each step she climbed, she closed her eyes and opened them only to see where her next step would land. Open . . . closed. Open . . . closed. Open . . . . Suddenly she heard a vile, soft whisper. "Hissssssss. Gohhhhh." Haven frantically looked around, below, and around again.

"Hisssssss gohhhhhh," she heard again. She quickened her pace until she reached the rooftop. She threw herself on the rooftop and exhaled with relief.

"Hissss gohhhh awaaaaaaaay."

Haven looked up. "Sol?" She heard a "clink, clink, clink" on the air vent a few yards away.

"Sol?" Haven heard a soft whimper.

From behind the vent, a voice whispered, "I'm not a monster."

"Sol, I'm coming!" Haven quickly got up and ran to the other side of the vent and found her best friend since the third grade lying on the floor. She was still in her waitress uniform.

"I can't do this anymore, Haven. I just can't."

"Sol, it's OK."

"No, it's not OK!" Sol screamed till her voice went hoarse. "He's a drunk. He can't keep a job and he's supposed to be the parent here, not me!" She pounded her chest. "NOT ME!! NOT ME!! NOT ME!!"

Haven wrapped her in her arms as she buckled to her knees.

"Not me."

"I've got you now, Sol. It's going to be OK. Hey, I've got an idea. Why don't you come stay with us for a while? Get away from all of this?"

"No, not again. I don't want to stay with you again; bring my problems to your house."

Haven held her close. "Hey, do you remember the time you came to the fair with me and Mom?"

"Yeah, so?"

"You threw up, remember?"

"Ok, that's just gross." Sol replied. "The point is I'm still glad you came with us. You got sick as a dog and we still had fun."

"Oh, yeah." Sol whispered. "What about Dad?"

"Your father can sleep it off."

"Alright," answered Sol.

"Let's go," said Haven.

"OK . . . OK," answered Sol.

From behind the vent, the mysterious voice whispered, "I'm your friend."

Sol felt the warmth of the fresh cup of tea, as she held it tight. She sat at the foot of Haven's bed flipping through Haven's photo with her free hand. She focused on one in particular. Beatrice, Haven and Sol at the fair. She noticed that Beatrice was leaning towards Haven and holding her tight, while Sol simply stood to the side of them.

"Lucky you," she mumbled.

The door squeaked open and Haven peeked in her open door.

"Hi," she said as she closed the door behind her and walked in. Gently, she sat down next to Sol. "So do you want to tell me what happened?"

"I asked the wrong question," answered Sol.

"Which was?"

"He had just come home and the interview didn't work out, I guess and. . ."

"You mean the job lead that my dad got for him?"

"Yeah, that one. Anyway, they told him on the spot that it wasn't a good fit and since he came home drunk, I asked him if he had stopped by the pub before or after the interview."

"He didn't hit you, did he?" Haven asked.

"He didn't mean to."

"Soledad, if he's hit you once, he'll hit you again! Is this the first time?"

"Yes, it really is Haven."

"Are you sure?"

"Yes, promise."

"You're staying here, Sol. I'll talk to Mom."

"Not tonight okay, Sis?"

"OK," answered Haven as she sighed deeply. "Maybe we can decide in the morning what the next step should be."

Sol sat up. "You know, every now and then my life is so crummy for so long and it feels like I'm on the verge of accepting things the way they are. Then I'll let myself get to that point of imagining being in that place, having given up, and then something pulls me back, makes me hope again that this time something will be different." Sol looked down into her teacup. "And then I'm disappointed and end up even more upset than before and I just sink deeper and deeper."

Haven looked down in pensive thought. "I try to convince my mom all the time to give up on Dad ever wanting to focus on us, on his family, because things are what they are, and it seems like nothing will ever change him. But after I tell her and go to my room and close the door, I hope that the light bulb in his head will go off. And then I hope that at the very least he could pretend that we're important to him. But, in the end, I just end up arguing with myself and going back to believing that his work is all that matters. But then Mom pulls me back into that place of hoping that something will change. She's just that way, always believing the best in people. I wish I was more like that."

Sol squared her shoulders at Haven. "That's the difference between you and me, Haven. Don't get me wrong, I'm grateful that you're always here, but in the end, you still have your mom. You still have the comforts of all this! Look around you. Have you seen my room lately? It's not even a room. I sleep on the couch in the living room while he has a decent bed to sleep on." She pointed around the room at the plush pillows, the antique bed and the illuminated liquid computer screen. "It's just different."

"Sol, the stuff . . . the money . . . it doesn't mean anything."

"Really?" Sol responded. "Do you remember about the earache I told you about that I had when was ten? When I was writhing in pain on the bed screaming in agony? He told me later that he couldn't take me to the doctor because he let the insurance lapse after mom left. Do you think my dad would be a drunk if we had the money to see a doctor? It's why he does it, Haven . . . to forget."

"It's a choice, Sol."

"It's a choice you've never had to make, Haven. God forbid something ever happened to your money or your parents. Where would you be? What if your mom got fed up and left all of a sudden like my mom did?"

Rob Dante left the chill of the outside night air and entered the front door of his home to a different sort of chill. He walked into the living room to Beatrice who sat in her favorite plush chair reading the back of the book Rob had given Haven.

'When I had journeyed half our life's way, I found myself within a shadowed forest, for I had lost the path that does not stray,' Beatrice quoted.

"I'm sorry," Rob simply said. "There was a problem."

"It's not me that needs to hear it," Beatrice answered.

"I still need to say it," Rob said.

"There's your problem," Beatrice said.

"Where is she?" Rob asked.

"In her room, Beatrice answered.

Beatrice stood up and walked out of the room.

Rob could hear the girls' chatter just beyond Haven's door. He gently knocked. No answer. "Listen, honey, there was a problem." The door squeaked open. Haven's stare pierced Rob's soul and cut it in half. "There is a problem," she said. "You lied."

"But if I had left. . . I'll make it up," Rob said.

"There's no such thing as making it up, Dad." And with that, Haven closed the door and sat back down with Sol.

"You OK?" Sol asked.

"You need to rest," Haven said.

Sol put her cup down and sighed deeply. "You're right. I'm sorry. Here you are helping me and . . . I shouldn't have said those awful things. I'm so sorry."

"It's OK, Sis. Don't worry about it."

"Crap, I hope your parents didn't hear all that." The door opened again. Beatrice smirked and winked at Sol. "Hear what?"

"Oh, Mrs. Dante, I am so sorry."

"Oh, don't worry about it. I totally understand. Just get some rest. I have to step out to run an errand, but I'll be right back. You girls better be asleep when I get back."

Sol jumped into bed. "Yes ma'am."

Haven stood up and walked towards Beatrice. "Hurry back, mom. You know my co-dependency really flares up when you're not around."

"Oh stop," said Beatrice. "I'll be back soon. Good night, girls."

Haven looked into Beatrice's eyes and held her tight. "I love you Mom."

"I love you too, sweetheart."

Beatrice walked out of the room.

Sol said to Haven, "I'm sorry I missed your tournament today."

Haven brushed off the concern. "Don't worry about it." After putting on her pajamas, Haven lay down and covered herself. "This is almost like the backyard campout we had in the third grade. You remember that?"

"Yeah, I remember," said Sol. "Made me hate snakes after that one crawled into our tent."

Haven chuckled. "You have a home here, Sol. Tell you what. We'll fix up an extra room just for you. How does that sound?"

"Really? Even after what I said?"

"Don't worry about it," Haven answered. "I'm sure Mom will be fine with it. This can be your home, too, and I'll always be here for you."

"Promise?"

"Promise."

Decadere (Descent)

The night air in the city of Charity Vane was as crisp as a fresh-fallen leaf. Cool to the skin and soothing on each inhale. Each breeze whispered the sweet saying to those who sought refuge here that they were safe and well-cared for. She was the "City of Good Deeds" and she was majestic. Each tower within her veil sought to outshine the next. The city had shown to the world that it could take care of its own quite efficiently and without prejudice. Whatever sins she bore were buried deep in a sea of forgetfulness never to be heard from again -- at least not from the general public. Even so, Charity Vane had lost its soul in the show of good deeds. It wasn't the good deeds themselves that brought the city to corruption but its self-deceiving pride. This pride caused it to justify achieving goals by any means necessary under the guise of caring for its own. Corruption was acceptable as long as it brought about a good outcome in the eyes of the bureaucrats. Secrets thrived in abundance between the government and her people, politicians and their constituents, and husbands and wives.

Tonight, the night sky held its own secret.

From 10,000 feet, a figure dressed in a black jumpsuit wearing a black helmet and a backpack streaked downward from the sky, shooting through the clouds at breakneck speed. The closer the figure came to the skyline, the heavier its breathing became.

A deep male voice chirped in the helmet intercom, "Artemis, do you copy?"

A female voice responded, "I copy, Gardener. Approaching visual range."

"Copy that."

From inside the helmet a targeting scanner homed in on the well-lit sign on the highest tower in the city.

Dante Tech.

"In visual range, Gardener."

"Copy."

The human missile descended rapidly as her internal altimeter began to beep an alert. It was time to deploy. As she chopped through the high winds, she pressed a button on her wrist. A small panel swished open. After pressing a coded combination, her black chute deployed.

"Chute deployed, Gardener." The release jerked the intruder into the night sky and slowed her descent. She took in the view.

"Copy that, Artemis." With the detection systems on the roof, its best you land on the adjacent building.

"Copy that, Gardener."

"Artemis, someone wants to talk to you. You can speak freely now, I've secured the channel."

"Put her on."

"Love?"

"I'm here."

"Please be careful. You still have a daughter at home waiting for you."

"I'm always careful . . .you know that," she responded.

The intruder landed with a loud thud, and after rolling on the ground, came to her feet. She swiftly disengaged the chute, which landed gently on the roof. Removing her backpack, she ran to the edge of the roof where she sighted her target building. The intruder then removed her helmet.

"Love, if careful is anything like your CIA records show then concern is warranted."

"Action trumps caution where Harry is concerned," retorted Beatrice. "I need to see what Harry is really doing with the Chinese and what my husband has chosen to ignore. If you didn't want me to do this, you wouldn't have asked for my help."

"The Virgilian Order simply asked for information that you might already know," said the elder voice.

"I know," added Beatrice, "but now I must know more."

Beatrice dropped the tool she had just retrieved from her satchel. "There is a deal involving powerful seismic technology and Harry is at the helm of that deal." Beatrice proceeded to unpack the necessary tools from her backpack. "And I've lost whatever faith I had in my husband's ability to tell right from wrong. I am doing this," she whispered. She lifted the needed tools up on her shoulders and ran over to the ledge.

Beatrice propped one leg up on the ledge and lifted the grappler onto her shoulder. She could see through the targeting system straight into the Dante Tech building adjacent to her secure perch and into the offices of the top brass.

Empty.

With no one in sight, she activated the targeting scanner and fired three shots from the weapon.

Thoomp! Thoomp! Thoomp!

Three projectiles left the device and found their home on the triple-layered, tempered glass. Each projectile ejected spider-legs which embedded into the glass and emitted a high-density heat beam into the glass, melting it away. As the glass turned to liquid, each spider simply folded up its legs and dropped to the ground below. With the obstacle out of the way, Beatrice loaded a larger attachment onto the grappler and fired. A larger projectile made its way through the night air and landed on the glass just above the newly formed entryway. Attached to it was a long thin tether that made its way back to Beatrice. She quickly unhooked it from the grappler and turned to face the opposite side towards the stairwell exit. She fired another shot. The projectile went right through the cement and expanded on the other side. The rope was now tight and ready for the onslaught. Beatrice hooked her harness to the rope and took her second step onto the ledge.

She looked down. As the night winds blew through her hair, she pushed the thought of any consequences of being caught out of her mind . . .

And jumped.

Beatrice flew through the night air between two high-rises. It had been a long time since she had done anything like this and as the wind gusts rocked her back and forth thoughts of Haven filled her mind. She hoped that she would never have to do something like this again. She hoped that she would finally put to an end the secrecy that Harry Reeve brought to the company and her family through her husband Rob. She hoped that Rob would finally see that you can save the world if you can save your own family.

Beatrice landed in the offices of Dante Tech in a quiet thud, ending in a roll. After rolling to her feet, she quickly ran to the office door which held the secrets she had come looking for. She pulled out a vial that contained a clear liquid and shot it onto the door lock. The drops of liquid adhered to the lock and trailed towards the inner workings of the lock as if each drop had a mind of its own and bonded within. It then morphed and motioned the lock to disengage and the door popped open. Beatrice hurried into the office where the liquid screens lit up the dark. She sat at one of the consoles and pulled out a black glove from her satchel. After putting it on, she placed her hand in the vat of clear gelatinous fluid. She waved her hand in the water seeking access to the com system.

The water turned red. Access denied.

She pulled her hand out of the water and pulled another glove out of her satchel and quickly put it on. After placing her hand in the vat, the water again turned red.

"No," she whispered.

"Artemis, report," said the male voice over the radio.

"Stand by, Gardener," Beatrice manipulated the illuminated water once again.

Green.

"Gardener, I have access."

"Copy that."

Beatrice moved the water in the large vat in order to find the images for hidden files that lay deep in the archives. Intensely focused, she honed in on one file of interest.

Project Armades.

"Armades?" she whispered to herself. She moved the file to open. Contained within were ten sub-folders. The first one, titled R&D, was her first target. She moved on the edge of her seat as she opened the folder containing a video record titled, *Alpha Test, Location: Sichuan province, southwest China: May 12*. The video began to play. What she saw horrified her. A large dome with tentacles seemed to produce a magnetic resonance wave that shook the earth, turning every sign of civilization into a sea of rubble. More text appeared on the screen.

8,500 Dead.

"Gardener, are you seeing what I'm seeing through the link?"

"I see it alright," he answered. "But I'm not believing it."

Beatrice sank back in her chair and tried her best to accept what she had just seen. The gentle wind from the outside made its way into Harry's office and pushed her hair aside.

"Hissssss, ssssssssstop."

Beatrice jumped to her feet and ran to the door. She looked around to see if there was anyone around. No one. She quickly ran back to Harry's desk and pulled out a storage device and placed it in the water.

"Hisssssss, sssssss. STOP!" the voice roared as the glass in the office shook.

Beatrice froze. Her heart raced and the sweat began to form on her brow. Every breath was quicker than the last.

The screen came up. Beatrice looked down at the screen, shaking.

File download ready.

Her hands shook as she moved it towards the screen. She tapped the water once again.

Download proceeding. 10% . . . 15% . . .

"Hisssssssssss die."

Download proceeding. 35% . . . 45% . . .

Beatrice could hear a door in the hallway slam open. The sound of footsteps running towards her became louder and louder.

"Gardener, do you copy?"

"We read you."

Download proceeding. 65% . . .

"I'm not alone."

Beatrice was about to yank the storage device.

"Abort," she heard in her ear.

"Copy that."

The footsteps stopped and all Beatrice could hear was the darkness and her heavy breathing.

Beatrice slowly rose from the chair and walked towards the glass wall that separated Harry's office from his assistant. A hint of black made its way across the other side of the glass. Beatrice took two steps closer.

A pair of yellow, glowing eyes appeared in the darkness. Beatrice gasped and took two quick steps back. Another pair appeared . . . and another. *Click, click.*

Just as the gunfire erupted, Beatrice pulled a device from her satchel that lit up as she tossed it towards an adjacent wall. The explosion created a doorway of escape, at least for now, and Beatrice ran for the hallway. She ran out into the corridor and even more gunfire erupted at her heels chipping away at the carpet behind her feet and the pictures on the walls. The gunmen with the yellow, glowing eyes followed. Beatrice turned a corner and headed towards an outer glass wall after throwing another explosive device at it. The explosion shattered the thick glass outward and sent pieces falling to the pavement below. The three gunmen made their way around the corner, but just as they did, Beatrice catapulted into the night sky and away from the building. Shooting through the crisp air above Charity Vane, she pulled a fastening tab on her chest, exposing the chute lever. The three gunmen kept racing towards the open glass wall, but just before they reached the edge, three demons catapulted from their human hosts, leaving the bodies of the three gunmen to tumble and roll towards the opening. Two of the gunmen smashed into the window beams while the third shot out of the window and fell towards the ground. The three demons flew like projectiles through the air. After expanding their wings, they shot directly towards Beatrice, who had just pulled her chute.

Beatrice looked up. "Oh my! Gardener! They're demons! Repeat . . . hostiles are demons!"

Beatrice's descent was not fast enough to outrun the flying harpies. One of the harpies shot through the chute and ripped a hole in it. Beatrice began to spiral out of control.

"Gardener, they've ripped my chute! I'm in freefall! Rose . . . help me!"

"Artemis, what is happening?"

Beatrice fell toward an adjacent tower with a glass angled roof.

"They're not human! They're not human! I'm going to hit the building!"

She hit the glass with a loud thud. The glass kept and didn't break. She slid down the angled roof, the demons still in pursuit.

Her descent ended in another loud thud on the ledge of the building.

One after the other, the demon harpies landed and surrounded her. Beatrice lay on the ground and, after trying to get up, she noticed that a metal rod had pierced her thigh. She screamed in agony.

"Hisssss . . . where isssss it?"

Beatrice spit blood onto the roof. "Where is what?"

"Hissss . . . the data." Another harpy took flight and hovered over Beatrice. "Yes! We need it now!"

"I don't know what you're talking about!"

"Hissss . . . you will give us the plans for the Arm of Hades and you may yet live to serve the Aristocracy. Now, once more, . . . WHERE IS IT!?"

"Arm of . . . Armades?"

"Hisssss . . . she knows."

The flying harpy landed in front of Beatrice and picked her up by the collar and threw her against a ventilation shaft. She landed on the roof. After spitting out more blood, she breathed her next words . . . "Go to hell." And all at once, the demons flared their wings and descended upon Beatrice. As one of the harpies flew past Beatrice in a close taunt, she grabbed its wing and brought it crashing down into the glass which gave way. The demon squealed as if summoning the other. That one descended upon Beatrice's back and bit her shoulder. Beatrice screamed in anguish as she pulled the beast off and flung it down. Before another could launch its attack, Beatrice pulled out the rod from her leg and shoved it into the eye of one of the demons as it approached. Her screams of pain and battle cries filled the night. As the sun peeked over the horizon, a cloud of harpies descended upon her and enveloped her. As she gave her all to fight them off, she thought of her Haven . . . her little girl. The sorrow of secrets held back flashed through her mind but gave way when the rush of memories flooded her heart. And with all the rage of a mother's love, she pulled the strength from the deepest part of her will and mettle and gave her last breath up to the night sky with the last words that would leave her lips.

"You've already lost."

And with those words, she collapsed while triumphant, proud and loving. The three demons looked at each other and then towards the shattered window of Dante Tech where Harry Reeve stood watching. His mouth moved with orders from a distance. The demons raised the body of Beatrice Rose Dante and tossed it to the winds below. Harry sighed and turned away from the window, not noticing a blinking message that read on the screen of the desk of Jinx Jenkins, Rob's assistant.

Download Complete.

Desolare (Shattered)

Just as a warm blanket of sunlight rose over the skyline of Charity Vane and trickles of light reflected off of towering steel and glass, Soledad Alden gently woke. Haven was still asleep as Sol pulled out her overnight bag and laid it on the bed. After pulling out her pink and white waitress uniform with Mickie's Pizza Place written on the name tag, she quietly placed it on the bed being careful not to wake Haven. She removed her working shoes from her bag and bent over to gently place them on the floor. As she stood up, the uniform caught her attention. Sol sighed deeply and then looked up and around the room at all the signs of modern convenience. She stepped towards the trophies on Haven's table. *First Place Kata. First Place Sparring, First Place Bo Staff and Student of the Year.* Then she moved towards Haven's closet and opened the door to a hallway with clothes sectioned off by type. She removed a beautiful red dress that sparkled even in the dim light. Still on the hanger, she held it close as if to try it on and gazed at herself in the mirror behind the door. A half-smile found its way to her chapped lips. Then all of a sudden, the joy fled her soul like a child scared by a ghastly beast. She dropped the dress to the ground. After putting on her shoes and uniform, she quietly exited the room without looking back and marched downstairs. Sol passed the library on her way to the front door when something . . . someone caught her eye. She gasped and then took two steps back. Rob Dante was sitting in a wingback chair by an easel with an unfinished canvas painting of Beatrice playing a flute. There was an empty barstool on the other side of the canvas with Beatrice's flute still on it.

Beatrice often came to this room to unwind and to catch up on reading. Other times she would play the flute. She had been playing since she was in the eighth grade. When she graduated from high school she was offered a music scholarship. She would later share with Rob how she wanted to change her major from music to linguistics analysis because she felt she could do more meaningful work with the latter while still enjoying her music. As she would play and unwind, Haven would work on her painting, developing her craft.

Sol approached Rob, who sat catatonic in the plush chair staring at the painting. "Mr. Dante?"

Rob's cold stare did not move its gaze.

"Mr. Dante, are you OK?"

Rob slowly turned his head and stared at Sol, who was taken aback by the bloodshot eyes that met hers.

She gasped. "What's wrong?"

Rob did not blink, but after a moment's pause, he gulped and looked down. "Something terrible," he uttered. "I'm sorry, Sol but you have to leave now."

Sol straightened up, turned and went towards the door. After he heard the door slam, Rob stood up slowly and straightened out his untucked shirt. He paused and looked up the stairs. He could feel the sickness in the pit of his stomach rising up through his throat. The first step was the hardest for him and he wondered how he was going to be of any comfort to his alienated daughter. He slowly opened the door and noticed that Haven had just opened her eyes.

She looked at him in surprise and asked, "Where's Sol?"

Rob opened the door the rest of the way. "She had to go to work. She probably didn't want to wake you." Haven looked over at the extra bed and then back at her dad. "OK, I guess. Did you bring your work home today?"

"No," answered Rob. He sat down on the bed. "Something's happened." Haven sat up in her bed.

"What? What is it? Where's mom?"

"Haven . . ."

The dread of all the nightmares ever dreamed took hold of Haven's heart and shattered it like glass. Hours of writhing sorrow shook her stomach as she held her blankets to her chest and cried in grunts of pain that were seared in her memory forever. Lying limp on her tear-drenched pillow she passed the day pouring unmerciful grief from a barren soul.

Procedimento

"The Sovereign Concillium of the Virgilian Order will now address the violation of the edict. Consulo Rose Marina Maro . . . Consulo Antonio Patricio Annucci . . . step forward." The two robed figures stepped into the soft light of the Council Room, surrounded by the hierarchy of the Virgilian Order. Since the inception of the Aristocracy, the Virgilian Order has kept watch over the many descendants of the Dante family line through the years in an effort to guide those who may be chosen for the mantle without direct intervention. Their job was to keep the line intact through the ages so that it would continue without end. The Order was founded by Father Thomas Alberto Carlino de Maro, a descendent of Publius Virgilius Maro and close friend of Benjamin Dante, who shared quarters with him during his voyage to the New World on SS Unity in 1638.

During the War of Independence, Father Carlino established the Order to render medical aid for the soldiers of the Continental Army. It was not until a skirmish with an army under the command of General Cornwallis that Father Carlino learned of Dante's responsibility and importance in the family line. With the aid of grateful colonists, he built the majestic castle as a monastery known as *The Sons of Virgilius* on the rocky coast of Charity Vane, which houses what is today known as the Virgilian Order.

Sovereign Paolo, the High Sovereign of the Concillium, conducted himself according to the Order's code of conduct concerning the affairs of men. His tall stature and glaring stare made him a very imposing figure. He made few friends.

"Consuls, you have violated a direct edict of non-interference," he said.

Sovereign Valerio, who was a kinder, gentler sovereign, interjected, "Consuls, please tell us how the untimely death of Beatrice Rose Dante came about."

Insulted at the assumption of the keeper of order on his behalf, Sovereign Paolo turned towards Valerio.

Consul Rose took a step forward and looked up at the Concillium of Twelve seated on the edict-engraved bench and began her report. "Sovereigns, the order I had received contained information on an agent of the Aristocracy possibly operating within the hierarchy of Dante Technologies. As you are aware, the company is in development of potentially dangerous seismic technology and the information could not be retrieved without direct intervention. Sovereign Paolo leaned forward. "You were not ordered to intervene. You were ordered to obtain further information from the Dante. You have violated the sacred edict of non-interference! We watch and guide, only guiding with action when absolutely necessary and to keep them from harm. That is all!"

"High Sovereign," began Rose, "respectfully, her name was Beatrice, and she was already concerned about the technology being developed which could find its way into the hands of the Aristocracy. At first, I tried to persuade her to confirm the severity of its impact, but her past history and experience made it impossible for her to ignore what could be potentially dangerous, not just for the world, but for her family. She knew that her family was a target. She had already lost a son and did not want to lose her daughter to whatever schemes the cabal was conjuring. Her suspicion was that the technology that Dante Tech is developing could potentially be a dreadful weapon in the arsenal of the Aristocracy."

"We don't know that!" barked Sovereign Paolo.

"Which is why we need more information," Rose replied.

Sovereign Paolo leaned forward to address Rose. "Your course of action was reckless. It seems your friendship with Beatrice has overshadowed your judgment. This is why the order forbids attachments to the Dantes."

"And yet," replied Rose, "this edict is not found in the original texts written by Father Carlino. It is our friendships that define us and makes us who we are. They give us a reason to stand for what is good and just. Sovereigns, have we become so entrenched in our traditions that we've become a shell of what we were initially intended to be?"

"And what is that, Consul?" asked Valerio.

"A vessel of God's protection and a guide from all danger, sovereigns. Evil swallows up the righteous and we stand by and watch. Beatrice laid down her life for others. Why should we be above that? We say that we do this for the love of mankind and the protection of destiny, but if we simply watch and do nothing then our love is nothing but a clanging cymbal."

"How dare you!" Paolo interjected.

"It is because of us that the evil of the Aristocracy is embedded in every level of society," added Rose. "Should we simply stand and watch as the Aristocracy makes great advances toward their goal?

Gardener chimed in. "I'm gonna have to say no to that one." Valerio smiled slightly but then asked, "Consul, were you able to obtain any verifiable information?"

"The data has been lost, I'm afraid."

"All of this for nothing then," High Sovereign Paolo interjected. "What of the Dante child? Is she aware of your role in her mother's life?"

"No, Sovereign," Rose replied. "She is not."

"Consul, this incident also goes to show that the edict of nonviolence should be upheld at all costs," said Paolo. "We are here to influence indirectly, to nudge them into the path that they should follow . . . not to add to the ills of this world."

Rose snapped toward the Sovereign. "Should we simply stand and watch as the Aristocracy makes great advances towards their goal? Do we simply stand and watch as children are abducted, and wives are beaten? While all we do is wait to see if one of the Dantes in our care is the holder of the mantle?"

"I'll vote no on that one too," Gardener added.

High Sovereign Paolo turned on the deep-voiced, bald, African American and pointed to him. "Consul, while we appreciate your gardening skills and the fact that you've given us this magnificent display of beauty to behold during our days at the order, we will not condone violence in any way, shape or form! Your technological aptitude does not grant you the right to interfere in the affairs of the Dantes. Your skills are for the betterment of mankind, not for its destruction. You have disgraced the order by your actions . . . both of you." The imposing stature and musculature of who had become known in the order as "The Gardener" seemed intimidating to some, and especially to High Sovereign Paolo, who sat back in his bench seat upon the Consul's approach.

"I really appreciate everything that you all have done for me, I really do. You took me in when my parents abandoned me." Gardener pointed to Rose. "And Consul Rose has been like a mother to me. But I don't see where any of you has bothered to look into this matter to see whether or not what she is telling you is the truth. Does the truth mean anything anymore? I've seen some weird stuff, but what I saw here scared the hell out of me! Do you have any idea what the Aristocracy could do with that kind of tech? We still need to find out what they're doing!"

Valerio interjected, "Consul, that's enough."

Gardener stood defiant, "That's what I thought."

High Sovereign Paolo picked up his gavel and slammed it on the table once. "The Concillium will discuss the consequences of your actions. Judgment will be rendered with haste. That is all." As the sovereigns rose, a bell tolled signifying the end of the proceeding. Their burgundy robes with golden sashes trailed as they exited.

Rose and Gardener looked up at each other. "I'm sorry, Rose," said Gardener. "I shouldn't have shot my mouth off like that."

Rose closed the distance between them. "You've been like a son to me and I'm proud of what you've become. You spoke your heart and that is what matters." Rose gazed out of the vast stone window overlooking the gardens that the sovereign had previously mentioned. "You know, when your mother brought you to me as an infant, barely a week old, she told me that her father had told her that you were an accident to be corrected. In her heart she knew that you were not an accident that you were here by design. Oh, how I wish she could see the man that you've become: a brilliant young man of strong conviction. I cannot consider what would have happened to you if she had not brought you here." She faced Antonio. Rose attempted to comfort herself. "We'll get through this together. As we always do. I cannot believe that the sovereigns would even consider expulsion given all the heart that we have poured into the Order . . . into you. In fact, it was Paolo who named you when you arrived."

Gardener rubbed his bald head. "I don't know. I'm pretty sure I ticked him off real good this time."

Rose cracked a smile. "Yes, love. You probably did."

Someone knocked at the door. It was Sovereign Valerio. A tall, thin man in his late seventies, Sovereign Valerio had a kind face, aged with wisdom and intuitiveness. As he entered the reflection antechamber, he clasped his hands and beamed and smiled at Rose with the affection of a father. "Rose, my old friend. Our years together are many and you have graced these halls with your love of humanity and selflessness." He paused a moment, sighed and looked away. "But your methods are of great concern."

Rose stood in front of the sovereign, wanting him to look her in the eyes. "Sovereign," she said, almost raising her voice.

Sovereign Valerio turned his gaze upon her once again.

"This is all I've known," said Rose. "This is my home. My family's blood lines the very walls of this place and is the brick and mortar that built it. I too am full of years of service just as you are. Surely, the Order is not considering expulsion."

Valerio moved away from Rose. "High Sovereign Paolo is of the line of Maro, just as you are. His influence is great, as are his ambitions."

Rose waved her hand in exasperation. "How can a man be so ambitious, yet bullish in his efforts to prevent any change at all?"

Valerio strode back to her, put his hands on her shoulders and fixed his eyes upon hers. "You will always be my sister." With those words, the bell tolled once again, signaling the collection of the sovereigns to the hall. Sovereign Valerio squeezed Rose's shoulders. "It is time, my friend."

"Consuls," began High Sovereign Paolo. "Step forward." Rose and Antonio stepped into the light of the tribunal. "It is the judgment of the council that as the architects of the operation that led to the death of the woman Beatrice Dante, Consul Rose Marina Maro and Consul Anthony Annucci also known as Gardener be disfellowshipped from the Virgilian Order for violation of the Edicts of the Line of Maro. You will be reassigned to the general population effective immediately and ordered to serve the neediest of communities in Charity Vane in the southeast region also known as 'The Mire.' There is a homeless shelter there which has fallen into disrepair. You are to restore and operate it. This mandate begins immediately."

Sovereign Valerio raised his head towards Paolo in surprise and disappointment. "High Sovereign Paolo, given the Consuls years of service to the Order, I must protest. As testified, it was the Dante mother who decided to pursue a path of intelligence, even prior to her friendship with the Consul."

High Sovereign Paolo turned indignantly at Valerio. "The decision of the High Sovereign is final."

Rose took a step closer to Paolo. "Sovereign, what of the Dante child? Surely, she will need more than what her father is able to give. She needs someone to care for her at this horrible time in her life."

"The Dante child is the responsibility of the Order now," Paolo ordered. Rose's heart and shoulders sank as she heard the Sovereign speak. "There is still a need for the consuls as there is a need in the community, so it is best that their services be directed there. We are not only here to uphold the sacred edicts, but also to offer help for consuls who have lost their way"

"You mean control," murmured Gardener.

"Consul Annucci, you are ordered to discontinue the search to locate and retrieve the data files that were lost during this unauthorized operation. Violation will result in expulsion for life, unless there is an objection."

Sovereign Valerio looked down in resignation.

"Very well," said Paolo.

"High Sovereign," interjected Valerio. "May the consuls be readmitted back into the Order at a later date should they prove to be a benefit to the community?"

High Sovereign Paolo cringed at the notion, but hesitantly said, "The Order may choose to recall the consuls at a later date. This meeting is adjourned."

"Antonio Patricio Annucci," said Rose, "you simply could not help yourself, could you?"

Gardener had a quirky smile on his face. "Nope. And, from now on, call me Gardener. I've always hated 'Annucci'. Sounds like a cologne."

Rose grabbed his large hand and placed it inside of hers. "That's only because it was Paolo who named you."

Antonio placed his large, muscular arm around Rose as they left the tribunal. She gently brushed her hand against the ancient stone walls as they strolled and gazed pensively at the corridors filled with the memories of her childhood. She pointed towards a balcony overlooking the ocean and paused. "Standing over at that perch, I asked my mother why the ocean was blue and you know what she said to me?" "Tell me," he answered.

Rose took a deep breath and exhaled. "'It's not,' she said to me. 'It's a reflection of the sky above.' I then asked her why God would make the ocean reflect the sky. She said, 'To remind us that things are not always as they seem.'" She picked up a rose from a bush planted inside a pot on the windowsill. "Like this rose: beautiful to the senses, but painful if you pick it up incorrectly." As she plucked the rose, a thorn pricked her finger, drawing blood. She whipped out a handkerchief and wrapped it around her finger. "I suspect there is a plan for something monstrous that we have stumbled upon, my friend."

"You're cookin' something, and it smells like trouble."

Rose smiled up at her friend of 28 years. "I read the Chronicle this morning and noticed that there was an opening for a biotech consultant at Dante Technologies. I think you should apply."

Gardener shook his head. "Aaah, yeah baby. They got toys I'm gonna get to play with, heh heh."

"Ah yes," Rose added. "You do love your toys, don't you?"

Sussurare (Whispers)

Haven could hear the whispers behind Purcell's, *A Funeral for Queen Mary*. "She was so pretty, so devoted." A flood of anguish rose up in Haven's mind. *What do you know?* As she sat in the pew of the majestic cathedral, she cringed while the whispers around her drew up the walls of her soul. "God must have had a reason." *Why couldn't it have been him instead?* she thought to herself. The massive choir pierced the walls of the cathedral but stopped short at the core of her soul. Haven's heart throbbed with muzzled pain. I wish they would just shut up. She clenched her teeth and prayed in her mind that the ones surrounding her who did not truly know Beatrice would stop living so that she didn't have to listen to their hollow words. Make them stop. Make them go away. Time had never been this slow and the beating of her heart had never been louder. With hands folded, she looked up at the open casket bathed in roses. She breathed in deeply and stood up slowly. She caressed the pew in front of her as she strolled past it and towards the last image that she would ever have of her mother, her joy. Lost and never to return. This was the third time she had experienced such grave finality. The first time was when her grandfather passed. If not for him, she never would have known what a father's love was like. It's a shame that a heart for his family was not passed on to his son. He would sit her on his lap and make her count his grey hairs. Instead, she'd pull them out, which, for any other grandpa, would be quite painful. But not for him. She took the last few steps that would bring her face to face with the echo that was once her mother and, as she did, she closed her eyes and breathed in through her nose. She laid her hands on the casket and opened her eyes. Beatrice was still asleep and was not going to wake up. Haven whispered, "Mom? Momma? Get up, Momma."

Her desperate plea went ignored.

"Momma, please get up," she whispered again.

For the first time in Haven's life, a daughter's cry for help to her mother went unanswered.

With tear-filled eyes, Haven noticed her dad a few paces away. He was talking to Harry Reeve, his business associate. Her dad had brought work to the funeral. I don't believe him! Harry looked over at Haven while Rob kept talking, not noticing Haven's pain. What are you doing here? A completely bald, tall, lanky man stood next to Harry. He was thin to the point of seeming anorexic. The man looked over at Haven while Rob maintained his focus. Harry soon turned his attention back to Rob while the thin man focused on Haven with squinting eyes. Don't look at me freak! She turned her gaze back to her mother.

"Oh Momma. . ."

A hand found its way on her shoulder. "Haven?" She turned around. It was Harry. The anorexic man was not with him. Haven turned her gaze back onto Beatrice. "Haven," Harry said. "I know how difficult a time this must be for you and your father. I just want you to know that if you need anything, anything at all, please don't hesitate to call."

Haven did not turn around. "I'm a little concerned about your father with this loss."

Haven lifted her head but did not meet his gaze. "I'm sure he can take care of himself," she said.

Harry turned Haven gently to have her face him. "With this loss, I'm just not sure that he can take care of you, and I just want to make sure that you know that I'm here should you need anything at all." Harry reached into his jacket pocket, pulled out a rose which he placed on the casket. Later, as Soledad stood with Haven, Harry caught Sol's eye. Harry gave her a half-smile as he passed her on his way out of the church. Sol put her arm around Haven and stood with her as Haven's tears pushed their way out, releasing a stream of loss and an acknowledgement that Haven's life would be very different from this day forward.

Rob approached the casket solemnly and stared at his beloved's face. The longer he stood, the heavier he breathed until he could only mutter in a subtle whisper, "I'm sorry, B."

∞

The buzzing of Haven's alarm the next morning was of no use since she had been sitting up on her bed against the wall hugging her knees staring into the void that was her room. She laid her legs down flat on the bed and held on to her stomach which was still cramped from a night of wailing in sorrow. She wiped the hair from her puffy eyes and leaned back. She looked over at the picture of Beatrice holding Cameron and wondered if she was holding him now. *I wish you could hold me now.* She looked over at the bulletin board that her mom had made for her with ribbons held down by buttons shaped like stars. She focused on a picture of Beatrice holding her as a baby with a caption underneath that read, "My little star." Right next to the picture was a cross. Haven clenched her teeth and voiced a subtle, "Where were you?" and swiped it off the dresser, sending it crashing against the wall.

There was a knock on the door, which squeaked as it opened. Sol poked her head around the door. "Sis?" she whispered. "Your dad let me in. Hope it was OK."

Haven sniffed and grabbed a tissue to wipe her nose. "Sure, come on in."

Sol sat down next to Haven. "Did you get any sleep at all?"

Haven sniffed again.

"Guess not. I guess you and I are a little more alike now."

Puzzled for a moment, Haven uttered, "Guess so."

Sol ran her fingers over a small, gold-laced statue of a Chinese dragon sitting on Haven's dresser. "Your dad said you were going to stay with your grandmother?" Sol asked.

"Yes," answered Haven.

"Why?" Sol asked.

Haven sat up on the edge of the bed. "Does it matter?"

Sol snapped her head around. "I could stay here with you."

"With your dad's last tirade, that's not likely to happen."

"It's not like my dad is going to come looking for me. He's supposed to check into rehab today. The place he's going to won't let him out unless he shows signs of recovery, so he'll probably be there for a while."

"Sorry to hear that," Haven responded.

"No, it's fine. He needs it. And honestly, so do I." Sol hugged Haven. At first, Haven was hesitant, but then gave in to the warmth of her friendship.

"You're all I have now, Sis," said Sol.

Another knock on the door. "Honey?" It was Rob. Haven didn't answer. "Haven?" Rob peeked into the room. Haven got up and started putting her clothes in a suitcase without sparing her dad a glance. "I'm just about ready."

Rob moved away from the door. "We've got to get a move-on, Haven. It's time."

Haven zipped her bag and lifted it off her bed and, as she turned around, she met Sol in a quick embrace. "I'll see you later," she whispered.

As they drove off, Sol stood in the driveway watching them go and waving goodbye.

Haven stared out of the passenger's seat window, watching the trees go by and the normal lives of the people of Charity Vane unfold. They drove by Mackenzy Park and saw parents cheering for their daughters in the little league all girls' baseball game. She stared intently and swallowed a sigh of hopelessness.

After keeping his eyes on the road for some time, Rob finally looked over. "How are you doing?" Haven ignored the question. Rob said, "Just wanted to try and..."

Haven interrupted, "Why am I being dumped off at Grandma's place?"

"There are some things that I have to take care of at the office."

"Like what?" Haven asked.

Rob spared her another quick glance. "Your mother and I had planned that should anything happen to me, she would be given unrestricted access to my files and assume the position of CEO of the company. Now that she's gone, I need to have someone in place should that still happen. Don't worry, you're not a prisoner. Your old motorcycle is still in their garage. We'll meet up at the ceremony."

Haven stared out of the window again. "What about your assistant, Jinx? She seems nice."

Rob was surprised that Haven had actually expressed any interest in the topic of the company. "I was thinking it should be Harry. He's been in the decision-making process anyway."

Haven did not turn her head. "He's creepy."

"He's been instrumental in accomplishing good things for the company in the ten years he's been there, so I'm sure the company would be in good hands."

"Hey, by the way, I'll be fine too," Haven said sarcastically.

"Yes," replied Rob. "It'll be good for you to spend this time with your grandmother anyway. She just lost her daughter, so it might be good for you both."

"Yes, and Willy the Leach as well. He creeps me out too."

"I think a lot of things creep you out. Anyway, he's harmless. Just keep to yourself and help your grandma out, and I'm sure you'll be fine."

"Mom didn't like him either."

"I know," said Rob. "I wish my parents were still here. Dad was sure nuts about you. What was his nickname for you? Flicker?"

"Yes, that was it. He was fun," said Haven. "What happened to you?"

Rob shot her a mean look and shook his head.

Rob and Haven arrived at the small cottage of Anna and Willy Holman, Beatrice's parents. Memories of hide and seek through the hedges, knocking over ugly gnomes and licking strawberry shaved ice filled her mind. But the same memories that warmed her heart brought heartache as she also remembered her grandfather. Willy had married Anna years after Haven's grandfather David passed away. Willy had been there for Anna, tending to her farm and taking care of major chores after the farmhand she had hired skipped town with her money. After six years of this, they decided to marry despite the fact that Willy had no income of his own. The way he saw it, the work that he now did on the farm should be counted as work. Beatrice had argued with Rob to help Anna financially, but Anna wouldn't have it. She believed that if you don't work, you don't eat, so that whatever happened to them was a natural consequence of their decisions. That is, until her health started failing her. She still did some gardening, but only exerted herself as much as one lung allowed. She lost the other from pneumonia complications.

Anna sat in her rocker crocheting as Rob greeted her from the frail, wooden stairs. Willy sat in his chair, reading the Chronicle. "Anna, I really appreciate you having Haven here while I tie some things up. There may be some late nights, so I figured this would be the best place for her."

"Well, of course it is," cried Anna as she moved towards Haven. "And how is my sweet girl doing this afternoon?" Haven opened her arms to receive the one who had taught her mother to love so well. "I'm OK, grandma. I guess."

"Sweetheart, you stay here as long as you need to. I've already fixed the extra bedroom for you, so why don't you go on in and put your things away. Tomorrow is a big day for you." Haven retrieved her suitcase and slowly went back up the stairs.

Rob placed his hand lightly on her shoulder. Haven brushed it off and went inside. Rob's shoulders slumped as he exhaled. Anna gently placed her hand on Rob's shoulder.

Willy said, "Well, there ya go. That's what workin' nights will get ya."

Rob snapped his head towards Willy. "Really? What will living off of a widow get you?"

Willy stood up. "Boy, you done better watch what yer flappin' 'cause ya ain't got room to talk unless you can remember last time ya got yer pretty manicured fingernails dirty."

"Enough!" cried Anna as she stomped her foot on the wooden porch. "Neither one of you are in a spot to judge the other. Now if you'll excuse me, I have some real work to do, like tending to my granddaughter."

After Rob got in the car and left, Willy picked up his outdated newspaper and began to read. Willy picked up his pipe, lit it and uttered a grunt. "Chump."

Anna found Haven unpacking. "Are you hungry?" she asked.

"No, Grandma. Just tired. By the way, Dad mentioned you wouldn't be able to go to the ceremony tomorrow. Please don't feel bad about not going because the school is recording it. I'll bring a vid back for you."

"Oh, Sweetheart, you are so kind. Doc won't let me two feet away from the house with one lung and all." Anna opened a dresser drawer. "I'll be there in spirit for sure." She pulled out a keepsake box hidden underneath items that once belonged to a very young Beatrice. She held it close and breathed in deeply. She held it out for Haven as she sat down on the bed.

"This was your mother's," she softly said. "Take it. It's yours now. I know it may not be what you wanted as a graduation present."

Haven opened it up and saw that it was a child's jigsaw puzzle. Anna placed her hand over Haven's shoulder gently. "It was her very first puzzle. She used to love putting these together."

Anna fought back the tears as she wrapped her arms around Haven.

Haven looked up into her gentle eyes. "I love you, Grandma."

Anna held her a little tighter. "Try to get some rest, sweetheart. We are all going to be so proud of you when you walk down that aisle in your robe and all." Anna brushed Haven's bangs aside from her forehead before she got up. "And your momma is going to be looking down from Heaven smiling at her little girl and being so proud." Anna closed the door behind her.

Haven sat down on the bed to the squeak of an old spring coil. She sat still for a moment looking around the room her mother had grown up in. All of Beatrice's childhood keepsakes were still there. Her first canvas painting, her porcelain doll collection, her art books and her many puzzles. Haven took a deep breath and put her head down on the pillow. Being emotionally exhausted, it was easy for her to doze off these days. The ticking of the clock by the doorsill became louder and louder as her eyes got heavier with each blink. It wasn't time to fall asleep yet. *Still need to unpack*, she thought to herself.

A scratch, scratch from the floorboard startled her awake.

Haven stood by the other side of the bed. Scratch, scratch. She went into the adjacent bathroom which shared a wall with her bedroom. Nothing.

Scraaaaaatch! Like fingernails on a chalkboard, the high-pitched scratch pierced her ears and sent her running out of the room. "Grandma? Willy?"

"We're in here, honey!" Anna cried from the kitchen.

Haven frantically ran into the kitchen. "Did you hear that?"

"Hear what, honey?" asked Anna.

"I thought I heard some scratching on the floor."

"Thas prolly some critter under the house makin' a nest or somethin', said Willy. "Ain't nothin'. If ya gonna be out heres, ya gotta get used to the farm noises, girl."

Anna frowned at him. "You could have said it a little nicer than that, Willy." She turned to Haven. "But he's right. You just have to get used to it. I used to go to the pond to relax and just sit and watch the water. Why don't you go watch the sun go down?"

Haven smiled. "Sounds nice." She dashed through the hallway and out through the back porch and headed towards the pond. She hadn't quite noticed Willy sitting there reading his newspaper. After she got out about 20 feet, she stopped and turned around to face him, her jaw dropping. "What the . . . ? Weren't you just inside?"

Willy put his newspaper down and yelled out, "Don't go swimmin'! Heh, heh."

Instead of going to the pond, Haven rushed over to the side of the house and entered through the garage door. She ran into her room and locked the door. She didn't notice the mist that almost made it into the room with her when she shut the door. Anna's faint voice could be heard in the kitchen.

"Honey, are you all right?" she shouted.

"Yes, Grandma. I think I'm going to turn in for the night."

"OK. Let us know if you need anything."

"'Night, Grandma."

Haven laid her head down gently on her pillow and pulled the covers over her as she lay in a fetal position. She hugged her blanket tight as if it were a life preserver and closed her eyes. As she breathed in through her nose, she could still smell the scent of her mother's perfume on her soft hand when she caressed her as she rested. She remembered long ago when Sol's father had gotten into a drunken rampage, and she called Haven to come get her out of the house before something terrible happened. Rob had maintained that she shouldn't let herself become involved and that the terrible things that were happening there would soon visit the Dante household should she choose to go. "Choose love," is what Beatrice lovingly told her. Haven hopped on her motorcycle and raced over there as fast as she could to find the fire department already there tearing down the wall behind the stove after Mr. Alden had fallen asleep on the dining room table. Haven did not regret bringing Sol home, but she did miss those comforting words.

Choose love.

Haven smelled something burning . . . almost like brimstone. *They must be burning a fire,* she thought.

The door slowly creaked open. A figure in the shadows poked his head in. A low gruff voice whispered, "hhh-hhhHaven?" Haven turned around to face the door. "Who . . . ?"

"Thought I heard somethin' like you talkin' to somebody.

"Willy?" Haven tried to keep the light out of her eyes.

"Just come to make sure you all right is all." The shadowy figure came in and closed the door behind him. "Don't you worry now, li'l girl. You'll be all right."

"I'm fine. I was trying to get some sleep."

"You sounded worried." He stepped closer and sat down on the bed.

"What do you want?" Haven demanded. "Where's Grandma?"

"Sshhhhh." The man placed his hand over Haven's mouth. His face moved into the moonlight. He looked like Willy but it was not. The air surrounding his face was cold and vile. A wickedness so abhorrent that the absence of light within its shell was palpable. "People know me around these parts, and they all think o' me as a good man." Haven went to move his hand from over her mouth, but Willy clamped down even harder.

Haven squirmed. A cold chill shot through her and she was paralyzed with fear.

"Mm mph!" she cried.

"Now, now li'l girl," Willy said as he exhaled a cold mist. Lightning struck. For an instant, Haven could see the face behind the human mask. The yellow eyes, the pointed ears and the long hair wrapped on the top of the head of this beast whose monstrous physique bore down on Haven's diminutive body. She tried to speak but the words would not form on her lips.

Grandma . . . help me . . . someone . . . . Oh God! Momma!

The rooms inside of Haven's heart echoed with the sounds of anguish. From deep within, her muzzled pleas were met with silent abandonment as all that she was came crumbling down. All defenses against a violation were destroyed in mere moments. The walls of her soul fractured and, in its place, grew the stone and mortared walls that would remain. Haven Irena Dante was forced to leave behind who she was, now and forever. The person that was Haven was no more and replaced with a torment of days.

And she might never see her again.

Mostro (Monster)

The mid-afternoon sun cast its warmth over the graduation ceremony for the senior class of Charity Vane High. Dressed in the school colors of red and gold, the graduates stood in the midst of spectacular regalia to commemorate their achievement in the company of family and close friends. Soledad Alden stood in the midst of the well-dressed, and well-to-do students and pulled her gown down as far as it would go to hide her tattered and torn tennis shoes. She scoured the graduates in search of Haven. Out of the corner of her eye, she spotted someone standing by the rear entrance of the stage, looking away from the others. Even though she never went in search of it, Haven was usually in the mix of any festivities, so she doubted that it was her. In fact, Haven did not have one ounce of party animal in her. But one thing Sol knew for certain – Haven did enjoy people. Sol looked down at the person's shoes: bright new heels that sparkled in the sunlight. *That's got to be her*, she thought to herself. She walked up to the girl and put her hand on her shoulder. "Haven?"

Haven immediately jerked her shoulder away and spun around to see who had just startled her. Shaken, Haven reactively belted, "Hey!"

"Haven, what are you doing? We're lining up!"

Haven blinked rapidly as if coming out of a trance. "Yes, I know. I'm coming. Just don't do that again. You scared me."

Sol took a step back as she said a simple, "Sorry" half-heartedly. "Are you all right?"

"Yes, I'm fine. Let's just go."

Haven led the way as they both walked off to join the line-up. Haven stood in front of Chucky Flegman who was an obese, curly-head boy about an inch shorter than Haven. She noticed the smidge of what looked like mayonnaise on Chuck's lip and even though she was disgusted by it, she didn't make a big deal out of it. "Um . . . you've got something on . . ." She pointed to his lip.

He nervously removed his hand from inside his gown and wiped it off. "Thanks. I had an accident when I was a kid when I fell, so I'm missing my back teeth and I get stuff . . . "

Haven could hide her disgust no more as she shrugged, she unknowingly looked at Chuck with disdain. "Oh . . . uh sorry," Chuck said. "Too much?"

"No," Haven said. "I'm the one who is sorry."

As the presenter began to read off the names of the graduates, Haven looked back at Rob, who sat typing on his communicator pad. She rolled her eyes and shook her head. *Workaholic*, she thought to herself. What she didn't notice was Sol typing in her compad as well. Sol stashed her compad back inside her gown. Rob put his down and watched Haven as she made her way up the side of the audience and towards the stage.

Noticing Haven's forlorn and wrinkled brow, Rob stood up and made his way towards Haven. Seeing the detached look on her face, he reached out for her.

She reacted immediately and pushed his hand away. "Don't touch me!" she demanded. Her fellow graduates were taken back by her outburst.

Motioning her away from the line, Rob escorted her away and insisted, "Haven, what's wrong?"

"Nothing," she responded. "I just don't like people touching me."

Puzzled, Rob asked, "Since when? Your mother was tucking you in and lying on the bed next to you right up until the accident. And you weren't acting like this yesterday." Rob paused. "What wrong?"

Haven looked down. "Nothing, Dad. I don't want to talk about it."

Rob insisted. "You don't want to talk about what?"

Haven's shoulders slumped. "It's embarrassing. I just . .last night . . . Willy. ."

Rob's eyes widened. He put his hand on his mouth and took a step back.

"Dad, wait. Please don't say anything. Please," she begged.

As his face turned red and his hands started to shake, Rob took a step closer to Haven. "What did he do?"

Haven looked up at Rob with tears welling up.

"Why didn't you tell me?" he asked anxiously.

Haven clenched her teeth. "Why!..? Are you serious? When was the last time we had a heart-to-heart, Dad?"

Rob shook his head. "I'm your father."

Haven rolled her eyes. "Right. You're my father. Well lookee there. That's just the solution to all of our problems, isn't it? Look 'Dad,' I really don't feel like dealing with this right now, so just drop it and we'll talk about it later. I have to get back in line now." Haven was about to walk away, but instead turned to face Rob. "And Dad, all you have to do is sit there and smile. So put your compad down and just stare at the stage and just smile, OK? Can you do that? I'm not asking for much here."

Rob's shoulders relaxed and he sighed. "Yes."

Haven went back into her line. Chuck said, "Me and my Dad don't get along much either. Not at all -- especially when he calls me Tubby. It's not like I don't want to like him, because I do. It's just that he says dumb stuff, so when he's around I just kinda go to my room and

maybe . . . I . . . oh forget it."

"It's ok, Chuck. I get it. Trust me, I get it."

Rob swallowed and returned to his seat. The presenter continued to call out the names of the graduates.

"Kristen Cameron."

Haven curiously turned to see Rob who sat staring into space. Haven went up the ramp.

"Lindsey Culbreth."

She turned again and could see his face turning blood-red.

"Michael Culbreth."

It was her turn next. One last look.

"Haven Irena Dante."

She marched up to the presenter and with a forced smile, held out her left for the diploma and her right hand to shake the presenter's hand. She turned to face the audience one last time.

The wind blew the program off of Rob's empty chair and onto the ground while an onlooker stepped on it on his way to his seat. With teeth clenched, Haven gripped the hand of the presenter and held it tight. Her heart sank beneath a wave of hopelessness.

Willy Holman sat in his rocking chair in the living room watching the evening news as the sun began to set. Anna was picking some ripe tomatoes. His favorite anchor was on, the one with the blonde hair and green eyes whom he stared at intently. Drops of sweat began to form on his brow as he watched. He wiped his forehead with his handkerchief, then used the remote to shut the TV off. He went to the bathroom to wash his face. As he turned the cold water on, steam immediately formed on the mirror. He stooped down to rinse and, when he came up, he was startled by the steam. Slowly raising his hand, he wiped a streak onto the mirror.

Then he saw it.

The yellow eyes and skin, and the pointed ears and evil smile. He gasped and took three steps back, backing into the bathroom door. His breathing became shallow and quick. He ripped his glasses off and threw them on the counter. Feeling sick to his stomach, he reached for the sink and threw up. When he opened his eyes and put his glasses back on, he looked into the sink and there was nothing there. He heard a knock at the front door and ran out, only to find the very same newscaster standing in his living room.

"Hi Willy," she said, in a low sultry voice.

Willy gasped. "What in . . ."

"Sshh." She stepped closer. "You watch me night after night and I just wanted to meet you in person."

"But . . ." was all Willy could say when she moved in and kissed him.

Rob's car came to a squealing halt in front of the Holman house. The newscaster turned around and calmly stated in a lower, grim voice, "It's him."

Willy's eyes were still closed when the newscaster morphed into a pile of snakes and dropped to the ground, scattering just as Rob ran through the front porch door. All the snakes, except for one, disappeared into the ground. The snake that was left had a ring around it. It was gold with what could have been a symbol on it. Just as the snakes disappeared into the floor, Willy began to shake profusely. All he could muster as a cry for help was, "Oh God!"

Rob grabbed him by the collar as the one snake made its way out the front door. It slithered through the ring and into the ground.

"What did you do?" Rob demanded as he shook Willy, who was still shaking on his own.

"Get your hands off me, boy!" A puff of yellow smoke came out of Willy's nose, which startled Rob. He coughed and more yellow smoke came out of his mouth in a large puff. While Willy was still shaking, blood began to trickle from his nose and ears. He screamed as he shook and then dropped.

Rob caught him halfway to the ground knocking over a vase. "Willy? Willy what's happening?"

Willy gurgled a faint "I'm sorry" and surrendered his last breath. Hearing the commotion, Anna came rushing in.

"Willy? Willy are you OK?" She saw Willy's lifeless body in Rob's arms.

On her motorcycle, Haven raced through the streets of Charity Vane at breakneck speed. *Jerk*, she thought to herself. Dodging traffic, she made her way onto the feeder road which led to the countryside, just outside the city limits. Being that it was typically a quieter, gentler part of town, she was shocked to see the flashing lights of the police cars and ambulance upon approaching the Holman household. Stunned, she parked her bike and made her way through the police officers with their blaring radios, only to find someone completely draped in a sheet on a gurney, blood seeping through from the person's face.

"Excuse me," she heard from the officer behind her. "Are you family?" he asked.

"Yes. What happened here?"

"I'm sorry, but one of the residents was fatally wounded."

Haven put her hand over her mouth. "Who?"

"Willy Holman. Mrs. Holman is fine but we're taking her to the hospital to have her checked out. Was he your grandfather?"

"No!" Haven shot back and angrily ran off to the prisoner transport vehicle to confront her father. She could barely see inside the vehicle through the glass shielding. "Dad?" she asked as she placed her hands on the glass. "Dad, what happened here? What did you do?"

Rob got as close to the glass as he could without pressing his face against the window. "Listen to me. Go to Sol's house. Don't stay here!"

Haven shot back a quizzical look and as she took two steps back, the squad car sped off. Haven slowly turned and dropped to her knees, holding in her breath with both hands. She wiped the first few tears that made their way down her cheek. She caught a glimpse of something glimmering in the light of the streetlamp. She reached out her hand and picked up the small, round and shiny object. It was the gold ring. When she held it close, it vibrated between her fingers. Startled, she dropped it back onto the grass. She thought to herself, *Willy's wedding band?* She picked it up again and took a closer look and noticed an inscription of some kind on the inside of the ring. It was a rather macabre, dark letter "A" with a circle around it.

She immediately placed it in her pocket, mounted her motorcycle and sped off.

Named after Dr. Judas Cradle, who was seen as the pioneer of criminal psychology, Judas Cradle Maximum Security Penitentiary was the dungeon where the dark souls of Charity Vane were kept hidden and tucked away. Since Charity Vane had become known as the "City of Good Deeds", the refuse within the prison walls of Judas Cradle would only bring shame to the city that had become the beacon and symbol of hope. The shame of corruption had to be hidden behind these walls. Charity Vane bled internally like a badly sutured bypass. This was due to the fact that the good it did was performed for the wrong reasons, such as notoriety and prestige, instead of authentic altruism. As such, Judas Cradle became the muzzle for the city that would hide its sins at all costs. Having her father in mind, Haven once called Charity Vane a "city of hypocrites" and wished that the hidden sins of this harlot could be shouted from the highest rooftop. Even so, Charity could not reveal to the rest of the world that she had flaws beneath the surface tucked away in the darkest parts of her heart and this was where those secrets were kept…away from the public and away from the "upright". The prison warden, Dominic Reins, believed having offenders be the victims of their own crimes was the only way to repay society. He was once accused of torturing the inmates using experimental behavioral modification techniques that he developed himself. The prosecution could not produce enough evidence against him, so the charges were dropped. The facility, located on an island off the southeast coast of Charity Vane, was far enough away, but not too far for Haven to come to for an answer.

"What happened?" she asked her father, who sat on the other side of heavy glass. She would only have five minutes with him and no privacy. The prisoners sat in half-booths with a small panel between them and their neighbor.

"Honey, just listen to me. I know what this looks like, but you really need to stay away from me right now."

Haven insisted. "Did you do this?"

Rob exhaled. "No. I know it appears that way but . . ."

Haven interrupted. "You were angry."

"Yes, I know, but I did not do this. Haven, listen. You have to stay away from me right now."

"Why?" Haven asked.

"Just trust me, for once. I know things are tough with us right now but I'm begging you please. Stay away. Harry has already called the company attorney and Joe's on his way, so I'll be fine." Neither of them noticed a thin bald man smoking a cigarette in the next booth, being questioned by the prison warden. The warden wore a long black leather jacket and round-rimmed, thick eyeglasses rested on his beakish nose, framed by his long, black hair.

"Go to Sol's house," Rob said. "Don't tell anyone where you're going, OK? Please?"

Haven sighed. "Fine, Dad . . . whatever."

A prison guard escorted Haven out of the prison. As she mounted her motorcycle just outside the gothic prison gate, she reached for her helmet, taking one last look at the prison that held her father. Haven pushed her helmet on and raced off. As she did, the stone, wingless Malebranche demons mounted on top of each of the gate columns came to life and took to the skies to pursue her. As Haven rode through the part of town known as 'The Mire', she passed a homeless person passed out on the curb behind a convertible, still holding a whisky bottle. As the wake of wind pushed his ragged jacket open, one of the Malebranche demons leaped into the vagabond. Immediately, his eyes glowed and he shook violently but for just a second. He then leaped to his feet and let out a thunderous growl as he landed in the driver's seat of the hot rod. After a quick hotwiring, he ramped up the vehicle and sped off after Haven. As he left the scene, the other demon leaped into a man selling drugs in an alley. The dealer dropped his money and jumped on his nearby motorcycle and sped off as well. They followed her up the onramp and onto the four-lane highway. Through her helmet, Haven heard the squeals of the monsters closing in and gasped in horror as she shifted gears and accelerated. When she noticed, in her rear-view mirror, another motorcycle closing in on her, she turned her head over her right shoulder to get a better look when she caught a glimpse of the rider's yellow glowing eyes. "Oh crap!"

The beast tried slamming her bike into an oncoming truck to no avail. Haven's quick reflexes came to bear as she swerved around the 18-wheeler and made it back onto her side of the road. Her chest pounded like a freight train on a frail wooden track. She swerved away and then came back in towards the monster in an attempt to throw him off the overpass they were approaching.

She yelled, "What the crap?" and revved her gas and punched it. The man-beast's motorcycle flew over the overpass, and just as fast as the demon entered the man, it exited in mid-air, landing inside of a drinking truck driver. The alcoholic's eyes glowed and he gave chase. With the mammoth machine at his disposal, he plowed through other vehicles with sounds of twisted metal, screeching tires, and shattering glass filling the air along with Haven's screams.

Haven's breathing became heavier and quicker. The other man-beast driving the convertible came darting up Haven's side, but not knowing the road, he drove his car right into the off-ramp divider. A news helicopter hovered above the off-ramp as the car flipped over the divider, ejecting the driver. The demon immediately left that poor soul to fall into the river and entered into the helicopter pilot. After letting out a raucous laugh, the demon pilot raced after Haven, who had just exited the highway. Haven could hear the loud rotors approaching her from behind as the pilot inched the blades closer and closer towards Haven's neck. Haven grunted, switched gears once again and pushed the gas even harder. She made her way through a narrow alley on the east side of the city after knocking over vendors on the sidewalks. The pilot, unable to navigate the tight space, veered off. Haven did not, however, plan for an escape route once she arrived onto the city street on the other side. *This road dead ends into the mall*, she thought to herself.

"Got nowhere else to go." She sighed and hit the gas once again, setting a collision course for the food court of the palatial Grand Mall of Charity Vane. "There's no way they can follow me in there," she said under her breath. After smashing through the glass, Haven came to a screeching halt at the end of the entrance walkway, which led to a 100-foot drop to the lower level.

While she stood for a moment to catch her breath a monstrous 18-wheeler came crashing through the mall entrance. In shock, she spun off toward the adjacent walkway. The truck barely missed her, sailing over the balcony to crash on the lower level. Just before the cabin hit the ground and burst into flames, the Malebranche exited the driver and leaped onto the ground, entering a security guard. As the helicopter hovered above the skylight, the guard pulled out his gun and began firing at Haven.

"Is this ever going to end?" she asked herself. After missing her, the guard took off on foot in pursuit while Haven sped up the escalator to the third floor. Finding the roof exit, she rammed through it and sped up the stairs to the rooftop where she was face-to-face with the helicopter.

"You want to play?" she screamed. "Do you?" And she hit the gas, setting course for the helicopter. Just before she hit the ledge, she jumped off, sending the motorcycle into the helicopter. The flying machine burst into flames and came crashing down onto the mall parking lot.

Haven got up and dusted herself off. She waved her fist at the wreckage and let out a big "Eat Harley!"

Haven tossed her helmet and came down the stairs of an adjacent building making her way to the parking lot. *Sol's house isn't far,* she thought to herself. 'The Mire' was comprised mostly of public housing where gang members, trapped in a mentality of defeatism, claimed territorial rights. The youth had been handed down a philosophy of entitlement and, choosing not to strive for a better life, they became bitter and angry about what they inherited, thus propagating the problem. They wanted someone to come in and take care of them, and when no one did, they were quick to accept their circumstances, laying all hope for the future as a sacrifice at the altar of anger.

Haven dodged the trash cans that had not been picked up for a week and made it up the stairs to Sol's apartment. *Glad we swapped keys*; she thought to herself as she frantically let herself in. She didn't think that Mr. Alden would be home. Sol said he was in rehab. If Sol was supposed to meet her at the apartment there were no signs of her ever being there. She walked down the hallway entrance and felt a cold chill go down her spine.

"Sol?" There was no response. When she entered the living room everything seemed to be right where it should be, which was in complete disarray. There was a pile of dishes in the sink right below the empty bottle of dish soap. She exhaled a cold shot of air and walked into the living room. She heard a door creek open and turned. "Mr. Alden?" No response. "Sol?" she tried one last time. "Guess she made a detour," she muttered to herself. *I'll wait for a little while*, she thought. Haven walked over to the window and stood pondering the events of the day. She tried to calm herself by breathing in deeply and exhaling. As she placed her hands to her side, she felt the ring which she still had in her pocket. She pulled it out to take a closer look.

"Beautiful, isn't it?" said a rumbling voice from behind.

Haven gasped loudly and turned, backing up against the wall next to the window as she shoved the ring back into her pocket. All she could see were the yellow eyes . . . those terrible yellow eyes that seemed familiar to her.

"Who are you?" she asked, terrified. Moving in the shadows she could feel the thud of each step on the wooden floor ring from her feet up through her body. She jumped with each step as the eight-foot, monstrous satyr stepped out of the shadows and showed himself. His pointy ears, yellow skin and hoofed feet sent Haven into a deeper state of shock. "Wh . . . what are you? Wh . . . what do you want?"

"Why, more of you, my dear. Your cheeks, your smell, your . . . friendship," replied the creature. He moved in closer. "Oh and I would like my ring back, soft one?" The satyr approached her.

"My name is Hedonis, prince of lust and ruler of the second circle of the Aristocracy."

"Stay away from me, monster!" Haven screamed.

Hedonis chuckled. "Oh, you human girls are all the same, your yes means no, and your no means yes. Can you simply just say what you mean?"

Haven stood defiant. "Don't come any closer."

More yellow eyes formed in the darkness behind the creature.

"Or what?" rumbled Hedonis. "I do not take threats lightly, my dear."

More creatures emerged from the shadows. A red dragon-like beast that stood upright lunged at her and put Haven in a chokehold. With his long, red, leathery arms he held her still as Hedonis moved even closer. She could feel his cold breath of ash on her cheek. That smell. That's what Willy smelled like. His voice echoed in the apartment. "I was hoping we could be friends . . . get to know each other even better than before. Get closer."

"Like hell," Haven answered.

"Like hell then," thundered Hedonis.

The red beast slammed Haven against the wall and, as she tried to get up, a ghoulish shade creature appeared from the shadows. He showed his fangs in a wicked smile and then dealt her a blow to the stomach. She spit up blood as she tried to compose herself. The dragon picked her up and threw her into the kitchen. Landing in the sink, onto the pile of dirty dishes, she managed to catch her breath and grabbed a kitchen knife. She could hear the heavy, hoofed steps approaching and, as soon as she saw the yellow eyes, she threw the knife, hoping to at least distract the monsters long enough to escape. Surprisingly, the shade dodged the knife and lunged at her before she could catch her next breath. Instead of striking, the ghoul grabbed Haven by the hair and threw her back into the living room. At that moment,

Haven's training kicked in and she rolled on the floor and rose to her feet.

"Enough!" she screamed. The shade lunged at her again but this time she grabbed the monster by the arm and, moving out of its path, she hurled the demon into the next room using its own momentum. The red dragon ran towards her. She spun a rapid-fire outside crescent kick to his jaw, catching him off guard. She spun around for a back fist, but the dragon was too fast. He blocked the arm and grabbed her by the neck. Her legs went limp. He reached inside of her pocket for the ring. "Goodbye, my dear," uttered Hedonis. "And this," he said as he held up the ring, "is mine."

Haven gasped for air.

Hedonis moved its face closer to Haven –his noxious breath gagging her. "With this I am able to remain merged with a human host outside of our realm. So you see, my dear, you won't be needing it, because you'll be dead soon." The red dragon grabbed Haven by the collar and lifted her up. Just as it did, Haven reached for the ring and grabbed it right out of Hedonis' hand.

"Finders, keepers, "she said.

The beast then flung Haven through the glass and into the night air.

"No!" Hedonis screamed.

The cold sting of the night air met her bruises and open wounds with no mercy as the glass shattered outward. Her rapid descent seemed to last a lifetime as her thoughts filled with the warmth of her mother's memory. "Mo . . . Momma?"

She could almost hear her voice. "Yes, sweetheart. I'm here."

"I miss you, Momma."

"I know you do, Sweetheart. Are you scared?"

"Yes, Momma."

"It's going to be OK, Honey. I love you."

"I love you too."

"Choose."

"Momma?"

"Choose love."

Haven closed her eyes, accepting the inevitable, in the comfort of knowing that she would soon be reunited with her mother and that all the pains of love and life would soon be behind her. She embraced herself as if it were Beatrice, in expectation of the joy of being with her again.

But then . . .

Rays of light began to emerge from beneath her, slowing her descent. The energy surged and enveloped her with warmth that she had never known and began to surround her until she came to a slow stop. She was resting. Feeling herself ascend she gave way to exhaustion and fell asleep. Something had caught her, and it was beautiful and warm. She paid no attention to the crackling sounds of light that kept her safe.

Hedonis, the ghoul, and the red dragon had come to the window to gloat over the death of a Dante, but instead were met with a brilliant, blinding light. The demons stepped back as the light drew closer and closer and its heat became more than uncomfortable. Its sound was deafening. The light rose higher and higher until it was face-to-face with Haven's assailants.

A booming, thunderous voice gave orders to the monsters, who were now trembling in fear. "Return to your abyss. The line has been called upon once again!"

As the curious demons moved closer to the window, the massive, bright-winged archangel repeated his command from his white horse with his sword drawn. He roared, "To your abyss! Now!" As the archangel repeated his command, his head changed into that of a lion while his wings gave way to a red cape that flowed in the wind behind him. He towed a blazing white chariot which held Haven. As the thunder of his voice faded, the demons morphed into bodies of snakes, dropping and then disappearing into the floor.

Haven rested in a warm blanket of light within the secure chariot as the chariot pierced the starry sky above Charity Vane.

Prova (Evidence)

The press, along with dozens of spectators, gathered at the steps of the Cabanela Courthouse as Roberto Bonifacio Dante was dragged in chains up the stairs and into the courthouse for his arraignment. Given Dante's public status, Chief Meiko thought it best to try and get him through the back door with as little risk as possible. However, the news had leaked out, and everyone rushed to catch a glimpse of the solitary man who had provided the city with all of the best technology that his company had to offer, now stood an accused man. He was brought in through the secured corridors with their liquid screens that displayed the identity of every person in the transport unit as they walked by the scanners mounted on the walls. The only other people allowed in the vast, marble-floored courtroom were the press. Rob was brought to the middle of the courtroom and directed to stand on the very scanner his company invented. Clerk Walker manipulated an interface vat.

A floating readout appeared with all the charges filed against him.

Charges: First Degree Murder, Breaking and Entering with Intent to Harm, Assault.

Evidence: DNA of Willy Holman found on the person of Roberto Bonifacio Dante; front door found broken in, evidence of a vehicle's rapid stop in front of home, signs of struggle within the Holman household.

The clerk manipulated the vat once more and brought up Rob's psychological profile.

Psych Profile: Recluse, aloof, borderline antisocial and/or avoidant behavior.

The evidence seemed insurmountable as the clerk brought up more information.

Medical History: Depression, Anxiety Disorder, Eating disorder.

It was then that the bailiff looked up at the courtroom witnesses and said, "All rise!" Judge Murray walked in and addressed the spectators as he sat down on a massive bench that was high above the spectators like a heavenly throne. "Be seated."

Joe Brazil approached a sensor pad and his credentials immediately appeared on a floating readout screen in front of the judge and the press.

Joseph Brazil, Defense Attorney on behalf of the accused.

"Mr. Brazil, the evidence has been submitted for assimilation by this court. Does the defendant wish to enter a plea?"

"Yes, your honor. The defendant wishes to enter a plea of not guilty." There were murmurings in the courtroom from both sides.

"Very well."

Judge Murray placed his hand in the vat interface and the liquid crept up his arm like spider legs crawling up a wall and stopped midway up his arm. His eyes turned white as the sensor interface was activated and he was instantly able to assimilate the information contained in the files. After a few seconds of this, he removed his arm and addressed the defense attorney.

"Bring in your first character witness, Mr. Brazil," ordered the judge. Joe Brazil reached into his pocket as a platform rose from the floor. He pulled out what appeared to be several vials. After inserting one of them into an interface attached to the platform, he opened one of the vials allowing a stream of water to come pouring out into a vat located on the platform. The water came alive and rose, forming a screen with Harry Reeve's image. The judge smirked when he saw the image on the liquid monitor. Harry folded his hands and made his statement as the word pro appeared on the left-hand side of the screen.

"Mr. Dante has built Dante Technologies from the ground up and has given not just this city but the world tools that have made our planet a better place . . . a safer place. Then the word con appeared on the left side of the screen as Harry continued. "I have been concerned about his state of mind with the loss of his son many years ago and now his wife. I understand that his daughter may have gone missing and has not been heard from in days."

Joe Brazil pulled out another vial and added it to the interface. "The defense calls Jinx Jenkins, assistant to Mr. Dante." Jinx was Rob's assistant for the past 20 years and was loyal to the Dante family and a friend to Beatrice and Haven. Her image appeared on the screen with the word pro as she began to speak.

"Mr. Dante has been a wonderful man to work for as well as generous to me. I've learned a great deal from working with him." The word con appeared on the screen. "I know the family issues have stressed him out a bit over the years and although he seems to want to do the right thing in spending more time with them, he feels his first priority is to his responsibilities at Dante Tech."

The judge tilted his head back. "Are there any other character witnesses?"

"No, your honor," said Mr. Brazil. "No other witnesses."

"Mr. Brazil, a verdict has been reached. Do you have anything to add?"

"Yes, your honor. I ask the court to please consider the history of contributions that my client has made to our city. The very technology used in this courtroom, a more expeditious system of disseminating the law, was invented and donated by my client and has revolutionized the legal system. And although it is true that Mr. Dante has a history of insensible behavior, even with his own family, I recommend that the murder charge be reduced to involuntary manslaughter. He has given much to this city and I ask that the city not turn its back on him now. That is all, your honor."

"Thank you, Mr. Brazil. This court has weighed the evidence and has found the defendant guilty of all charges." The courtroom press erupted with shouted questions.

Judge Murray immediately slammed his gavel on the bench, and it resonated through the courtroom. No one noticed the gold band on his right ring finger with a macabre inscription on it. "Order! There will be order in the courtroom!"

"Should there be another outburst I will have the press removed from the courtroom. I take it I make myself clear?" The press immediately calmed down to hear the sentence.

At that moment, animated water began pouring into the courtroom on both sides as if to create a circular barrier between the accused and the outside world. Once they reached behind Rob a wall went up with energy shooting through it as a measure of safety both for and against the accused. Then, the judge read the sentence.

"Roberto Bonifacio Dante, for the charge of First-Degree Murder, Breaking and Entering with Intent to Inflict Harm, and Assault, I hereby sentence you to death. You are hereby remanded to Charity Vane

Maximum Security Prison until sentence is carried out. May whatever god you serve have mercy on your soul."

Rob swallowed hard and clenched his teeth in utter despair as the judge read the verdict. He never thought in a million years that he would ever find himself in such a place of losing everything that he had ever worked for; everything he had ever fought for was gone in the blink of an eye. Tomorrow didn't matter nor did what the future held. All was lost forever and there was nothing more that could be taken from him.

The bailiff once again ordered, "All rise!" As the press stood, the judge walked off of the bench and caught himself almost tripping as he came down the stoop. The bailiff caught him in time, but just as he did, his jaw dropped, and his eyes widened at the judge's yellow, glowing eyes. He blinked twice. The judge' eyes looked normal again. The bailiff shook it off and reluctantly, cleared the way for the judge to exit the courtroom.

The guards approached Rob and, using a grappling device, they hooked on to Rob's chains and escorted him out of the courtroom. The press tried to follow, but the guards stopped them. Weighed down with shame, Rob kept his eyes on the ground as he was taken out of the courtroom.

The press corps turned around and was already gathering outside of the courthouse, waiting for a comment from Harry Reeve, who apparently had one prepared.

"I am in as much shock and disbelief as the public is about the sequence of events that have culminated in today's verdict. I personally wish to state that despite the hardships that Mr. Dante has had to endure in the past, this action is out of character for him and as such I stand by my belief that he is not guilty of the crime for which he has just been convicted. I also wish to express my concern for his well-being and that of his missing daughter, and I ask everyone to please keep them in your thoughts. I want to assure everyone that Dante Technologies will continue normal operations. The value of the company has not changed and its impact on the world will not diminish. The staff can also rest assured that there will be no changes to operations or personnel other than myself and we'd like to thank the public for their support during this difficult time. Please refer any questions to public relations. Thank you. Good day."

Jinx Jenkins slammed her fist on her glass desk almost shattering it. "Do you really expect me to believe that garbage?" Gardener backed away slowly from Jinx' desk. Noticing his reaction, Jinx collected herself and leaned back in her chair, folding her hands across her desk. "Mr. Gardener, for the past four months you've grown to become an exceptional asset to the Research and Development group, and it's been a joy to have you here, but you do get why I'm so skeptical about what you're telling me." Jinx had helped Rob start Dante Technologies. When Rob hired Harry, Jinx was pleased that he had found someone to take some of Rob's load off, but after getting to know Harry, she became more and more concerned about things that he kept private, even from her. She was not jealous, but she did not want to see everything that Rob had worked for destroyed by someone who had come out of nowhere and who might not have the company's best interests at heart. Gardener, too, had come out of nowhere, so Jinx was apprehensive about trusting him just yet.

"I know what it sounds like Ms. Jenkins. It sounds crazy. I belong to a group called the Virgilian Order. They've been watching the Dante family for centuries, primarily to keep them safe from harm, but the night that Beatrice died, we failed. Even though she was a Dante by marriage, she was still a big help to us, and we messed up by allowing her to go in and look for evidence of the Aristocracy operating inside this company by herself. She had previous training, but when you're fighting these monsters, sometimes it's just not enough. We should have stopped her. Now we're trying to backtrack and find out what it is that she was about to uncover here. There was a file that I was able to trace back to you."

"What is the Aristocracy?" Jinx asked.

Gardener hesitated. "All I can say is that they are very bad people -- if you want to call them that."

Jinx stood up slowly and walked to the window. Jinx had curly red hair and stood six feet tall. Even her stride exuded confidence and was, to some, intimidating. "I was so happy when Harry came to work here, because it meant that finally Rob could start spending time with his family and leave things to us. But after a while, Harry started leaving us out of the loop on things; me first and then Rob. I thought it might be because he wanted to show Rob that the company was in good hands, but then when he started reaching agreements without Rob's consent with people that we knew nothing about, my suspicions grew."

Gardener moved closer to Jinx' desk. "It's him, it's gotta be," he said. Jinx turned around.

"The Monday after Beatrice died, I found a file in my system files which I had never seen before. Since Harry had pulled out all the stops to keep me out of the loop, I can only assume that it was placed there by someone else and I'm sure it wasn't Rob. I had no clue where it came from and I couldn't ask around either."

Gardener moved even closer. "I'd like to see it. It may be what we've been looking for."

Jinx looked over at her desk and thought for a moment. Then she turned around facing the sunshine. "No," she said calmly.

"Why?" asked Gardener. "We have to find out what the Aristocracy is up to!"

Jinx turned back around. "Look, you've only begun to earn my trust, I'm not there just yet. You say that you're here to protect the Dantes, then great. Go and find the one that's missing. She's out there somewhere and if you had been doing your job, she wouldn't be lost."

Gardener looked down. "We don't know where she is."

Jinx moved closer. "Then go and find her. You find her and I'll give her the file. She is, after all, a Dante. I'll provide whatever assistance I can from here. Feel free to discreetly use whatever resources you may need from R&D."

"Thanks, Ms. Jenkins. "We'll find her," Gardener said.

Rose entered the courtyard of the beautifully renovated shelter which she had named, "Desert Rose." Even though it was located within "the mire", the shelter for battered women and discarded children of Charity Vane was shaped and crafted like an oasis. Freshly bloomed roses adorned the walls. Green vines wrapped around the benches and stone structures that surrounded the courtyard and a waterfall arched over the walkway leading out from the courtyard. Those sheltered here could walk underneath a dome of water and reach up to touch the cool crisp flow. Those who were kept safe here since everyone who came here for safety were encouraged to develop their talents or skills in order to keep the shelter running. Rose continued through the corridor and was met by Gardener on the other side.

"Are we ready?" she asked.

"Yup," he responded. "Ready to fire it up."

Rose looked up at Gardener. "It's been nine months since we've begun our search for her. Do we know how the order is doing in their search?" Gardener turned his head. "They're not saying much these days."

"Oh dear," Rose said. "What will come of this world without someone to intervene?"

"I try not to think about it," Gardener replied.

Gardener walked towards a waterfall.

He calmly walked into the waterfall but did not get wet. He stood there and looked back at Rose with a grin on his face as the water bounced off of him like drops of light.

"Come on in, the water's fine," he said wryly. Rose held out her hand and each droplet bounced off her hand like a pebble skipping on a calm lake. There was a cool calmness in the air that spoke to her soul and reminded her that they were on the right path. As they went on Gardener continued, "Do you think they know something and they're just not telling us?"

"That is very plausible, my friend," Rose answered.

The sub-level elevator lit up as the doors opened and they walked into its ambient light. The floor of the elevator was clear as were the floors below. The elevator began its journey downward. Workers filled each level like busy bees in a hive. Education and training level, BioMech research, sonics, and others that were filled with complex organic technology.

They came to a slow stop. The doors opened to a dimly lit area. Workers with headlamps scurried about to get to their stations prior to activation. As Gardener tapped his pad, Rose exited the elevator.

"It's beautiful," Rose said as she gasped.

The lights came on, accompanied by a low, thunderous buzz that quieted to a hum. Immediately, halls lit up that extended out as did the command center walls, the liquid monitors filling the room with fluid light. Gardener motioned towards a very messy work-table he had obviously spent some all-nighters on. "Check this out."

"What is it?" Rose asked as she moved towards him.

Gardener picked up an incomplete, makeshift device and showed it to Rose. "This is something I've been working on for a while. It's a static gun. It uses highly charged, static electricity to separate a host from a demon. One shot from this bad boy and its instant exorcism. Cool thing is that it won't jack with a person who's clean. I'm also working on a stat bomb."

"Very clever," Rose exclaimed. "You've worked so hard," Rose said as she looked around. She took a moment to take everything in. "It's breathtaking what you've done here."

"I can cook, baby," Gardener chuckled.

"So, what are we calling it?" she asked.

Gardener turned to Rose and simply replied, "The Garden."

Missione (The Mission)

As the sparks of energy that supported her began to disappear into the morning light, an ensnaring peace wrapped Haven in a tight, warm blanket. Craving rest, the sense of solace surrounding her made it difficult for her to open her weighted eyes. The last glimmering flicker faded into the bright sky, adorned with four virtuous stars known as *Prudence, Fortitude, Temperance, and Justice.* These stars had shone in these foreign skies for millennia, casting their light upon those who would make it to the beginning of their journey to this place here and would sprinkle them with just enough starlight to begin their quest, with some help along the way.

As she opened her eyes, Haven sat up slowly and her heart melted at the beauty that overtook her soul. The cool, crystalline water that washed upon the shore just a few yards away reached out like fingers onto the white sand, almost touching the bright green grass that Haven rested upon. The surrounding snow-capped mountains and peaks formed a mouth that guided the water to this resting place of souls. The trees on the rolling hills surrounding her were lush and green and their blossoms showered the air with seeds of new life that flowed in the wind as if following a current. Even the grass was alive here, as was the landscape that was adorned with colorful blooms of red, blue and yellow. Haven stood up and looked around, wondering where she was and how she had gotten to this wondrous place. She raised her hands to see if they were scarred, bruised or otherwise damaged. After being relieved that they were unscathed, she noticed that she could not only feel the wake of air, but she could see it. She gasped as she waved her hand around making designs in the air, which would dissipate rapidly upon completion of each movement. It was like standing underwater.

She then heard a loud squeal from overhead, and when she looked up, her jaw dropped at the massive size of the giant eagles flying overhead. Each had six wings instead of the normal two, as did the row of lions that came swooping in to circle them. The lions headed off in another direction with thunderous roars. She shivered at the thought of one of them landing on and devouring her when she heard someone talking just beyond the trees behind her. She turned and hollered, "Hello?" As the faintly visual sound wave of her bellow left her mouth she gasped again and quietly uttered, "Wow." She walked closer to the sound of the voice, and when she peeked through the trees, she saw a man draped in a long, white robe talking to a bull.

"Hello?" she cried again. Upon hearing her call, the man and the bull scattered in two separate directions. Just before they left her field of vision, they sprouted wings and flew away, leaving Haven in disbelief.

Curious, she decided to take a look around and took two steps up the hill she had just laid on following the faint sound of a song sung by a light voice carried by the brisk wind from somewhere nearby.

"Twinkle, twinkle little star,

How I wonder what you are…"

Haven snapped her head to look around, curious as to where the child's voice was carried from.

"Up above the world so high,

Like a diamond in the sky…"

At the base of a mighty oak tree Haven saw a little girl at a picnic table.

The child was focused on her task and didn't hear Haven's call. Haven walked further up the hill towards the child. Haven repeated her greeting, which went ignored. When she moved closer, she could see the reason for the child's intense focus.

It was a jigsaw puzzle. The girl was about five years old and wore her dark brown hair up in two pigtails. Under her blue denim overalls, she wore a simple white t-shirt and plain sneakers for running and jumping. She had been working hard on the puzzle for some time and was intent on finishing it, until Haven caught her attention. Very matter-of-factly, she got up and walked over to Haven and hugged her tightly. Then she ran back to the table and sat back down. Haven never knew what hit her. Haven sat down next to the precious girl.

"What are you doing?" Haven asked.

"I'm doing my puzzle," said the girl.

"Well, what's it of?"

"Oh, I can't wait to show it to you. You're gonna like it."

"I am? How do you know?" Haven asked.

"Because it's really pretty."

"Hmmm," Haven muttered under her breath. "What is this place? Am I in Heaven?"

"No, silly," answered the child.

"Is this . . . purgatory?"

"Nooo. It's the choose."

"You mean shoes?"

"You're funny. I said the chooooose. Like when you choose to do one thing for yourself or you choose to do something else for another." She tilted her head and bobbed her shoulders. "It's a gate, too."

"Sure looks like Heaven," Haven said.

"Heaven is lots prettier!" Excited, she jumped on her chair. "Do you want to go there? We can play lots there and nobody's mean. And the best part is you can play with all of the animals. Even the big ones like lions and tigers." She made tiger claws out of her hands and made a growling sound. "Rawr!"

Rushed with euphoria, Haven breathed in the beauty of her surroundings. "You're saying I can go there if I choose to? That I can decide for myself?"

"Yup," replied the girl as she jumped down. "But if you do, you can't come back!"

"I don't know. My dad. He's alone now." Haven answered sadly. "It sure is beautiful here, but I just don't know. I know he's not been the greatest dad in the world, but he's by himself now. My friend Sol is a mess, and she can barely take care of herself, let alone her dad."

"If you need to go it's OK."

"Why is it OK?" Haven asked.

"So you can stop the bad people."

An image of Harry flashed through her mind, but he was different. His eyes glowed yellow.

"Bad people?" Haven asked in a monotone voice.

"Yeah, they do mean things."

"You've been playing with puzzles too long up here because I don't think one person can stop all the bad. It's like...bad, bad. There is bad oozing out of people's butts. And then, right before I got here, things had just gotten a whole lot worse - as in more bad."

"Well, you can do the choose but before you do, you have to get dressed."

Haven was perplexed. "If you think I'm going to put on a dress, you're out of your mind."

"No, no, no. You have to get dressed on the mountain," she said.

Haven was now getting frustrated. "I don't understand any of this! What am I doing here? What do you mean by getting dressed?"

The little girl placed her hands on Haven's face to calm her fears. "A boat is coming. It will take you to where you have to get dressed. Don't worry. It's gonna be OK."

A loud thunderous roar shook the earth beneath their feet as a large shadow eclipsed the sun and cast its darkness over the grassy plain.

The young child smiled from ear to ear and shouted, "Here it comes!"

Haven looked up at the massive wooden clipper ship that tore the veil in the sky and bore down on them like a monstrous whale piercing an open sea. Its bow stem alone was about seventy-five yards long and as the bow broke the sky it left a sky wake that swayed even the largest of trees in the valley. As it tore through the sky, the porthole cannons came into view and they were equally massive. Haven gasped and stared intently as she noticed there were no sails on the airship and no mast. The ship was called the *SS Cato*, as inscribed on its side. An archangel stood majestically in the center of the ship's deck with its outspread wings serving as its sails. Directing the vessel downward, he pointed towards its destination. As the winds rippled through the feathers of its wings, the archangel stood mighty, strong, and silent. Despite its monstrous size and thunderous sound of wood bearing against the wind, the ship maneuvered effortlessly on the sky waves. The archangel signaled an all-stop with a motion of his hand and the ship decelerated to a hovering position over a field. Massive chains let a large wooden ramp down onto the ground where it landed in a loud thud, shaking the earth beneath.

Still in awe, Haven turned towards the child. "That's a big boat."

The child blinked and smiled. "Yes!" she exclaimed. "It will take you to the mountain where you can get dressed. But before you go, I have a present for you."

"What is it?" Haven asked.

The child walked over to the oak tree and reached into a pile of branches and pulled out an old, short-withered branch. She walked back over to Haven and handed it to her.

"What is this for?" she asked.

"It's the key for the choose. It opens gates and does other neat stuff," she said. She grabbed it back from Haven and playfully swung it back and swung it back and forth and then lunged it like a sword. "Heeya!" she shouted. "See?"

"Well," Haven began. "I'll try to put it to good use." She turned and breathed a heavy sigh as she gazed at the airship and exhaled bated breath, "OK."

The child clapped her hands in excitement and cheered for her with a "Yipee!"

Haven cautiously walked towards the ship and, the closer she got, the more massive it grew. She approached portside thinking surely there would be someone there to greet her. She gently caressed the guardrail. "Looks sturdy enough," she mumbled to herself as she walked up the ramp. She walked onto the deck and twitched at the sound of the thunderous clanking door chains. Haven then walked to the rails and looked down at the little girl who was waving and smiling. Haven waved back. She could barely hear the little girl screaming at the top of her lungs, "Choose love!"

Haven put her hand to her ear. "What? What did you say?" But by this time the clanging chains and shifting of the boat drowned out the little girl's departing message.

The doors shut with a loud thud and the archangel pointed towards the sky. Haven grabbed a hold of the rail as the ship jerked to take off. The wooden ship shook and vibrated but cruised safely above and beyond the bright skies.

Haven ran to the bow of the ship to see what wonders were ahead. As the winds pushed the giant wings of the Archangel, she turned to him. "Are there any others on the boat?" she asked the giant navigator. There was no response. "Sir?" she asked. "Excuse me?" Silence was her answer. Giving up on ever having any conversation with the brilliant archangel, she turned her attention forward. The ship carried her quite a distance and, in the journey, she was able to gaze upon creatures never before seen by man. A gargantuan griffin flew next to the ship close to the port rails. Haven gasped when she saw it, but as it moved closer, she could see the warmth of his eyes, so she edged closer. The griffin coasted closer as well, and Haven reached out and ran her hand over his side. The griffin let out a deep, thunderous bellow, which scared Haven into taking three steps back. More griffins pierced the clouds above and flew over the ship, hovering just above the deck. Haven reached up and touched the beasts which spun in contentment. In unison, they all veered off into the clouds just before the mountain came into view, beyond the horizon. Haven moved closer to the front rail to get a closer look when it came into full view.

The mountain was engulfed in night with bright shining stars floating in its hold. The ring of fire that circled the top third of the mountain looked like a crown of blazing fire. Terraces wrapped the mountain from bottom to top and the stars shined their light between them.

The archangel changed his hand position to motion the ship to slow for descent and, as they slowly dropped altitude, the ship grunted and groaned. The archangel signaled all-stop and the ship safely hovered just above the shore leading up to the valley. As the giant chains clanked loudly to let the door down, Haven's greeter came into view. The tall man was dressed in an ash tunic and a red cloak that gently waved in the wind. He stood regally against the canvas of clouds. A sword handle with no blade attached was snugly secured in his leather belt. The door landed on solid ground with a loud thud. The man came towards Haven as she strolled down the ramp and onto the shore.

"Greetings, I am Argelius and heir to the mantle of guide."

Haven stood there, eyes squinting in disbelief at his attire. "You're joking, right? Why are you dressed like that?"

Argelius motioned Haven to walk with him. "Jesting is not in my nature, young one. This is the attire of my time and since here we stand outside of time, it is quite acceptable that I dress as such. I was a soldier once, a knight called upon to defend king and country. That is, until I was called to this wondrous place where a thousand years is like a day and a day is like a thousand years."

"And where is here?" Haven asked.

"Here is where your journey of choice begins. It is my solemn duty to be your guide through this purging of human weakness as well as your training."

"Being human is not a weakness," Haven stated as she walked with Argelius.

"Ah, but it is when your weakness dictates your decisions. When you respond in haste with hate in your heart, you are unable to see the truth of the matter. You have not only been sent here to begin your training, but also, to begin a journey. A journey that will test both mind and spirit and reveal what is in your soul. Only when you know the secrets of your soul are you able to make an informed choice. And that choice being . . . to return to your earthly realm or to ascend into paradise and forever rest with all who have gone before you," said Argelius as they walked up the steep hill. It was difficult for Haven to keep up, being so much shorter than the lanky Argelius. "You will travel up the Mount of Judgment where you will find the river of choosing," Argelius said.

"I met a child," Haven said. "She said something about getting dressed."

Argelius smirked. "This carries a different meaning than what you may think, child. To be dressed in this realm is to be clothed in the virtues of selflessness, humility and love for others, and shed the clothes of envy and wrath. These are the garments she is referring to."

"How does that happen?" Haven asked.

"As with all living things, with trials by fire. By revealing those things that corrupt the soul can we choose wisely."

"Then what?" asked Haven.

"Once you reach the river of choosing, you will plunge the staff given to you by the child into it," answered Argelius. "Should you choose to return to your realm, you will do so with all of the pain and sorrow you have ever known returned to you and you must weather these with the full knowledge that you passed on the chance to never experience them again. For, should you choose paradise, you will enter in to be with your loved ones who have gone before you," he explained. "But make no mistake. The trials will test both mind and body. Come now, we must be on our way."

"Wait," Haven said. "What is your part in all of this? Why you?"

Argelius paused. "For centuries, we have been charged to protect and guide those of your family line and it is my duty to do so now." Argelius removed a branding iron from his cloak. Once it hit the air it heated up. "But first..."

"Oh no you don't," Haven said. "So help me if you touch me with that, there's going to be..." But she was too late. Argelius branded her arm with an ancient letter "D". Haven screamed. "I hate you already," she added.

"By trials and fire," Argelius answered. "You are now recognized as one of the Dante line."

"What I've always wanted," Haven answered. She continued to rub her arm. "That really hurt." Argelius grabbed her arm and passed his hand over the burn. The sizzling stopped immediately.

"Feel better?" he asked.

"Still hate you," she said. "How did you do that?"

"The gifts are irrevocable," he said.

"I don't even know what that means but fine. Let's do this," she said.

They continued on and entered a vast region void of life and full of ash, as if something horrible had happened there many years before. Haven looked around the barren wasteland as they moved on.

"What is this place?" she asked.

"It is the Valley of Rulers, child. Once this was a lush, green landscape teeming with life."

Haven snapped her head around to him and asked, "OK so first, don't ever call me 'child'. And second, if this is the 'Valley of Rulers' then where are all the rulers?"

"Some have gone to the mount while others were lost."

"So they're all . . . dead? If this is a realm beyond death how is it that they've died twice?"

"Not a death . . . but a limbo which is a fate much worse than death," he answered. "Come, child. We must make haste."

"You really need to stop calling me that," Haven said as she rolled her eyes.

Suddenly, the ground beneath their feet began to shake and the earth rumbled and roared.

"What is that?" Haven asked.

"This valley is not as barren as it seems," he said. "We must move fast!"

Haven turned to gauge where the noise could be coming from.

"Argelius?" Haven glanced around the terrain finding no trace of her guide. "Argelius, where are you?" A low rumble shook the ground beneath her. She gasped and steadied herself. "Argelius! There's something here!" No one answered her call. A crack immediately opened from the ground beneath where she stood, leading to a clearing a few feet away.

She gasped and said, "What the . . . ?"

A grayish smoke began to creep up from the fracture. Curious but cautious, Haven took a step forward and paused. Eyes fixed on the smoke, she tried to reassure herself. *It's just smoke. That's all it is. Nothing more.*

The ground exploded, revealing a monstrous serpent that shot straight up into the sky and towered above her. With debris still falling from the sky, the massive serpent curled up over Haven, ready to strike. Haven took two steps back and gasped in horror with eyes wide. Poised, the serpent's mouth opened and let out a stream of fire scorching the sooty ground. She dashed behind a boulder when the fire serpent turned to fire another blast. Then she peeked around it at the creature. Haven jumped to her feet and climbed a nearby rock face, before the serpent could discover her location. When she reached what she thought would be a safe distance, she moved behind some loose rock directly above the serpent's head and, grunting, heaved the rocks as hard as she could. The rock came tumbling down upon the head of the serpent and he let out a deafening roar and lit up the sky with his fiery breath. Knowing the location of his intended victim, the serpent took in every ounce of breath possible.

A war cry came from behind a nearby cliff. Argelius jumped down from the ledge and in mid-air he pulled out his sword, which lit up in a fiery flame. He descended onto the serpent's head and landed on it, causing the beast to sway in a frantic frenzy. The serpent's hiss was deafening as he rocked back and forth, trying to shake the warrior off. Not able to keep his grip on the serpent, Argelius was thrown off, landing on the side of the cavern. He plunged his flame sword into the rock, which instantly slowed his descent onto the ground while destabilizing the rocks above. Realizing the ground beneath her was becoming unstable, Haven leaped onto an adjacent rock face and then down to a rolling stop on solid ground. Argelius narrowly escaped the falling debris but managed to pull Haven away just in time. The falling rubble came crashing down on the monster, who gave up his fight and rushed back into the ground before the mountain came crashing down where he once stood.

Out of breath, Haven asked, "What was that?"

"The fire serpent," Argelius replied. "The beast appears at the scent of a new arrival. Come, we must not remain here lest the beast perform an encore. Are you hurt?"

"No, I'm fine . . . I think. By the way, thanks for the disappearing act. Nice to know you have my back,"

Haven said. "Guess we know what happened to the rulers."

"We need to continue. There is something I wish to share with you before we proceed to the first terrace," Argelius said.

Haven shook the dust from her clothes. "Can't wait," she said.

"Come. We are almost there."

The two travelers continued on the dusty gravel and soot deeper into the valley and through a rocky corridor. When they emerged, they found themselves on a grassy field at the base of a castle just outside of its massive, iron gate. At the entrance stood a statue of an angel with his hands outstretched as if telling those who would try to pass to stop and those inside to depart. The angel's other hand held a sword pointed outwards from the gate.

At the base of the statue there was an inscription:

Do not weep for the dead king or mourn his loss; rather weep bitterly for him who is exiled, for he shall never see his native land again.

They walked passed the gate and towards the courtyard. "You lived here?" Haven asked.

"The Castle of Isola Del Cantone," Argelius began. "My home in Genoa many years ago. It is very isolated. Very peaceful." Haven stood in the middle of the courtyard and took in the majesty of the castle, its tall stone walls and the green landscape that surrounded it. Argelius walked away from her and sat on a stone by the castle wall. "Did you grow up here?"

"I did," Argelius said. "But we are not here to relive my past."

"So why are we here?" she asked.

"To fight," Argelius answered.

Black, faceless demons began to emerge from the walls of the castle and ran towards Haven. They had arms, legs, hands and feet like humans but no features. And they were fast and fierce.

"These are the shades," Argelius said. "They are demons of the mist. Watch their tactics."

"Heh," Haven said to herself. "Welcome to my world." Haven jumped into a fighting stance but did not wait for a shade to reach her. She rolled forward, stood up in a kicking stance and thrust a sidekick into the shade. When the shade hit the wall, it phased right through it.

"What the…?"

Noticing her surprise, Argelius chimed in. "In this realm, you must cast off the chains of your understanding. Whatever you believe is what will manifest. Whatever manifests is what you believe you are capable of. Out of the abundance of the heart come your beliefs about yourself and your surroundings."

Another shade phased through a wall behind her and pulled her in halfway. Her eyes widened when she noticed she had phased into the wall along with the shade. "Works for you…" She pushed away, grabbed the shade by the head and plunged it into the ground. "Works for me," she said. Another shade swooshed to her and threw a punch but missed. Haven returned the strike, but it went right through the shade. "Come on!" she shouted in frustration. She threw another one and missed again. Another shade landed a kick to Haven's back and sent her to an adjacent wall. The stone on the wall crumbled upon impact. As more shades ran to her, she punched the wall to test it and sent pieces flying everywhere. "Hard as stone," she mumbled. Haven turned as the shades reached her. She punched on and sent it soaring through the air. "Yes!" she shouted. Another kicked and she blocked. "That's right, keep it comin'!" she said. More shades appeared. Taking turns, they all threw punches at Haven at lightning speed. But soon, she began to pant. "Yeah, I can keep this up all week," she said. The more they struck, the slower she blocked.

"They're wearing you down," Argelius said.

"Jump in and help anytime!" Haven shouted back. One shade landed a punch to Haven's gut. She collapsed and held her stomach.

"Stop!" Argelius shouted. The shades disappeared. Haven was now hyperventilating in a fetal position on the ground. He reached down to help her up. "Come. Stand." He walked her over to a wall to sit upon until she caught her breath.

"Better?" Argelius asked.

"I'm fine," Haven said. "Just used to fighting six-foot narcissists, not demons that phase through walls."

"I understand," Argelius said. "I'm sorry if I pushed you too hard. The fight that awaits you is one that will require all of you - heart, mind and soul. You are the beloved's chosen."

Haven smiled. "Beloved's chosen. Kinda like the sound of that."

"It is true," Argelius added. "But you'll only see the fruits of it when you believe it for yourself." "What is it?" Haven asked. "Oh, it's nothing," Argelius replied. "Let's get some rest."

"No, I want to go again," Haven said.

"That's my girl," Argelius said. Haven looked up and smiled. "Stay awhile and watch me take the trophy."

"You will be victorious!" Argelius shouted as he raised his fist in the air.

He reached down to help Haven stand but as he did, he noticed something in the distance. "Interesting," he said to himself. Haven stood ready. "OK, keep your eyes in the ring and your fists raised high," she declared.

"Ready?" Argelius asked. "Begin!"

Two shades phased through a wall. Haven slid between them, grabbed one by the head and smashed it into the ground. The shade smashed into a hundred pieces and slithered between the stone bricks on the ground. She then spun around, jumped back to her feet and plunged her rock-solid knee into him. That shade burst into pieces then likewise, fell to the ground and seeped between the cracks.

"Yes! Eat brick!" Haven shouted.

"Stop!" Argelius ordered. "Well done! Very well done, indeed!" Argelius said as he clapped. Haven took a bow. "Thank ye," she said. "Thank ye kindly." She looked over and noticed a beautiful pool of water just outside the walls. "Race ya!" she said as she took off.

As she plunged her face into the crystalline pool that reflected back at her, Argelius walked over to a massive tree. He looked down to the ground at the base of the tree in a moment of silence. After satisfying her thirst, Haven walked up beside Argelius.

"You fought well," Argelius said. "Your parents would be proud."

"My mom was always proud," Haven said.

"Was?" Argelius asked.

"She passed away not too long ago. 'an accident' my dad called it. I still don't know what really happened. The investigation had barely begun when whatever this is started happening to me. She always made things a little clearer for me even if I bucked her at first. She was good about pushing back but in her own little subtle way. I miss her. We'd stay up late fighting over pieces of a puzzle that we were putting together."

"I grieve for your loss. And what of your father?" Argelius asked.

"It's complicated," Haven answered. "So does this tree mean anything?"

"It is the final resting place of my parents."

"I'm so sorry," Haven said.

"It was a long time ago," Argelius said. "My mother had passed years before my father so for many years it was he, my six brothers and I."

"Wow, six. Never a dull time in that castle, I guess."

"Never," Argelius answered. "My brothers and I were hired by the French in their battle against England. The 'hundred years war' is how it became known. We defended well in the battle of Crecy, but our bows would not reach our invaders. The English had the range and the advantage. They all perished. Only I survived. It was more than my father could bear. He would soon take ill and pass. Then came the Black Plague. God's wrath on the guiles of war."

Haven placed her hand on Argelius' arm. "I'm so sorry," she said. "I don't know what to say."

"No matter, child," Argelius said. "As I said it was many lifetimes ago." He turned to Haven and smiled. "May there lie better days ahead," he said.

"Come on teacher. Let's go on to the next lesson."

"Yes," Argelius said. "Onward!"

Verdetto (The Verdict): The First Terrace

Two prison guards dragged Rob's limp body back into his jail cell. Although he was still alive, he could barely lift his head. The sweat on his brow dripped through the filth on his cheeks. His shirt was torn where the straps had held him in place. The impression of the brace that had held his head in place during his interrogation was still deeply embedded in his cheeks. The guards placed him on the cold, metal slab. The new recruit nervously looked over at the older prison guard. "Hey Jeff, do you think we need to get the doc to come in and take a look at him?"

"Naw, he'll be fine."

They both turned and locked him in. He groaned and grunted and then turned over to face the wall. His muscles cramped from being still for more than nine hours. In the cell next to his there was a man sitting with his legs crossed on a hard steel bed. He was completely bald and so thin that when he held his cigarette to his mouth even the joints in his hands were visible. He sat there quietly studying the new inmate.

"I take it you've just had your first visit with our beloved warden, Mr. Reins? What method did he introduce you to today, the corkscrew or the ear drops?" he asked.

Rob moaned and said, "Ear drops."

"Ah, the ear drops," said Anorexic Man. "Hot oil on the ear drum does not a pleasant experience make."

Rob waved his hand. "Please, I'd rather just lay here. It hurts too much to talk."

The man took a puff from his cigarette. "Oh, come now. We're going to be in here for a long time. You might as well get to know the commoners."

Rob was barely able to lift his head. "I don't even know you, so just let me be."

Anorexic Man stood up and moved closer to the glass wall. "Ah, but I do know of you, Mr. Dante. The technology you've created turned Charity Vane into the thriving technological wonder it is. You've saved us all!" he said sarcastically.

"None of that matters anymore," Rob said.

"And you have a beautiful family."

"I did . . . once," said Rob.

"Ah, traded them in to save the world. Not an equitable trade, my friend. In any case, I'm sorry to hear of your loss . . . your wife . . . your son."

Rob turned around. "My son died years ago. How do you know of my son? Who are you?"

"Just a friend. That is all. All I know is what I saw on the networks." Leaning on the glass with his right hand, Anorexic Man placed his left hand in his pocket as he inhaled. "Tell me what really happened. How did your son really die?"

"He was born with a hole in his heart." Rob's voice began to crack. "He was here just long enough for us to take a picture with him."

"Did you bury him?"

"Yes!" cried Rob. "Yes, of course we did!"

"Are you sure it was him?"

Rob sat up. "Yes! I said yes already! Why are you asking me these questions?" yelled Rob.

"Sometimes the road to healing is paved with memories past," answered Anorexic Man.

"Really?" asked Rob sarcastically. "And what was the crime that you committed that brought you here? By crossing the road to healing and reliving your mistakes?"

"No," replied Anorexic Man. "I kidnapped someone and then left him in the storage room of a train station."

Rob stood up and ran towards the glass wall. "You're lying! That wasn't you. That man was executed years ago for that crime!"

"Oh, was he? You know," he said as he ran his hand over his bald head. "I used to have hair."

Rob pounded the wall repeatedly, in a frenzy. "Shut up! Shut up, you sick twisted bastard!" screamed Rob at the top of his lungs.

"Calm down. That wasn't me. I only wanted to see if you had gotten passed it."

Rob slammed the glass wall with his fist. "You! You sick freak!"

"I killed someone, you killed someone. What's the difference?" Anorexic Man moved away from the glass wall.

Rob turned away. "I'm nothing like you."

"One thing that you're going to have to come to grips with, my friend, is the truth."

"I don't care anymore," Rob said.

"We all have monsters living inside of us. Some of us have learned to embrace them."

Rob sat back down on his cold metal slab, turned his head to the wall and lay down.

"God, help me," Rob whispered.

Soledad approached her boss behind the counter of Mickie's Pizza Place and stuffed her hat in her purse. "I'm heading out, Mickie," she said.

Mickie turned around to address his star employee. "They ever find your friend? How long's it been now?"

"No and nine months," Sol answered.

"Still no idea where she is? Just up and disappeared?"

"Yes, we've gone over this. She disappeared and no one has seen her all of this time."

"So you've been back home all this time 'cause you were staying with her right?" Mickie asked.

"I was," answered Sol. "Not anymore. I can't."

"So where you goin'?"

"Home," answered Sol.

"Listen, I got a room in the back, if you wanna bunk in there for a little bit."

"No, that's OK Mickie. Thanks, though." Sol opened the door, and, as it chimed, she walked out. "Good night."

Sol walked through the trash-riddled streets of 'The Mire' toward home. She noticed the door to her apartment was open. She slammed through the main entrance door and ran in to investigate. As soon as she came to her floor, she could smell the gas that filled the hallway. She frantically ran to her door and pulled out her keys.

"Dad? Dad are you in there?" she yelled as she fumbled to find the right key.

She banged again. No answer. After zipping through her keys, she found the right one and opened the door. Sol ran in and gagged at the strong smell of gas that was inside. She ran through the dining room towards the kitchen. She saw Trevor sprawled out across the kitchen table. There were beer cans all across the floor and two bottles of whiskey on the table with him.

"Dad get up! Dad!"

She walked towards the kitchen and out of the corner of her eye she spotted an eviction notice on the table by her dad's knee and paused. Shuffling through more papers on the table, she found a letter from a subsidiary of Dante Tech with an offer to interview. She picked it up and read the note just to make sure. Sol glared at her dad one last time and then looked into the kitchen. The oven had been left wide open with gas spewing out. Sol reached into her dad's pocket and pulled out his cell phone, which was off. Sol pressed the on button. After seeing that the phone was booting up, she dropped it on the kitchen table and left.

As Sol walked down the sidewalk, she pulled out her phone and hit speed-dial #2.

Still groggy, Trevor moved to pick up his cell phone after a few rings. "Uh. Hello?" Trevor mumbled.

"Goodbye, Dad."

The explosion blew out the entire floor of the apartment building, causing the roof to cave in a loud fiery crash.

Sol had just hung up her phone and placed it in her pocket when it rang.

"Hello?"

"Yes, is this Ms. Soledad Alden?" said the crackling voice on the other end.

"Yes, who is this?"

"Good day. This is Dominic Reins. I am the Chief Warden of the Charity Vane Penitentiary. I'm so sorry to disturb you, young lady but I've heard some wonderful things about you from one of our "guests" if I may refer to him as such. I believe you know him. A Mr. Roberto Dante?"

"Yes, what about him?" Sol asked.

"Well again, so sorry to be a bother, but I've been looking for someone to fill the shoes of my last assistant since she has gone on to other things and given what

Mr. Dante has related to me it would seem that you may be an ideal candidate for the position. I was hoping we might speak on the matter," explained Reins.

"I already have a job," retorted Sol.

"My dear, there would be substantial pay involved," said Reins. "Would you be interested?"

"OK. Sure."

"Oh splendid, my dear. Please come and visit our facility. I will have our guards waiting to escort you. I assure you that you'll be quite safe here," said Reins.

"Sure. Whatever. Thanks."

"Oh, to the contrary, my dear, thank you!" said Reins.

Sol closed her phone. She could hear the police sirens blaring and on their way. She took one last look back at the blazing inferno and stared into the fire.

La Prima Terrazza

Haven struggled to climb the steep steps of the mountainside on the way to the next terrace. "Are there no elevators in heaven?" she asked Argelius. Argelius looked out from the mountainside into the vast night sky. Haven paused for a moment to join him in appreciating the stars that danced so close you could almost reach out and grab one. She leaned against the mountain and took it all in.

"Are we there yet?" she asked.

"Close," Argelius said.

"So, whose ass am I going to have to kick to get through this test?" Haven asked as she panted. "All I need is a swig of something to drink and I'm ready to go again."

"You have good reason to be confident," Argelius said. "And all the more to muster humility - the missing link in all of humanity."

"You look plenty human to me," Haven answered. "Smell like one too." Argelius shot Haven a look of disdain. Haven scoffingly nodded. "Yeah," she added. Argelius turned away and smiled. "Made you laugh," Haven said.

"Let us continue," he said. "Aye, aye, captain," Haven answered.

Haven and Argelius reached a massive iron gate with beautiful, white pillars on each side. Within the gate stood a tall red curtain that reached into the clouds above. The bottom of the curtain was laced in decorative gold that reflected the light around them. On one of the gate posts that held the iron hinges there was a plaque with an inscription on it.

Enter into His courts with praise to stand on the day of atonement.

In the ground there was a keyhole.

Haven looked to Argelius. "I left my keys at home," she said.

"The staff," Argelius said. "The staff that the child gave you is the key." Haven reached for the branch that was hanging on her belt. As she held it in both hands, the branch grew just a little - enough to fit into the keyhole. She placed it into the keyhole. "Ok let's see what this does," she added. She snapped it in and turned it. The massive gates creaked and groaned as they opened.

"Open sesame!" Haven said. She looked over at Argelius. "It's just something us humans say."

Suddenly, two angels landed with a loud thud at the entrance gate. Each was clothed in brilliant light and adorned in the purest gold belts and stood around 8-feet tall, at least. They pulled their swords and pointed them at Argelius. In unison, they both said, "Only the beloved may go behind the veil." Argelius bowed and stepped back. Confused, Haven looked back at Argelius. "Wait, are you not going in with me?"

"It is as the guardian decrees," Argelius answered. "You will have to go into the courts without me. Fret not. I will be waiting for you on the other side."

"No, no." Haven said. "I'm not going in there alone. You got me started on this, you need to come with me. Come on, let's go." Haven started walking towards Argelius when one of the angels touched her on the shoulder. Haven closed her eyes in order to not be blinded by the bright light that suddenly surrounded her. When she opened them, she was no longer at the gate.

Haven stood on a platform in the center of a white marble courtroom. The seat where the judge sat was white marble stone that was crystalline with a bright white energy that emanated from it. Embedded in the walls of this great white hall were voices from a heavenly choir that sang holy, holy, holy over and over again in a frequency Haven had never heard. When the choir began, she grabbed her chest as if the soundwaves had reached deep within the cavity of her heart and gripped it tight. To the right of judge's seat was a greyish, old lectern whose wood was cracked. Even the glue that kept it together was rotting from within.

Suddenly, the choir ceased their worship and in one voice sang, all rise.

The judge then appeared before them sitting in the judgement seat. Two majestic guardian angels stood at his feet. His face was so brilliant that his features were untraceable. His hair flowed like rivers of light that danced on his shoulders. He looked down at Haven… and he smiled.

One of the guardian angels stepped forward. When he spoke, the floor beneath Haven's feet rumbled. "The court of the heavens is now commenced," he said. "Speak the oath," he ordered.

Haven's face turned flush and white. Her breathing was deep and heavy. "I don't understand. I don't know any oath. What is happening?"

The angel continued, "Blood cries out. Bring in the accuser." As ordered, a short, pudgy demon with bulgy eyes and leathery skin walked out from behind the curtain to the rotten lectern.

"What the hell?" Haven asked. The guardian angels reached for their swords, but the judge waved them down. "Sorry," Haven added.

The book the demon brought with him was so heavy that he had to pull it with a rope. Leaving greenish-brown slime in his wake, he dragged the book to the base of the lectern and stood on a box. He was so short that he could barely see over the top. He pulled the book up with the rope and set it on top of the lectern. After opening it, he read aloud in a raspy voice.

"The beloved stands accused of murder," he said.

"What are you talking about? I haven't killed anyone! I'd never kill anyone!" Haven shouted. The faces of the choir on the walls then disappeared and, in its place, came an image of Haven at Beatrice's funeral. As she looked over her mother's casket, her words rang through the hall.

"Why couldn't it have been him instead?" Behind the curtain from where the demon emerged, other demons cheered. The accuser chuckled to himself and closed the book.

"I didn't say that!" Haven shouted. "Even if I had, I wouldn't have done it. For crying out loud, he's my father. I may have thinking that, but I didn't say it. I wouldn't have done it. What kind of jacked up court is this?"

In unison, the angels cried, "Raca!" and the hall shook. A scroll appeared in front of them and in unison, both read to the court, "But I say unto you, that whosoever is angry with a beloved without a cause shall be in danger of the judgment and whosoever should hold rage in his heart is guilty of murder."

One of the angels stepped forward. "Does the accused speak the oath?"

Haven threw her hands up. "I told you, I don't know any oath. I didn't kill my dad. In fact, he's rotting in jail as we speak." The demons cheered louder.

The judge leaned forward. A tear came down his cheek. The guardian angels turned to the judge who simply nodded.

In unison, the angels declared, "Judgement is decreed. The accused will stand the trials." The demons hissed but the guardian angels had had enough of them. They turned and with one look, the demons ran.

"What does that mean?" Haven asked. The guardians said nothing. One of them walked up to Haven and touched her on the shoulder.

"Choose well," he said. A brilliant light enveloped them and once again, Haven closed her eyes to protect them from his brightness. When she opened them, she was on a grassy field on the side of the terrace mountain. Argelius was there waiting. "You're here which means you've fared better than some. Are you well enough to continue?"

"I've done nothing wrong," she said angrily. She then turned and continued on her journey with Argelius leading the way.

Fierrezza (The Proud): The Second Terrace

"Copy that," Gardener whispered into his head microphone. He walked in stealth-like manner making sure each step he took would not cause too loud a wake as he made his way in the sewer beneath the streets of Charity Vane. The six-foot-seven Gardener carried a makeshift but ominous weapon almost as tall as he was. It had a long barrel and what appeared to be a pressure tank on top of the barrel. His hand held the pistol-grip tightly with his finger just off the trigger, ready to fire at a moment's notice. Because he was beneath the city streets, communications were garbled.

"I do hope your new toy fulfills its purpose," stated Rose over a static-filled line.

"Ain't nobody hopes this thing works as much as I do," answered Gardener. "Believe me, I'd rather be up there stuffing my face in front of my big screen."

Gardener came around a corner looking before he went. He was over-cautious since no one had his back. "By the way, you sure this is the place?"

"The information Chief Meiko supplied to us seems to point to this location," answered Rose.

"Then how come he ain't down here looking himself?" asked Gardener as he rolled his eyes.

"They have, but they don't have the experience that we do," Rose answered. "It didn't turn out so well."

"And you trust him?" asked Gardener.

"No. Not just yet. The less he knows about us the better. For now, we'll allow him to believe we're simply a humanitarian cause seeking to reunite homeless children with their parents. Keep going, Gardener. Haven must. . ." Rose's last sentence became too garbled to understand. "Rose? Rose, are you there?"

Nothing.

"Aw, great. I'm on my own," Gardener moaned.

Unexpectedly, Gardener heard what sounded like someone humming a song. Not just someone, but a young boy. Gardener's abrupt turn caused water to slosh against the walls of the tunnel he was in. The humming became louder and louder. Gardener turned a corner. The light on the weapons he created, illuminated a short, heavyset boy with curly-red hair and freckles. In spite of the young-sounding voice, he was clearly about seventeen, possibly even eighteen. He stared at Gardener while holding a sewer rat by the tail.

"I saw it first!" the boy cried.

"Just what the heck are you doing down here?" asked Gardener.

The boy turned and sprinted away through the tunnel splashing water and making waves.

"Hey!" Gardener yelled as he ran after him. "Wait up!"

"I saw it first!" echoed through the tunnel.

Gardener came to an intersection in the tunnels. The boy was gone. He looked in all four directions. Blackness. All he could hear was the water dripping off of his wet suit. Where'd he go? he asked himself.

Gardener put his weapon down.

"Rose, can you hear me?" Nothing. "Crud, I'm too deep." Gardener backtracked to his previous position. "Rose, if you can hear me, I'm going to backtrack." He received no response. Then, he heard a whisper. Gardener stopped in his tracks. A low, soft whisper came from behind.

"I found it first," said the voice.

Gardener raised his weapon and turned to find the boy once again simply standing there. This time he had nothing in his hands. Upon closer inspection Gardener noticed the rat's tail in the boy's mouth as he slurped it back in and swallowed.

"That's messed up," Gardener said. "What's your name, son?"

"Chuck. Chuck Flegman. Nobody likes me because I'm fat."

Gardener tilted his head. "Chuck, I'm gonna take a wild guess and say that nobody likes you because you eat rats. What is up with that?"

He heard a crackling in the walls of the tunnel, so he slowly raised his weapon's light to the ceiling of the tunnel. What seemed to be several dozen people crawled on the walls in the darkness towards Gardener.

"Oh crap," uttered Gardener.

Chuck opened his eyes wider and yelled, "I saw him first!" and he lunged towards Gardener along with his sewer-mates.

"I guess now we'll see if this baby works." He aimed his makeshift weapon at one of the persons. "Come on, baby. Work."

He fired. A sphere of light shot out from the weapon striking the would-be attacker who had lunged in front of Chuck. The man immediately started to shake. In a flash, a demon was separated from its host, who landed in the water in a loud splash. The man stood up and screamed in horror, not knowing how he got there.

"Get out of here!" cried Gardener. "Head to the surface!" The man nodded and dashed to the nearest manhole cover behind Gardener.

Gardener fired a volley of shots causing several to hit the water in a loud splash.

"Ah yeah, baby! Let's get it on!" he cried as he fired away. Person after person was instantly separated from its possessing demon leaving the hosts dazed and confused.

Chuck began to throw people in front of Gardener to block his shots, releasing demons from each in turn. When Chuck jumped on the side of the tunnel to push off toward Gardener, he was not able to raise his weapon up in time. Chuck slammed him up against the wall, causing him to lose his grip on his weapon. They struggled to and fro violently crashing into walls and sending others slamming against the aged brick. One of the hosts saved by Gardener turned back around as if second-guessing her escape. Although she was scared, the young woman crept back over to where Gardener had dropped his weapon. She picked up the heavy machine and tried as best she could to aim it at the boy attacking Gardener. She screamed as she fired. In a loud thundering roar, a large gelatinous demon which looked like a blob, fell out of the young man and into the water. Panicked, the woman dropped the weapon and waved her hands in the air frantically.

"Nice shootin'!" exclaimed Gardener. The water beneath began to bubble and then boil. Gardener moved back but the woman stood motionless. Gardener propped himself up slowly. Then, a large bulbous mass began to emerge from the water. The massive gelatinous mass began to form enormous arms and legs. Like an unfinished clay monster, the beast stood with eyes glowing yellow before Gardener and the woman. One of the formerly possessed who had been trapped in muck, attempted a last-ditch effort to escape when the massive, rotund glob of jelly picked him up with one hand and swallowed him whole. After his meal, the jelly-like demon known as Voratum, moved towards the young woman placing himself between her and Gardener. When he finally spoke, his voice was just as gelatinous as his form. He spoke agitatedly.

"I am Voratum of the Third Circle. You will leave this place. Yes, you will. I demand that you leave this very instant. And you will not return."

"You like to repeat yourself a lot," quipped Gardener. "But I'm only going to say this once. I'm not leaving without the girl."

"The girl you may not have. I am still hungry. Yes. Yes. You may not take her."

"Hungry for what?" Gardener asked.

"Hungry for fear. Yes. Yes. I must feed on her fear. She provides much sustenance. Yes, she does."

Just then, a demon came out of the darkness from behind and slammed Gardener into the wall. Voratum ran towards Gardener and slammed his body against him crushing him against the tunnel wall. Gardener fell into the sewer water and came up gasping for air.

The young woman ran towards the weapon, picked it up and aimed it towards the monster.

She fired the weapon at the ceiling sending brick and rock tumbling down on their position. Just before Gardener and the young woman went out of sight, the beast re-entered the dazed, young man who leaned idly against the wall. The young woman helped Gardener up. "There's a girl here. I saw her in one of the tunnels not too far from here."

Gardener turned his focus back on the beast, who was now on the other side of the fallen debris.

"We need to move now!" Gardener yelled as he took the weapon from the daring woman. As they ran, they could hear the squeals and shrieks of demons on the other side fading away. "This way!" the young woman cried. They turned corners one after another with demons edging closer and closer. They came to a corner when the young woman yelled, "This way! She's in there!" They hustled into an open area with massive pipes keeping the streets above from caving in. Hearing a soft whimper, they looked at each other and turned a corner to find a girl tied to a pylon with a potato sack over her head. Gardener and the young woman ran over to her. Gardener threw his weapon on the ground and knelt down. He pulled the sack off of her head, revealing a young Asian girl who was about fifteen years old. Fresh tears streaked her filthy face.

"Gardener. Have you found her?" asked Rose, startling him.

"No," answered Gardener, resigned. "We found a girl though."

"Be careful," Rose said.

Gardener pulled the ropes off the young girl. "You're OK now. We'll get you back to your mom and dad, OK?" He brushed her hair aside. "Come on. Let's go."

They stood up and exited the tunnel. Gardener turned to the young woman. "This girl gets to live another day 'cause of you. Thanks for your help. Now you get to go home now, too."

"Thanks to you. Say. What were you doing down here anyway?" the young woman said.

"Looking for someone. She's about your age, actually," Gardener answered as he pulled out a holo-emitter.

With a press of a button, a holographic image of Haven popped up.

"I know her. She was a good friend. I heard about her missing in the newscasts. Maybe I can help you find her. I'll do whatever I can to help!"

"Thanks. That's mighty nice of you. Say, you seem pretty handy with tech stuff and I could use the help, so if you need a job or somethin' I can help there."

"Thanks. I actually just got a job. A good one, too. For once in my life I feel like what I'm doing matters. Like my life matters," she said.

"I know what you mean," Gardener answered. "By the way, what's your name? I'm Gardener. That's what my friends call me."

"It's nice to meet you, Gardener. I'm Sol. Soledad Alden."

La Seconda Terrazza

Haven and Argelius made their way up a steep slope of the mountain when they come across a chipped stone tablet set off to the side that was propped up on a rock. The large, weathered tablet measured about nine feet high and the carving was in Italian. As they approached, as if the tablet sensed the presence and of the traveler, the letters morphed into words that she could understand.

Pride is the veil that blinds the eyes of the soul.

After reading the words, Haven glanced over at Argelius.

"Remember, the message of each tablet will help you through your journey. Remember them well," Argelius instructed. After using her key once again, they made their way past the gate of the terrace into a landscape completely made of white marble with moving images appearing as whisks of wind on both the ground and the wall. She witnessed the falling of the Berlin Wall, the American Revolution and the passing of the first Dante through this realm. As they continued on, Haven noticed the carvings on the ground. She paused for a moment for a closer look. "Argelius . . . look at this."

He ignored her wish and pressed on. "Time is of the essence."

As Haven knelt down, the carvings began to move across the surface of the ground. Like a finger painting a masterpiece, a gentle wind motioned the carvings to take shape into an elderly woman wearing a blue-striped habit and a white robe feeding thousands of starving children. There was no sound to the carvings, only the wind. The children came running towards her from all walks of life and the more that came, the more food she had. Haven smiled lightly as she enjoyed the carvings. Argelius, now a few yards away, called for her once again. Then, the woman's withered face turned towards Haven as if she knew she was being watched and smiled brightly. Haven smiled back and stood up, waving goodbye to the elderly woman.

And the woman waved back.

Haven marched up the side of the mountain to catch up to Argelius and noticed more carvings on the side of the hill, except these did not move.

The first one she came across was a painting of a war raging between angels. On one side, Michael led an army of angels while, on the other, Lucifer led an army of blindfolded angels. In the background, the teary-eyed face of God shone above all and angels fell into the abyss as demons and formed the nine circles of Hell. Haven came to a lush, green paradise with two angels wielding fire swords against a man with a giant snake. She took a second look at the snake and then at the man. His face had been scratched out of focus. She squinted and brushed the dust away when she heard her name being shouted from the terrace. "Haven! Come!" She sighed and ran off to meet her guide.

When she came to a clearing, Argelius stood waiting for her along with wooden drays. Some were full of building materials like wood or large nails while others were filled with rotten vegetables or rocks. The wood the drays were made from was splintered and frail. Surrounding the carts were people of all ages, of all races pulling their carts, struggling with all of their might to pull the weighted dray, if only a few steps. An old man with a rock-filled dray fell over. Haven rushed over to help him up.

"There now. Are you all right?"

The man looked up with sad eyes. Haven covered her mouth and held her stomach. The man had no mouth.

"He cannot express his want to you, child. This is his burden to bear," Argelius clarified. "You have yours."

Haven turned to face Argelius. "He can't possibly pull that cart by himself! If he's on a journey like I am, then it's not a journey for him at all. It's more like a torturous punishment."

"Stay your tongue," Argelius ordered. "We all have our burdens to bear. And yours," Argelius said as he pointed away, "is over there." The bright light of the day shone upon a massive pile of dung that reached 8 feet high above the dray that contained it. Haven cringed at the smell of the excrement.

"That's a big pile of . . ." Haven began when Argelius interrupted. "When you reach the next terrace with your cart, the true nature of your burden will be made clear," Argelius said.

"It looks pretty clear to me right now. How am I supposed to pull this much crap? It's got to weigh 300 pounds! It's too heavy!" Argelius walked over to Haven's cart and easily lifted it with two hands as if he was lifting paper. "Not to me," he said.

Haven walked over to the cart. "Well, if you can pick it up then I'll give it a try." Haven tried lifting it. She heaved and puffed as she tried again to no avail. It was still too heavy.

"I can't pull this," she said. Argelius motioned towards the cart. "If this is your burden, tailored for you, then you must."

Haven took the harness and wrapped it around her waist and shoulder and pulled with grunts and groans.

She dug her feet into the ground beneath as she pulled until finally, the cart moved.

Haven heaved and pulled up the terrace. She made it around the corner, thinking of home. She grunted under her breath, "If my family had been a little more normal, I wouldn't be here. If Mom were still alive, I wouldn't be pulling this stupid cart. If Dad . . ." Haven felt the cart get heavier. "If Dad . . ." She was barely able to pull. "Aaaaahhhhh," she screamed at the top of her lungs as she collapsed. "Gotta keep going. Get up. Come on." She rose to her feet and pulled for just a few feet when she saw the very same tablet she had seen at the entrance of this terrace.

Pride is the veil that blinds the eyes of the soul.

Haven dropped to her knees gasping for air and looked up at the sign again to make sure it said what she thought it said. "That can't be. I was just there." She hunched over. "Oh Momma. I don't understand any of this." Haven looked up and saw a clear, crisp puddle of water. She ripped off her harness and ran over for a drink. She slid into the edge of the puddle and plunged her head into the cool, refreshing water. After taking a drink, she pushed herself up when she noticed her reflection in the water.

It was Rob.

Haven blinked twice and turned around. "Dad?" There was no one there. She looked down into the water again and there he was. She opened her mouth to speak, and it was his mouth opening in the reflection. Haven dipped her finger into the water to make sure the reflection she saw was not in her mind. Her reflection was still that of her Dad, confirming her fear. "In our hatred, we become the thing that we despise the most," said Argelius from behind.

Haven turned around. "I'm not him."

"And yet your reflection says something quite different. Is it such an evil thing to aspire to do good?" Argelius asked.

"Not at the expense of your own family," answered Haven.

"Well said," continued Argelius. "But in your just belief you have acquired a much more dangerous attribute: pride. It's not enough for you to be right. You take it a step further and despise those who have done wrong. Thus, you are lost in your pride, and in so doing, you convolute the truth and make it unrecognizable to others. And most importantly, the truth about yourself."

Still exhausted, Haven turned her head down in shame. "Let's try this again," she said as she walked towards the carriage. Haven placed the harness back onto her shoulders and waist and began to pull. She took two steps and then three and onwards and upwards she went.

"It's lighter," she said to herself. "It's getting easier to pull."

Haven's steps turned into a light sprint. She ran as hard as she could and could feel the mark of humility burning into her arm. Ignoring the pain, she kept going until she reached a clearing where Argelius stood. Huffing and puffing she came to a stop.

"Well done," Argelius said.

"Wasn't that something? I mean . . . I was running! Did you see that?" As she slowly turned around, she stopped and her eyes widened.

She looked up to the crystal statue of Rob holding both Haven and Cameron. Smiling from ear to ear, Rob held them close.

"That's my dad," Haven whispered.

"Your father it is," Argelius said.

Haven half-smiled and walked closer. She gently placed a hand on Cameron.

"Cameron," she sighed. She looked into the eyes of the representation of Cameron and noticed a tinge of light barely visible emanating from his eyes. She blinked and then looked over at the representations of Rob and herself. Those eyes were clear. She turned towards Cameron again and searched deeper and confirmed what she saw . . . light.

Haven's arms began to burn intensely. She held them until she could hold it in no more. "Aaah!" she screamed as the tribal marks on her arms surfaced. Just as her arms burned, her staff grew in strength and length. Haven had received the mark of humility. Argelius placed his hands over her arms to ease the burn.

"Thanks," Haven said.

"Onward?" Argelius asked.

"Onward," Haven answered.

Furja (The Wrathful): The Third Terrace

Haven and Argelius approached the third gate. But instead of a wrought iron gate, the entrance to this realm was an energy shield resembling a white curtain held up by two pillars. On one of the pillars, they saw a plaque with an inscription.

La Terzo Terrazza

Wrath is a shroud that covers the prayers of the afflicted.

As Haven inserted her staff, Argelius grabbed her hand. "On this terrace, you must contend alone," he said. "Once again, I may not go with you." Haven tilted her head. "You're supposed to be my guide," she said. "So far, the only thing you've trained me on is how to fight and most of that, I already knew how to do. Maybe not fight with the shades but still."

"This is a path you must take alone," Argelius simply said. "Ok but you haven't said why," she answered. "Geez, you're starting to remind me of my dad."

"There are some lessons that are best learned alone," Argelius said.

"Is this really one of them?" she asked. Argelius gave her no response. "Ok, fine. So what am I in for?" she asked.

"The 'Terrace of Contention' is a place where angels war with the shades that are trying to stop them from delivering the answer to the prayers received by the Creator," Argelius explained.

"What do I have to do?" Haven asked.

"You must learn to hear the voice of the Creator and act accordingly. Anger, wrath or unforgiveness will prevent you from hearing clearly. The Creator will hear the cry of the broken and send you on the mission to either slay the demon that is preventing the prayer from being answered or be the answer to the prayer."

Haven stopped him. "Look, I'm not even big on prayer, I don't even know if I believe in prayer, I don't even say grace so how am I supposed to…"

"You are the beloved," Argelius said. Then he turned and left. "I will await you on the other side."

"But…" Haven sighed as she watched him leave. "Some guide." She then turned the key.

The shield curtain that served as the gate reached out and enveloped her. Haven was on an otherworldly platform that floated in the dust of the stars. The black of space surrounded the platform with a floor made of pure white light. Every step she took let out a short burst of energy beneath her feet. She walked over to the edge and from there could see other terraces floating in the vastness with brightly hung stars behind each. "Oh," she said as she took two steps back. Suddenly, she started hearing whispering voices behind veils of light on her platform. And they did not sound friendly.

"You have no place," said an eerie voice behind a veil.

"You're not worthy of the mantle," shrieked another.

"Did you father ever care?" "You're all alone."

"Stop it," Haven ordered.

A shade appeared in front of her. It squealed, "She's dead and now you have no one!"

"Stop!" Haven shouted. As the word left her lips, an angel appeared behind the demon and slashed its throat. The shade evaporated into black dust. The angelic warrior looked at Haven and smiled. He then disappeared. Haven could sense movement behind her. When she turned around, she gasped at the myriad of angels battling demons. Angel swords whistled through the air with every strike. In every battle, a ray of light tethered from high above the fighting angel on the platform. Haven turned and noticed an angel strike down a demon with its sword. She turned and reached for the branch on her belt. "Great," she said to herself. She pulled it out and held it in two hands. "Better than nothing," she added. The branch grew a few inches. There were three marks on it that glowed. Just as quick, the marks on her arms lit up. "Whoa," she said. A demon jumped out at Haven. "You are not beloved," he shrieked. Haven smashed his face in with her weapon. Another demon jumped out in front of her.

"He never loved you," he squealed. Haven spin-kicked him in the face and followed up by smashing his head into the ground. He evaporated just as quickly as he appeared. Another shade grabbed Haven from behind. "You're not beloved," it shrieked. Haven bent her knees, popped the shade in the face, grabbed him and brought him crashing into the ground. More shades appeared and fiercely ran towards her, yelling words made to destroy her from within.

"You were always in his way."

"He just left you there."

"You're all alone."

Haven knelt down and covered her ears. Amidst the vicious verbal assaults, she remembered Beatrice's still small voice.

"Peace be still," she would say to calm Haven's fray. Haven took a deep breath. She opened her eyes. The shades were gone. Then she heard another voice. From far away she heard her father pray two simple words. "Help me," he said. And Haven heard it.

"Dad?" she asked. Then in the deep recesses of her soul she heard the unmistakable voice of another. Haven turned towards where she thought the sound came from. A vortex of mist formed and within, she could see an image. It was Rob in his cell. He was in a fetal position. His breathing was shallow.

"Dad?" Haven said. Rob could not hear her. Haven's lip quivered as she dropped to her knees.

"Oh Dad," she whispered.

Suddenly, a door leading to Rob's cell opened. It was Jinx. She held a case in her hand.

"Rob?" Jinx said. Rob did not move.

"Rob, wake up," Jinx said forcefully.

Rob turned. Jinx smiled.

"I brought you some soup," she said. Rob returned the smile. He turned and folded up a letter he had been writing.

"Prayer answered," Haven said.

A barrage of demons appeared. Haven stood confidently. Then she heard a voice.

"Go," He said.

She took a running start and barreled through the shades that were in her way. Of those that did not fall away, she side kicked, hook kicked and bombarded the hoard with punches and kicks. Even the angels began to take notice and joined her in the fight. One angel looked at her and nodded as if giving her his approval. Haven then turned and jumped off of the terrace. She flew down through the vastness of cold space like a comet. As she did, more marking burned into her arms and her weapon. She landed with a loud thud on the terrace below. She took a moment to catch her breath and stood up. A mist began to form around her. Onward she went. Alone. But with her first solo victory in hand.

∞

Sol marched through the dingy halls of Judas Cradle Maximum Security Prison passing inmates who scoffed and howled at her. All of them were in an uproar about her visit. She ignored the scowling and the profanities. Up the metal stairs she climbed to Dominic Rein's office, which overlooked the main hall of the prison. The large metal door to his office clanked when the guards opened it. It was more like a safe than an office, with books stacked as high as the ceiling from wall to wall. Most were psychiatric in nature, while others explained the science of chemistry. Vials and bottles of various sizes were on display on a large metal table to the left of his desk. Reins sat in his large wingback chair, still wearing the same long black leather jacket and round-rimmed glasses. He had an unusually wide smile on his face that, coupled with his thin lips, made his teeth shine even in the darkest of places.

"Oh, do come in, my dear. This is such a delight!" Reins exclaimed as he clapped his hands. "Please do tell me what you have found, you delicious little creature, you. Please. Come closer."

"You were right. The ones searching for Haven revealed themselves. Your friend's trap worked well to bring them out in the open," Sol reported.

"Oh, delight of delights!" shouted Reins. "Tell me scrumptious, who are they?"

"They run a homeless shelter called Desert Rose within 'The Mire'. It's close to where I lived, so I should be able to find it easily. There is one thing though."

"Tell me, my dear, what is it? What wonderful giddy, delightful query clouds your mind? Tell me."

"There is something I don't understand," Sol began. "I've known Haven all of my life and she's never mentioned these people. Why would they be interested in her?"

Dominic raised one eyebrow and slowly stood up. "Why, indeed. Why, why, why, why indeed, you say."

"There must be something more they're after. This isn't all about Haven," Sol said. "What do they want?"

Reins walked behind Sol and rubbed his fingers across her shoulder. As she cringed, she took a step forward.

"You're right. But if you are going to become part of this family, or should I say, lead this family, then you should know it all," he said. "You see, my dear, Mr. Dante has created a magnificent device that will allow us to dwell on the surface, open and free. Quite lovely, wouldn't you say?"

"I would," Sol answered.

Reins smiled slightly. "Of course, you would my dear. In any case, Mr. Dante has chosen not to use this device to its full potential. That is where you come in, my dear. We need the device to usher in our reign!" he said as he threw his arms in the air.

"And what do I get out of it?" Sol asked.

"Oh, my dear, you will be the beneficiary of our good will! You will have every need met and want for nothing! From that point on, you will live only to enjoy life! You will no longer strive for the evils of wealth, stature and significance. You will live life to its fullest at last!" he exclaimed as he clapped his hands.

"More than my father was ever able to give me," Sol said.

"Yes. So much more. You will finally be at rest, my child," Reins said. "You know, there is so much more to life than the human mind can comprehend if people will only embrace it."

"What do you mean?" asked Sol.

"Join us in spirit!" he exclaimed.

It was then that Hedonis stepped out of the shadows. "Embrace us and find your wonderful place of security!" Hedonis said. The massive satyr stepped in front of Sol who looked up and did not fear the dark. Hedonis looked down at Sol and his eyes glowed yellow.

"You smell delicious," Hedonis said. Sol smiled slightly and Hedonis returned the smile. Then, Hedonis began to morph into a pile of snakes and one by one each entered into Sol's mouth. Sol squirmed in discomfort as she turned away from Reins' view. Her grunts and moans soon gave way to deep chuckles of joy until the two became one, not noticing what was happening to Reins. Sol turned back around and her eyes glowed yellow.

"I feel so much better," she said in a low gruff voice.

"Oh wonderful, my dear," Reins said. "And now that we have let our hair down, so to speak."

Sol looked up at Reins, who was sitting in his chair in a catatonic state. She turned to face a dark corner of the office where the voice came from. A wry smile came to Sol's face as she looked up at Reins' demon who had shown his true form; a massive dragon with yellow eyes and 12-inch fangs and yellow plating that armored his underbelly. It towered over Sol and she showed no fear.

"You may address me as Lord Hordran of the Fourth Circle. I see the most delightful things in your future, my dear. Welcome to the family!"

"Thank you, Lord Hordran," Sol replied as she bowed her head in submission.

Misericordia (Mercy): The Fourth Terrace

Haven made her way through the mist. Although the fog was dense and obscured her vision, it was not overpowering or suffocating. She came upon a stone gate with an inscription written in stone overhead:

Mercy is carried on the sea of empathy but lost in the fog of enmity.

She used her key once again and passed through the gate.

La Quarta Terrazza

Haven heard raspy voices in the haze. She looked around but saw nothing. She picked up her pace and the voices became minutely louder the deeper into the terrace she went, until she could hear what each was whispering. "Seize," a voice said. Another emerged from the mist. "Seize." And yet another said, "Seize." She picked up her pace even faster until she saw a shadow beginning to emerge from within the smog. An extremely thin, bald man stood staring at Haven.

"I know you," Haven said. More men exactly like him began to emerge from the smoke, surrounding Haven. "What do you want?"

"You are not him," one of them said.

"I am not who?" she asked.

"Him. The one who betrayed us. The one who ran from us to join the destroyer," the man said. "We chased him here from the Valley of Rulers, but he was no more." Then, as if on cue, they formed an opening, giving her a clear path out of their mist.

"Go," another said.

Haven ran as fast she could back into the smoke. After a few yards she stopped to catch her breath. While she was stooped over, she heard it. Carnival music. And it was not far away. The music grew louder and louder as she walked towards it. Wanting to know the source of the music, she sprinted until she came to a clearing. It was the Charity Vane Carnival just as it was 10 years before. The bright lights, her favorite rides; the smell of elephant ears filled the air as did the dust beneath her feet. Her favorite ride was the parachute drop. Watching it come down, her heart filled with the joy of childhood. Here there were no worries, no cares, only fun and laughter. Wide-eyed and smiling, Haven ran to the carnival.

She ran past the main entrance into the center square and looked around to take in the sights, sounds, and smells of one of her favorite pastimes. When she stopped, her shoulders dropped, and she stopped smiling. She took a step closer to what she just saw.

"Mom?"

Beatrice couldn't hear her as she was comforting a young child who had just gotten sick from a ride. Next to that child was another. It was Haven 10 years ago. Haven watched as Beatrice lovingly stroked the child's hair and held a cup of water for her to drink. The young Haven stroked the child's back and comforted her with kind, encouraging words.

Wanting to reach out, Haven crept towards them until an odd bald man who looked exactly like Anorexic Man, except this one was covered in zippers, stopped her. Every inch of his tight-fitted, black, long-tailed suit was covered in zippers, even his zebra fur top hat. He smoked a cigarette from an elegant holder.

"Hold on there, lassie. Where do ya think you're going?" he asked in a thick Scottish accent.

"I want to go see my . . . " she turned before she could finish her sentence. Beatrice, Haven and the little girl were gone.

"Mom . . . Sol."

"Aye, they're gone ya see?" he said. "Have ya thought of stayin' close to yer loved ones, missy? Ya stand less of a chance of losin' them in the crowd. Say, speakin' of losin' someone, there was a chap who came through here some time ago. Not a very nice fella he was. Aye, we thought he was a good man, but he had a way about him. He left the valley in ruins and now everything is out of order. So whataya say, missy? Have ya seen him?"

"Who are you?" Haven asked.

"Well 'round here they just call me Mr. Zippers on account of me having all these. It's pretty obvious, don't cha think?"

"The man you're looking for. What does he look like?" Haven asked.

"Well, missy, he walks around like everyone should hear what he's sayin', ya know. I heard that somethin' happened at tha front gate and that things have nay been the same around here since. He wears a cloak like he's got somethin' to hide. So, enough with the chit-chat. Tell me, missy. Have ya seen him?"

"No, I'm afraid not," Haven answered while she looked away. When she turned back the point of Mr. Zippers' nose was right up next to hers. She gasped at his quickness.

"Question is, missy: would ya tell me if ya did?" asked Mr. Zippers as he waved his long, pointy finger at Haven.

"Um," Haven said, averting her eyes. "I have no reason not to."

"Aye, there's an answer for ya." Mr. Zippers pulled away. "Well then. Ya best be on yer way, little girl. Speakin' of, ya got quite the journey ahead of ya, so let me help you on yer way there."

"No, really I think if I just head straight . . . " Haven began. But before she could finish, the man opened one of the pouches on his chest and removed a vial of some sort of concoction. He then opened the bottle and poured a purple liquid into his hand, he blew it in Haven's face.

"When ya see the cloaked man, missy. Tell 'im I'm lookin' for 'im."

"Oh, that is disgusting! What is that?" The purple spray covered her face and blinded her. When it dissipated, she found herself back . . .

. . . in her bedroom.

Haven rubbed her eyes and looked around her room. The karate trophies were all there. Sol's waitress uniform hung on the door. "This is the morning he told me," she said to herself. Haven sat up. At the foot of her bed Rob stood motionless as if he had been there all night. His eyes were grief-stricken and his breathing was shallow.

"Dad?" Haven asked, knowing what was coming.

Rob turned towards her. "Honey. Something has happened. Something. . .terrible." Rob recounted how Beatrice had died in a terrible accident on the way home on that dreadful evening. He told her how the driver of the transport vehicle had fallen asleep at the wheel, sending him crashing into Beatrice's motorcycle. That she had died on impact.

Haven started to shake. "Why? Why was it her and not you?" Her lip quivered. She picked up her third-place karate trophy and threw it across the room. As soon as it hit her dresser mirror, the sound of the shattered glass snapped her back into the moment he stood at the foot of the bed. She was met once again with her father's resigned despondency.

"Haven. There's been an accident." Rob told his daughter. And he went on to relate to her how Beatrice slid off of a city side road and flew off of her motorcycle and onto an oncoming vehicle, dying upon impact. Haven clenched her sheets. "If you had been here, you could have stopped her from leaving!" Haven picked up a second-place karate trophy and looked at her father, screaming "I hate you! I'll always hate you! It should have been you!" Haven threw the trophy across the room.

When it shattered the mirror, Haven found herself right back where she started, seeing her dad, a man broken, standing at the foot of her bed.

"Sweetheart, it's just you and me now," he said.

She picked up a first-place trophy, but it wasn't for karate. The trophy said, Charity... First place. She held it tight. A hand reached out and grabbed the hand that held the trophy. Haven turned.

Beatrice sat next to her. Beatrice placed the other hand on Haven's back, comforting her. "I love him, and I know he loves you too," she said. Haven looked back down at her trophy and smoke filled the room once again. When it dissipated, Mr. Zippers stood unzipping a pouch on his arm. He removed a potion bottle. He opened it with care and sprayed the blue liquid in Haven's face.

"Don't forget, lassie," he whispered. "Tell 'im I'm lookin' for 'im." As the mist around her began to form, more markings etched into her arms and her staff grew slightly in strength and length. When the mist dissipated,

Haven found herself at the exit of the gate and Argelius waiting there for her.

"I lost track of you," Argelius said. "What happened in there?"

Haven lifted her arms which now had more burns on them. "This," she said. Argelius grabbed her arms. "Let me help," he said. He ran his hands over them, and the burning stopped.

"Onward?" Haven asked.

"Onward," Argelius said.

"Lord Hordran," began Sol, "I've seen the ones who strive against us. The ones who seek the one called from the line."

Hordran shook as he approached Sol. "Do not dismay, my sister. They will not find the one they seek, but if they do, we will use the opportunity to draw her into our realm by using her father as bait! Oh, how delightful this will be! Oh yes, yes!" Hordran frantically clapped his hands. "The daughter will come to the rescue of the father, who will operate our machine for us! Oh scrumptious!"

"Is this the device you mentioned earlier, my lord?" asked Sol.

"Oh, my dear, open your mind to the one who inhabits you now," Hordran instructed. "The knowledge is in he who created the device for human purposes but we, my dear, will recreate our lovely landscape here on the surface and we will rule over the human infestation!"

"I see the plan now, my lord," Sol replied. "I see everything more clearly."

Hordran walked around his office and brushed his hands on Sol's shoulders. "You, dear one, will reign with us forever. Oh yes, you will, and you will be granted every delightful wish and want you can possibly imagine! Think of it! No more wars. No more hunger. No more pain!"

Sol smiled, "I am grateful, Lord Hordran."

"Oh nonsense, my delightful one, it is you who should be thanked. You will be the key that will unify us all and bring about peace and stability. With a stable, unified authority we will lead a new era for change that will bring the countries of the world together as one in harmony and understanding."

Sol looked over her shoulder. "That will be a great day, Lord Hordran."

"Oh a delightful day indeed," he responded. "I want you to remain closely linked with this band, my dear. Help them, if need be. Become one of them so that we may know their plans and we may head them off. Do not let them be made aware of your loyalties, my precious one, and be patient and wise."

"Understood, Lord Hordran," Sol answered.

"There is something else, my dear child," Hordran continued. "Now that you have merged with Hedonis, I think that you shall have a new name. Oh yes, a new name, how delightful."

"What do you think it should be, Lord Hordran?" Sol asked.

"Oh. Let's see. Hmm. I think," Hordran said as he rubbed his hands together. "I think it shall be Solstice! Yes! Your new name is Solstice! Oh, how lovely your new name is."

"I like it," Sol said. "Solstice."

Rose leaned over the massive conference table and her concerned face shone in the light that descended from overhead. "What was her name?" she asked.

"She said her name was Soledad Alden," Gardener answered.

"Oh dear," Rose gasped.

"What is it?" Gardener asked.

"Bring her up on the monitor," Rose snapped back.

Gardener placed his hand in a vat of liquid and began manipulating it. Liquid screens descended from the ceiling and formed a display screen directly in front of him. Rose walked around the table to face the monitor.

Name: Soledad Cailey Alden
Age: 18
Parents: Trevor and Cailey Alden (both deceased)

"That's Haven's friend," Rose answered.
"What?" Gardener said surprised.

"Bring up each parent separately and cause of death of each," Rose ordered. Gardener manipulated the vat to bring up the information.

Trevor Alden. Date of Death: June 21, Cause: Accident.

"Bring up detail," Rose asked.

Aged gas line rupture sparked by an unknown source resulting in explosive reaction.

"Bring up detail on her mother," Rose asked.

Gardener complied.

Cailey Alden. Date of Death: June 21. Cause: Accident.

"Check to see if there is any video footage of the incident," Rose ordered.

"Checking," Gardener answered. "Found something." An image of a cross street came up on the screen. As they moved closer to the screen, the video showed a car crashing against a guardrail and coming to a complete stop. After a few seconds, an explosion from underneath the vehicle catapulted the car over the guardrail sending it crashing into an oncoming truck below.

Gardener took a step back and turned towards Rose. "No way that car hit the guardrail hard enough to send it flying. No way."

Rose pointed towards the vehicle just behind the one Mrs. Alden was driving. "Zoom in on the driver of that vehicle."

Gardener placed his hand back in the vat. The image zoomed in on the driver. His eyes were glowing yellow and he had a device in his hand that was pointed towards Mrs. Alden's car. Rose and Gardener took a step back.

"We should tag this girl," Gardener said.

"Agreed," Rose said. "But something tells me that she'll be looking for us . . . and for Haven. And when she does, we need not turn her away."

Gentilezza (Kindness): The Fifth Terrace

"Why is he looking for you?" Haven asked Argelius as they walked the narrow, stone road to the next terrace. "He sounded like he had a score to settle."

"This is a road full of spirits and unwanted diversions. Anyone on such a narrow path can find themselves distracted from their intended destination. You must be very careful about whose truth you take in, lest you find yourself swept away at any point in this journey. Even at the end of this journey, just when you think you are at victory's gate, there is a river that leads back to Hades should a traveler make the wrong choice. So put aside doubt and do not question."

Haven kept quiet and pensive, knowing that if she was to reach the peak of Mount Judgment she had no choice but to see this journey to its end. She looked up at her traveling companion and guide, and for the first time in this long, perilous journey, she allowed herself to arrive at a place in her mind where all possibilities were laid before her. And she doubted him.

La Quinta Terrazza

Haven and Argelius hiked on to the entrance of the fifth terrace, which was made of jagged-edged rocks. She read the inscription on the stone gate.

Kindness withheld is an evil unto itself.

Argelius asked Haven, "Would you come to the aid of another, even if it meant that your choice could be wrong?"

She snapped back, "How would coming to the aid of someone be the wrong choice?"

A brisk wind shot by them as if something flew by at breakneck speed, almost knocking them over. The wind came back and blew by them again, this time emitting a high-pitched sound that was alluring to the senses. Then another and another. Finally, a white mist hovered directly in front of them, moving from one side of Argelius to another.

Haven's staff had grown to a meaningful length by this point. She pulled her staff out from her back strap and tapped on the ground. When she did, the mist around the staff gave way to the sound of it hitting the ground. She tapped again - this time a little harder. The mist moved farther away from them. Far enough so they could see where the cry was coming from.

"It is a white siren," Argelius said. "Foul creatures."

"She doesn't look so foul to me," Haven said.

The creature had long stringy hair, bleach white powdery skin and black lips to match her dark eyes. She wore what looked like a thin veil that was ripped. Her hands and feet were contorted as if crippled and she was chained to a rock. They could see the song as sound waves emanating from the creature's parched lips. The Siren let out a deafening cry.

"Freeee meee! Freeeee meee!"

Haven swung her staff on the rock the siren was tied to. The chains and rock exploded into a million pieces. The siren was free. When the dust and soot dissipated, the siren was replaced by a beautiful young woman of fair skin, blond hair and brilliant green eyes whose inner light comforted Haven.

The young woman walked up to Haven and gently kissed her on the cheek. "Thank you," the siren sweetly said. "You've delivered me from my captivity."

From behind, the fire sword of Argelius penetrated the siren's back exiting through the belly. The siren screamed high-pitched squeals in utter agony.

"What have you done!" screamed Haven. "What is wrong with you? She was free!"

Unexpectedly, the siren's clothes ripped open, revealing a beast many times larger than her previous form. The White Siren had wings shaped like a bat and white hair and eyes.

"Freedom is not what she needs. The sirens are at war with the terrace inhabitants and they are resolute in their desire to lure those on the narrow path away from it. You must learn to choose wisely for whom you bestow your kindness."

That did not sit well with Haven. Not one bit. Haven reached for her staff. The White Siren flapped her wings and hovered over the guide.

"Yoouuuu will never reach yourrrr dessstination!" The siren screeched while pointing at Argelius. She then flew off with a deep gust of wind beneath her.

Haven glared at Argelius with her staff drawn. Argelius stood defiant as well, with his fire sword lit, ready to answer her defiance.

"You wish to challenge me?" he asked.

Haven put her staff back in her holster, realizing that she needed him for the rest of this trip.

"You must choose wisely upon whom to bestow your kindness," Argelius said.

"My kindness should not be withheld from anyone," Haven said.

"Including your father?" Argelius answered.

"She didn't do anything," Haven said.

"You will be proven wrong," Argelius said. "But for now, come. We must continue moving forward."

They came to a rocky hill overlooking a sea of muck and mire. "This is the Valley of Sloth," explained Argelius. "Here the sirens fight against the souls who lie buried in the mud. Souls who were indecisive in their moral convictions. The sirens lured them here using their songs of self-pity only to trap them using their sonic screams." Argelius turned to Haven. "The cycle is endless. These are the souls who blame others for their moral laziness. They believe that they will one day be set free, but they are wrong."

The eyes of the souls were opened slightly so as to witness what was happening just above them. Haven reached for the closest trapped soul buried in muck and attempted to bring her to her feet. Contrite, the weary soul simply looked up at her and smiled while remaining limp.

"Come on! Get up! I'll get you out of here!" Haven pulled and pulled to no avail.

"You must stay on the straight and narrow, Haven of Dante!" cried Argelius.

"What about the people?" she cried. "I can't just leave them here like this!"

"Do not stray from your path, my friend!" Argelius yelled. "Salvation for all lies in you accomplishing your goal!"

Haven tried to take steps towards her goal and the weight of the mud made it increasingly difficult with every step she took.

"I can't," she mumbled.

Argelius sighed heavily as if disappointed by his pupil's ignorance. "Haven of Dante, if you are not saved, none of us will be!" He stretched out his leg to take a step and his foot landed on the back of a soul trapped in muck. The slush of the mud underneath the trapped one made Haven cringe. Step after brisk step, Argelius made his way quite easily to Haven and passed her in the quest for safety. As he made his way to the other side, after dodging spears and sonic screams, he turned towards Haven and commanded her to follow likewise. Haven looked down at one of the souls who returned her stare with hungry eyes pleading for help. Argelius again commanded her to hurry.

Haven reached for the helpless one, pulling her arm as hard as she possibly could. The limp body barely moved in the sludge an inch before coming to a stop.

The sirens on the other end turned their song into screeching and flew towards Haven, who looked left and right, not able to see a way out. In the last moment before either side reached her, Haven disappeared into the muddy slime of the earth beneath. Haven was completely submerged. Suddenly, a vortex began to form in the middle of the massive muddy slush. Argelius looked closer and seemed bewildered by what was happening. The sirens shook as the earth beneath them trembled. In a sudden explosion, the mud and sludge shot out from the center of the field and formed two walls of sludge, leaving Haven standing with the end of her staff having cracked the ground. She was clean and strong in the midst of all those who, once lifeless wretches, now stood washed and unsoiled. The walls of mud kept the sirens at bay. Haven lifted her staff and motioned to the others to leave this place, and they indeed followed her to freedom. As she walked past Argelius, the guide stood bewildered.

"No one ever achieved greatness by walking on the backs of their fellow man," Haven said. She turned towards the first lost soul she had tried to remove from the muck, whose back was now turned away from her, and placed her hand on her shoulder, turning her around.

It was Haven herself, as a younger child. Haven gasped. "What is this?"

The child who was Haven spoke sweetly and lightly, "When you free others, you free yourself!" Then she and the others turned into a fine mist of light and, after dancing and circling around Haven, they floated upwards, fading into the sky.

Haven's arms burned once again, and her staff grew slightly in strength and length.

"Why are you doing this?" Haven asked Argelius. "Guiding me on this journey?"

"It is my duty," he answered.

"That's your only reason? Because it's your duty? Why you?"

Argelius turned a quizzical eye towards Haven. "Why would you ask such a preposterous thing? Do you not see the benefit of having a guide through such a perilous journey? I am here to ensure that you reach your final destination. I would have thought this would have been made clear by now."

"I'm not so sure," Haven answered.

The Wedding Feast

It was hard to see through the thick foliage. Withered vines and moss clung to the trees that seemed to tower endlessly into the sky. As they walked through the dark, murky forest, they could hear the swaying trees creak back and forth and dead leaves gently falling like the morning dew.

"Here we must be extremely careful, for we are in the Forest of the Nexus," Argelius said. "Many have come through this realm and have never left. One wrong turn and you could end up in limbo - the space between the spaces and the times between the times."

"It looks harmless enough," Haven said.

"It is much more," Argelius said. "The forest of the nexus is where all of the realms interconnect."

After a few hours of trekking on the dusty road riddled with rocks and dead tree branches, they came upon a clearing. A bowl of fruit and a cup of water sat on a tall tree stump. The bowl was dusty and worn, but the fruit and water were fresh, as if someone had just picked the fruit off of a tree and poured the water.

"That's odd," Haven said as she pulled out her staff. "But I'm really famished." She took one step and held her staff by the end with one hand, She pushed the bowl over, tossing it on the ground. She bent over and picked up a beautiful red, ripe fruit and turned around towards Argelius, who now stood a few feet behind her.

"Hungry?" she asked. She paused and looked beyond Argelius. An arrow now headed towards his head from behind him at breakneck speed.

"Get down!" she yelled. Argelius complied and fell to the ground. When the arrow came into view, Haven saw a rope attached to it. As it landed on the tree in a loud thud just behind Haven, the rope became taut. Haven reached up to touch the rope, stopping when she heard the sound a hundred, maybe thousands of arrows whizzing through the air. All at once, arrows with ropes tied to their nocks came from every direction hitting their targets until they formed a net just above their heads. Once the net was complete, the trees with the arrows embedded in them came crashing down all around them forcing Haven and her guide close to the ground.

"I can't move," cried Haven.

"I am immobilized as well," answered Argelius.

The rope was not thick, but it was strong, as Haven found out when she tried to push upwards in a feeble attempt to snap it.

"Can you reach your sword?" Haven yelled.

With grunts and groans, Argelius tried to budge his hand even an inch, to no avail.

A large thud shook the ground beneath them. Already gazing in that direction, she focused her eyes on the bowl of fruit, which lifted from the ground with every thunderous pound. These were the footsteps of a giant who came closer by the second.

Almost in a panic, Haven tried her best to turn every which way she could, but all she could move were her eyes. The giant's steps came closer and closer until they stopped. She heard creaking right behind her head, which slowly made its way around to face her.

It was the face of a tree, and not a kind one. Its massive nose was larger than Haven's torso. It moved closer and opened its squinty eye directly in front of Haven.

It moved away from Haven and said in a loud, thunderous male voice, "Who dares invade my forest?"

"My name is Haven. Haven Dante," she said hesitantly.

"Dante?" answered the tree. "How dare you desecrate my realm with your filthy presence?"

Haven's breathing became shorter. "I . . . I'm just trying to reach the peak of Mount Judgment."

"Silence!" ordered the tree. "Remove the prisoners and bring them with us!" he ordered. "Remove their weapons! Bind their hands!"

In unison, the trees wrapped Haven and Argelius up in a makeshift cage and removed Haven's staff and Argelius' sword. Then they marched through the forest in thunderous footsteps that could surely be felt miles away.

"I am Gnosius," the tree answered. "I am a descendant of the Tree of Knowledge of Good and Evil and whoever eats of my fruit will taste death! Rumors of the desolation of the Valley of Rulers have reached this far up the mountain. Those same rumors speak of the destroyer, the one who has brought about that destruction. Someone who goes by the name of Dante. This would not be you, would it?

"No. I mean, that's my name but I had never passed through the valley until recently. And I'm hoping I never have to again," Haven said.

Gnosius moved towards Argelius. "And who is your guide, this companion of yours?"

"I am Argelius. Guide to the Dante through the terraces," he answered for himself.

Gnosius pointed his lengthy finger at Argelius, "I have seen many a guide through my realm, but you I have never laid eyes upon."

Haven interrupted. "Gnosius. There was no sign of life when I got there, none at all. I promise," she said.

"Very curious," Gnosius replied. "You say you go by the name of Dante, yet you also say the valley's misery was complete before your arrival."

"That's not something I would do," Haven said as she sat in her cage.

Gnosius stopped in his tracks and gazed upon Haven closely once again. His voice boomed. "Curious indeed."

As the trees, with thunderous footsteps, hauled their captives through the dark forest, Haven heard a rustling of leaves and spotted shadows moving in the midst of the dense foliage on either side. This seemed to go unnoticed by Gnosius, as if he were used to the creatures that populated this realm. Haven peered through the net and saw a bald, short, rather round beast peeking out through the foliage. He had sunken eyes, a pug nose and pink skin. He briefly poked his head through, then tucked himself back into the foliage and out of sight. Haven could hear a minor rumble and saw leaves flying up in the path of whatever was rolling through the forest toward her. The creature halted and popped its head through the trees once more and then sped away.

The majestic giants crunched and thundered through the forest until they came to a clearing. Haven's eyes widened at the scene of complete debauchery. A giant centaur in a drunken stupor tripped over a chair and landed on a table laden with roasted meats and delicacies of many varieties that seemed to go on beyond human sight, stretching beyond this realm. His landing sent a silver plate full of fruits and meat hurdling through the air. Several of the round creatures with pug noses that Haven had seen in the forest surrounded the table. With food and drink dribbling down their pink hairy chins, they all stopped in their tracks and turned to face Gnosius and his captives. The interruption lasted only a moment before the creatures continued their gluttonous frenzy.

"I will address the captives now," Gnosius commanded. The cages landed on the ground with a loud THUD!

"Hey! Easy!" Haven tried to rub her sore bottom but couldn't reach with her hands still bound.

"Oh my stars," Argelius exclaimed.

Haven and Argelius stood up and moved towards the cage bars as Gnosius came closer to address them. From where they stood, they had a better view of the giant who stood before them with outstretched arms and long tangled fingers; long fingers that could touch the sky.

"Gaze upon the wedding feast," Gnosius declared as all the creatures of the realm cheered in unison. Gnosius plucked a piece of fruit from his own branch and held it up for all to see. "Here this fruit bestows upon those who are nourished from it an insatiable hunger for insight and wisdom, unlike they've ever known before!" Gnosius moved towards Haven with fruit in hand.

"Eat of this and become wise like the serpent." A massive centaur galloped up next to Gnosius as he motioned towards Haven to eat the fruit. The crowd chanted, "Eat! Eat! Eat! Eat!"

Haven noticed a smaller centaur next to the massive one. It held a sackcloth pillow with two gold wedding bands resting neatly on it.

Haven squinted and asked, "Who is getting married?"

The larger centaur pulled his shoulders back and stuck his chest out and declared, "I am Eurytus, my lovely maiden. I am your betrothed and you will reign with me at the Table of Longing where you and I will judge the travelers who pass through this realm. I have waited eons for a suitable bride to join me in here. All I've had for generations are these filthy, wretched creature servants that disgust me," he said as he pointed towards the pink-skinned round beasts feasting at the Table of

Longing. One such creature peeked from behind the bushes. Haven noticed him out of the corner of her eye as he peeked back down.

"You've waited that long and in all that time you've never found someone with four legs who'll marry you?" Haven asked sarcastically. Eurytus frowned while Argelius smirked.

"Generations ago I was to marry my true queen but the betrayer of the valley of rulers took her from me. Should I discover his identity, he will wish he had never been born." Eurytus leaned closer to Haven. "But with one who has travelled the realms, I may sit as judge to the travelers until the one who was the betrayer passes through this realm. And then, I will drink his blood." Eurytus tromped away from Haven's cage. "For now, we feast!"

"Lovely," Haven said.

As the carousing resumed Haven sat back in her cage pondering her next move. She looked over at Argelius. "Got any ideas?" she asked.

Argelius shrugged his shoulders. "We wait," he said.

"Figures," Haven said. She watched the pug creature staring at her from the bushes. Haven leaned over to the side of the cage where she could get a better glimpse at the creature. She reached into her pocket and pulled out the red fruit that she had previously confiscated and showed it to the creature.

"Psst. Hey. I know you're in there," Haven whispered.

Argelius looked behind him to see to whom she might have been speaking to.

"Come on out. I'll bet you're hungry. This fruit is not like the fruit that you have at your table. It's special!" The creature slowly crept out of the bushes and edged towards Haven's cage. The closer he got, the more he twitched.

"I . . . it's so so . . . beautiful," the creature stuttered.

Haven said, "It's yours if you get me out of here."

"Oh. Oh, but Eurytus is strong and . . . and . . . mighty."

"That horse-man? Don't let him control you. You're better than that. Look at how he treats you. You can be free of that. Set me free and I'll help you."

"Oh . . . but . . . I dd d ddon't know. Hhe is strong and he keeps us safe from hharm."

"What is your name?" Haven asked.

"SSSlog. I . . . I . . . I . . . am f . . . f . . . of the hhhoard."

"Well, Slog, your destiny belongs to you, not anyone else. He's probably got you believing that you can't fend for yourself and that you need him to take care of you and protect you. That's all a lie. You're just here to feed his massive ego."

"D d do you really b b b believe that?" Slog asked.

"Yes! You are the master of your destiny. Look, I'll prove it to you. I'm giving you this fruit whether you free me or not. Here, take it."

Slog looked down at the fruit and then up at Haven and finally took the fruit. As Haven watched, Slog gobbled the fruit down as fast as he could.

"T t t tasty," he uttered.

"Glad you liked it", Haven said.

Slog rolled up in a ball and sped off through the foliage. Haven threw up her hands, sighed and sat back in her cage. "And that's the thanks I get," she said. As her heart sank, she turned to face Argelius who was hunched over in a fetal position.

"Hey, Argelius. Are you ok?" she asked. He didn't answer. "Hey!" Argelius turned. The blood inside of the swollen veins of his neck were turning black. "What is it?" The white of his eyes turned black.

Suddenly, the skies became dark. Haven looked around and turned back to Argelius. "Are you doing this? Argelius! Stop it!" She slammed her hands on the bars of the cage to no avail. She turned when she heard the voices of the beasts of the realm gasp. They had all turned to gaze on the horizon. And just beyond their realm rose a blackness that slowly covered the sky. As the shadow of the black reached the beasts, they began to shake. Their skin started forming bubbles of pus and then burst as they burned. Haven turned to see Slog standing there with key and lock in hand. The door was wide open. But Argelius was gone.

"Good Slog." Quietly, Haven exited the cage and motioned Slog to follow her.

Haven and Slog snuck through the foliage, hoping to find Argelius without getting caught by the approaching black. While crouching, Haven turned to Slog. "You've got to get out of here. Get as far away as you can."

Slog whispered, "Y..y..yes. Oh but I . . . I . . . I h h heard him say s s s something about the black. And a rrriver."

"You have to run as far away and as fast as you can!"

"O O Ok. Oh but eat this first," Slog said as he handed Haven the fruit from the Tree of Knowledge of Good and Evil.

"Now's not the time," she said. "Go!"

"Oh, but you must," Slog said.

"Fine, give me that." She took it and ate. Instantly, she saw the conduits that ran all through the forest. It was a massive super-highway of passages that ran from the trunks of the trees and into the ground below them. "What am I seeing?" Haven asked.

"It is the nexus," Slog said.

"My God," she said. She turned and saw the black approaching. "Go," Haven said. "Don't be afraid."

Haven and Slog exchanged smiles. Slog then rolled up into a ball and sped off. Once he was gone, Haven darted through the forest to retrieve the staff from the trees.

As she snuck through the foliage, she heard voices just beyond the flora which seemed to open to a clearing up ahead. She crouched down even further. As she crept closer, the voices became clearer and louder. She saw the outlines of the owners of the voices and they appeared more familiar as she drew near. When she came to the edge of the clearing, she saw all that she needed to see.

It was Argelius. And he had the staff of Moshe. And he stood with Eurytus.

"You have what you need, Argelius," Eurytus said. "I have what I wanted, a bride. We have concluded our agreement and now you must take your leave. From here, I will find the betrayer."

Haven slowly began to emerge from the foliage. "You sure you haven't found him already?" Argelius turned to face Haven. "I see you found my staff," she said.

"Haven, trust me," Argelius said.

"Give me my staff," Haven said.

"Haven…"

"What?" she asked.

"Run." The black shot out from behind Argelius like a flash of darkness. The black consumed Eurytus in one quick burst. Haven turned and dashed back into the forest. Tentacles of black reached out for her. She waved off each reach after reach. But she wasn't fast enough. The black consumed her.

When the darkness cleared, Haven found herself standing on a floating rock in the center of a massive cavern that reached into the black below and darkness above. Embedded into the sides of the cavern, she could see where the walls that were lined with hundreds of alcoves with a human being wrapped in bandages inside of each. Just below her, were platforms with shades on them waiting to float near a connecting platform.

Her chest began to pound, and her breathing became heavy. "Limbo," she said to herself. The platforms beneath her began to float towards her. She walked over to the other side of her platform. "Nowhere to go," she whispered. And just when one of the platforms was close enough, a shade jumped off and landed on hers. She readied herself into a fighting stance. The shade charged. Haven ran towards it, and slid underneath it, propped her foot up and sent the shade flying over the edge. But it wasn't the last. Another made it onto the platform. She spin-kicked that one and sent it flying. Then another landed on her platform. It ran towards her. She turned but was met with another that caught her off guard. The shade kicked Haven so hard that she flew off the platform and into an alcove nearby. She pushed off the wall and caught a glimpse of the wrapped penitent. An eye opened. Haven screamed and moved back but almost fell into the darkness below. The penitent grabbed her and pulled her up. Shocked, Haven clawed his face, ripping the bandages off. It was Willy.

"Haven?" Willy said.

"Willy? What are you doing here?" she asked.

"Last I knew, I was on a slab. Next thing, some fella is wrapping me up."

"But how did you end up here?" she asked.

"No idea. But I know I ain't alone. I got free'd once but then those ugly demons caught me and put me back in here."

"How'd you get free?" she asked.

"Benny," Willy said. "We gotta find Benny!"

The shades on the platform jeered as their platform slowly moved closer. "We gotta find Benny and get you outta here. We gotta climb. Come on!"

Upward they went. They could hear the jeers and taunts of the shades on the platform, but they were too quick for the slow-moving rock.

"Willy," Haven said as they moved upwards.

"Did my dad do this?" she asked.

"Your dad ain't had nothin' to do with how I got here. I see these two men over by the house and then it all went blank," Willy said.

"So my dad...?"

"Like I'm tryin' to tell ya. He didn't put me here. The two guys. There was somethin' evil in them. Scared the crap out of me."

"My grandma?"

"Sure did love her. With all that's inside of me. "Now come on. We got to get you outta here. Benny can get us out. That's for sure." They came to an alcove. "Here is he is. Must got caught." They both reached in and started removing the bandages from this penitent. Underneath was a man in his 20s wearing a colonial revolutionary uniform." Willy tapped him lightly on the cheek twice.

"Benny! Wake up!" Willy said. The soldier came to. "William?" he asked.

"Yeah, Benny. It's me...Willy. Ain't no time for chit chat. We have to get moving."

The soldier looked over at Haven. "What angel has passed through the nexus unscathed to rescue her servant?"

"My name is Haven. Who are you?"

"My name is Benjamin Esteban Dante. Of the Dante family line."

Haven's eyes widened like she had seen a ghost. Benjamin turned to Willy. "William, you have done well to bring the angel to my midst. I can only assume she is an heir to the mantle. As such, we must climb to the chalice, my young friend. Before the betrayer seals the entrance. For surely, he has the means by now, to accomplish such a feat."

"Wait," Haven said. "Who is the betrayer? Are you talking about my guide? No, that's not him."

"Do not torture yourself," Benjamin began. "there was no way you could have known what Argelius' intent was. That one has cruel intent to seal in the limbo forever so that no more of the Dante line may inherit the mantle of knight."

Willy threw his hands up. "I done told ya man, speak English!"

Benjamin placed his hand on Haven's shoulder. "He is not who you think he is. Argelius failed long ago to hold the sacred mantle of the Dante family line...to defend against the unspeakable evil of the destroyer and his minions, 'The Aristocracy'. When he was stripped of the mantle, he unleashed the Black Death upon mankind and with his gift of healing, offered to heal them. He created a problem in order to solve it in an attempt to regain his mantle. But the Creator saw right through that and banished him here. He escaped and now wishes to win back his favor or rule the Aristocracy itself."

"Millions of people...dead?" Haven said.

"We must get to the chalice of the oath. There, you may drink from it and speak the oath. Only then, will you be set free from the black of limbo. Argelius has trapped many in this dreadful place. We must leave... now!" The three began their climb until they came to a narrow rock face. A platform below was close enough to the cavern wall that a few of the shades jumped and made it to the levels below. Willy looked down. "I don't know," he said nervously. "Don't look down, Willy," Haven said. "Just keep going."

Willy slipped and fell to the level just below them. "Willy!" Haven screamed. Just as she did, a shade reached up from beneath and grabbed him. It pulled him into an alcove, and they disappeared.

"Willy!" Haven screamed.

"Oh William," Benjamin said. "Come angel. We must continue. We must reach the bridge to the chalice." The sound of the shades rising up from the cavern below was thunderous. Then they saw it. A bridge reaching across to the center of the cavern where an enclosed platform was held in place by two other connecting bridges. The walls were solid rock with jagged edges pointing out like a deadly sea urchin. "There," Benjamin said. Just as they started crossing it, the shades reached it from underneath the bridges. They were cut off. Benjamin and Haven looked at each other in agreement.

"Onward," they both said. Benjamin pulled out his flintlock pistol and fired at one of the shades. It disintegrated right before their eyes. Haven spun an outside crescent kick and sent the shade over the bridge and into the darkness below.

"What manner of fighting is this?" Benjamin asked.

"It's called karate," Haven said.

"I see. A peculiar form of combat, this is. Effective but peculiar," Benjamin said. Haven smiled. "I'll have to give you a lesson some time," she said.

They barreled through the shades and made it to the entrance. Benjamin quickly turned and rolled a stone in front of the entrance to keep them securely in place and unharmed. Haven walked to the center of the chamber where there was a crystalline pool of water. Before it, on a stone, sat a golden chalice.

"Take the chalice," Benjamin said. With great care, Haven lifted the chalice, took a deep breath and walked over to the pool. "Look into the pool," he said. "Any last trace of unforgiveness and wrath must be purged here. See the face of the one you must absolve."

Haven looked in. Rob's face appeared but only for a moment. His face dissolved and, in its place, her own face appeared.

"Now forgive," he said. "And drink."

Haven dipped the chalice into the pool and drank.

"Are you ready to take the oath?" Benjamin asked. Just as he did, the shades began to pound on the outside walls. Within the hollow construct, their pounds echoes liked explosions.

"In taking the oath of the family line, you must accept the atonement of the blood of Christ which will rid your being of your sin nature, replacing it with his spirit and the desire to do good for others unselfishly and without fear."

"I understand," Haven said.

"Then speak the oath," Benjamin added.

Haven took a deep breath and repeated the oath after Benjamin.

"Surrender self, abandon all,

the blood atones a sinful fall.
To fight the dark and fill with light
I heed the call, As Dante's knight."

As soon as she uttered those words, the walls around her began to fade.

"I'll be waiting for your signal on Mount Judgement," Benjamin said.

"Wait," Haven said. "What signal?"

Rose walked into the large conference room of The Garden where Gardener sat at one of the liquid consoles manipulating vats and watching the readouts on the screens. She gently placed her hand on his shoulder. Her soft, worried voice whispered, "Anything?"

"No, not a thing," answered Gardener. "I've hacked into CVCU's system and they've placed her at the bottom of the heap as far as priorities go. At one point they had a lead, so I hacked the cameras all through the city and couldn't find any trace of her."

"Charity Vane Crimes Unit has always been lacking in investigative prowess," Rose said. "Keep at it. She must be found and I . . . "

The com system began to beep. Gardener and Rose looked at each other in amazement. No one knew they were here, and their operation had been kept secret since its inception.

"Let's see it," Rose ordered.

"Well alrighty then," answered Gardener. "Checking. Uh, you're either going to totally eat this up or fall over."

"Who is it?" asked Rose frantically.

"It's the Virgilian Order. They want to talk to you."

Rose hesitated and breathed in a heavy sigh. "Well, all right. Let's see what they want."

"Well, this ought to be good," smirked Gardener. He hit the transmit button and they both turned around to face the large conference table in the middle of the room. "Transmitting," Gardener indicated. A nozzle came down from the ceiling and from it came a simple drop of water. It hit the table in a large-controlled splash that turned into a self-contained vortex. Slowly the image of Sovereign Valerio came into view within the vortex. When it flattened out, Rose's eyes widened at the sight of her old friend.

"Valerio?" Rose asked.

"Yes, my sister," said Valerio. "It is I. I trust you are well?"

"I am, Sovereign," Rose answered. "I'm happy to hear from you, but I have to say that I'm quite surprised, old friend."

"It is against the wishes of the Order that we speak, Rose," said Valerio.

"To what do I owe this honor?" asked Rose.

"The Order is aware of your search for the Dante girl known as Haven. The Order knows her whereabouts and has chosen to shield you from this information."

"They know what we're doing. They want me to fail," answered Rose.

"Yes," stated Valerio.

Gardener stood up. "Why?"

"The girl will not be found on any place on this earth. She is presently undergoing the trials. I thought it would be prudent to advise you of this since your shelter would provide the perfect setting in which to shield her from harm upon the completion of her trials."

"I don't understand," said Rose. "Wouldn't the Order itself provide more than adequate shelter upon her exit from the trials? The Order has successfully received and cared for those who have endured the trials for centuries."

"You have been our most trusted Consul and I do not agree with the outcome of the decision to remove you from the order. I am not alone in believing that it was too hasty. I suspect there is an infiltrator in our midst."

"Any idea who?" Gardener asked.

"Yes. But not one that I want to discuss in a transmission," Valerio responded.

"You are a faithful friend, Sovereign Valerio."

"As are you, Rose. Gardener, Rose: watch over each other and the girl. We know of her whereabouts, but we do not know of the nature of her trials since they are individualized for each person who is called to service. She has been through so much already. Goodbye, my friends. I will not contact you again."

"Goodbye Sovereign," said Rose sadly.

The liquid screen dissipated upwards into the light. Pensive, Gardener exited the screen by manipulating the vat liquid.

Mount Judgement

Haven stood on the peak of Mount Judgement across from Argelius who had been waiting for her. He was holding the staff on his back much like Haven had.

"Robore Voluntatis," he said bitterly.

"I'm not impressed," Haven said. "Not anymore."

"It means, 'strength of will'. You emerged triumphantly from the Black. So, I, on the other hand, am impressed. But this is as far as your strength will get you."

"I trusted you, Haven said. "Why?"

"To stop evil once and for all."

"You can't," Haven said. "No one can. It's called, choice. And that you can't take away."

"Stupid child," Argelius replied. "You are too young to have any semblance of wisdom. I have witnessed the folly of man since before you were born." Argelius raised the staff. "And with this, I can seal the passage to the nine circles. Evil is vanquished. Problem solved."

"Favor restored?"

"You freed the penitent," Argelius said.

"You mean the prisoner," Haven responded.

"He's a fool," Argelius said.

"So was I," Haven answered. "Now, I'm just pissed."

Haven charged forward in a flying sidekick that landed on the madman's chest, sending him hurling through the air and crashing into the rock.

Argelius quickly recovered.

"So, you have chosen," Argelius said.

"Pretty early on, actually," Haven said.

"Foolish," he said as he barraged Haven with a series of blows to the head.

Haven met each one with the precision and experience of a trained student of martial arts. She turned and swept Argelius' legs out from under him. He landed in a roll, regained his feet and charged again towards Haven.

"Man cannot rule himself," Argelius declared.

Haven met each blow with a blow of her own. A side kick, a back fist, an upper cut. A spinning outside crescent kick sent Argelius to the ground once more.

"Not your call," she said.

"The beloved endured these trials day after day but is never free of them. Around the mountain they go and see their folly and yet they persist."

"We learn eventually," she said.

Argelius swept Haven's legs out from under her with her own staff. She flipped and landed on her hands and a bent knee. "Getting tired?" he mocked.

Haven looked up. "Just getting started," she said. She then looked down at her hands. A light glow began to emanate from them. The dust on the ground surrounding began to rise into the air. She took a deep breath in and slammed her fist into the opposite hand. A sonic wave shot out from her hands and spread across the landscape as they clashed in a thunderous boom.

"So, you did learn something," he said. "That's my girl."

"Not from you," Haven said.

"You think small. With the staff of Moshe, I can stop the ones responsible for all of the evil in the world. Think of it! I can send every demon that has ever caused any pain and trap them in the hell they came from. Don't you want to be rid of the pain of loss? Killing? War?"

Argelius took a step closer to Haven. "There would never be a need for another Dante to lose someone they love. With this staff I can contain the Aristocracy - the nine circles of hell itself!"

"You mean control," Haven answered.

Argelius' shoulders dropped. Haven moved closer.

"You have such a massive ego. You know, with an ego like yours why not kick it up a notch and have them worship you? Make you a god? Because if you're a god, you can't make the same mistake the Witness made when you were called from your family. This isn't about eliminating evil. It's about you deluding yourself into thinking you're going to save humanity so that you can be lifted up on a pedestal."

"I will seal the portal to this realm. And you will never be able to leave this place," Argelius said.

"Everything is a choice. And in order to win a fight, you have to choose to fight it," Haven added.

Haven rushed towards Argelius and grabbed the staff. "Never," she said. She then lifted her feet into his chest and tried to push him off. But instead, he slammed his forehead onto the bridge of her nose which pushed both of them backwards. Argelius fell into the River of Choosing. He stood up and lifted the staff.

"Humanity's deliverance begins now," Argelius declared. With all of his might, he slammed one end of the staff into the water.

Nothing happened.

"What?" He tried again. Nothing. "Why isn't this working?"

"You have to be chosen," Haven said. She rushed at Argelius, grabbed the staff with both hands and kicked him. Argelius landed in the water defeated and drenched.

Haven then spun the staff and slammed the tip into the water. The force of the blast pushed back the water and revealed a layer of black tar underneath. "No!" screamed Argelius. Haven spun again and slammed it down into the black. In an explosion of dark soot, the black opened up and revealed all of the penitents that had been trapped below. One by one, they emerged from beneath the dark tar. The shades could not touch the light above and were trapped in their realm while others were set free. Willy was on a nearby rock sitting down. "Get 'im girl!"

"That she will," said a voice from the shadows in the entrance.

Gasping for air, Argelius demanded, "Who goes there?"

"Your works of folly have released me from the black where you held me prisoner within the mountain," answered the voice.

"Show yourself, I command you!" Argelius shouted.

Haven frowned at Argelius then tried to pierce the dark with her eyes and identify the newcomer.

"Your commands have no weight," the voice said, "and your rule does not come from any authority but your own. The slavery you have imposed on those you have manipulated is at an end. I show myself of my own volition and with boldness, I come before you to shine a light in the darkness of your deeds. And you will rule no more, betrayer."

A tall, thin man dressed in the tattered blue uniform of a colonial soldier, bearing a cavalry sword, slowly left the shadows.

Benjamin lowered his sword. "Tell me, Argelius, how is it that you came to this place? Were you not truly the first that was given the charge to fight the great evil?"

Argelius removed his sword from its sheath and lit it. He then pointed it at Benjamin. "That I was. But when my family needed me the most, the witness took me and sent me on this wretched journey for the mantle charge. My family needed me! They all died because I was not there to fight alongside them!"

Benjamin took a step forward, "And so you brought about the Black Death on mankind? The disease that you brought killed millions of people!"

"There is no trial if there is no fire. Angels do not understand what it is to be human. Those who watch over us and do God's bidding are like mindless puppets! I've said it before and I'll say it again, humans cannot be trusted to rule themselves. With this mantle I can help humanity thrive and finally be set free from their own recklessness."

Benjamin raised his sword once again. "What is freedom without free will? Argelius, you are a Dante. I know of your agreement with the dark lord. You desolated the Valley of Rulers and killed everyone therein."

"Your flintlock and sword are no match for me, Benjamin."

"Your dark soul is no match for the light, Argelius."

Benjamin lunged at Argelius, who met his blows with blocks and counterstrikes. Benjamin managed to deliver a cross-cut across Argelius' chest. Argelius screamed in agony as he returned the blow with a thrust to Benjamin's abdomen, sending him flying into the rock. Dazed and bruised, Benjamin cried out, "Heir of Dante, make the choice."

Reluctantly, Haven acknowledged Benjamin's command.

Benjamin stood up as quickly as his injured body permitted. He lifted his sword and clashed with Argelius' fire sword. Each clash culminated in a burst of fire and the sound of lightning.

Haven lifted her staff and slammed the point into the ground. A shockwave went out through the land.

"No," Argelius said under his breath.

"The signal," Benjamin said. Their swords met once again.

Then all at once, the shades, the hoard and the white sirens appeared and pounced on Argelius. He swung his sword to keep them at bay but was only able to slay two of the shades. One of the shades grabbed the hand that held the fire sword incapacitating him. A deafening, high-pitched screech came from on high as the White Siren bore down on him. He swung desperately to keep them away but to no avail. They clawed and struck Argelius as he fell to the ground. While on the ground, Argelius turned and found himself facing a familiar accuser, Mr. Zippers who was now looking down on him. "Aye, thar ya be," Mr. Zippers said. "I've been lookin' for ya." He unzipped a pouch in his leg and whipped out a vial. He opened it and blew the contents in Argelius' face.

Argelius began to scream in horrid panic. "No!" He shook his head attempting to get whatever images that tormented his mind out of his head. He swung his fire sword in every direction with whatever remaining strength he had. As they moved closer to a nearby precipice, Argelius mustered enough coherence to lunge at Benjamin. They both went over.

Haven walked into the river and turned. "Goodbye, Grandpa," she said. She plunged the point of the staff into the water. "It's time to choose," she whispered. The water quickly receded and then returned. As the water began to overtake her, the light from the markings on her arms and the staff became bright as the morning sun. Mount Judgment disappeared in a flash of light.

Haven stood on a platform in the center of the same white marble courtroom where she had stood previously. The seat where the judge sat was white marble stone that was crystalline with a bright white energy that emanated from it.

Once again, the walls of this great white hall were embedded with voices from a heavenly choir that sang holy, holy, holy over and over again. Haven smiled and breathed it all in.

To the right of judge's seat was the same greyish, old lectern whose wood was cracked.

The choir ceased their worship and in one voice sang, all rise.

The judge then appeared before them sitting in the judgement seat. His hair flowed like rivers of light that danced on his shoulders. He looked down at Haven… and he smiled. Two majestic guardian angels stood at his feet.

One of the guardian angels stepped forward. "The court of the heavens is now commenced," he said. "Blood cries out. Bring in the accuser." As ordered, a short, pudgy demon with bulgy eyes and leathery skin walked out from behind the curtain towards the rotten lectern.

The book the demon brought with him was so heavy that he had to pull it with a rope. Leaving slime in his wake, he dragged the book to the base of the lectern and stood on a box. He was so short that he could barely see over the top. He pulled the book up with the rope and set it on top of the lectern.

"Does he need help with that?" Haven asked. The judge laughed. The court shook.

After opening it, he read aloud in a raspy voice.

"The beloved stands accused of murder," he said.

The faces of the choir on the walls then disappeared and, in its place, came an image of Haven at Beatrice's funeral. As she looked over her mother's casket, her words rang through the hall.

"Why couldn't it have been him instead?" Behind the curtain from where the demon emerged, other demons cheered. The accuser chuckled to himself and closed the book.

One of the angels stepped forward. "Does the accused speak the oath?"

Haven cleared her throat. "I just learned this so don't freak out if I mess it up. Ok here it goes:

Surrender self, abandon all,
the blood atones a sinful fall.
To fight the dark and fill with light
I heed the call, As Dante's knight."

The judge leaned forward. He smiled so wide it blinded the demon accusers. The guardian angels turned to the judge who simply nodded.

In unison, the angels declared, "Judgement is decreed. The accused is innocent." The images on the screen then disappeared and were erased. The demons hissed in protest. The guardian angels pulled their swords and sent them back to Hades with a swift stroke for each.

"Well done," the judge said. A brilliant light enveloped them and once again, Haven closed her eyes to protect them from its brightness. When she opened them, she was on a grassy field on the side of the terrace mountain.

Haven was sitting in the bright morning sky on the bright green grass beneath her when she heard the voice of a young child in the midst of the squeaks and creaks of an old swing.

"Up above the world so high . . . "

Haven walked towards the little girl who was rocking back and forth on a swing that hung from a nearby tree. The little girl noticed Haven walking up the slope and immediately smiled from ear to ear.

"You're back!" she exclaimed as she jumped off her swing and ran towards Haven. The child squeezed her neck tightly. She let go and held Haven's face in her hands. "I knew you would come back!"

"I had some help," Haven said.

"Yay!" the little girl cheered.

"I'm going back. I'm going to go stop the bad people."

"You chose love," the little girl said. "And you'll stop them all and save people! I know it!"

"My weaknesses will return, won't they?" Haven asked.

"Yes, but you'll hear the voice now. You'll be different."

"Different? How?" asked Haven.

"You'll see," the child answered as she approached Haven and hugged her tight.

As she uttered those words, the winds that first met Haven upon her arrival began to swirl around her. Haven could once again hear the sounds of the creatures of the forest. For a moment, she took it all in. "I'm really going to miss being here. With you."

The girl looked up at Haven with her big brown eyes and said, "I love you."

Haven's eyes twitched as the reality around her became distorted. She could feel herself getting sleepy and feeling strangely weighted. "Wait! You never told me your name! The young brown-eyed, brown-haired girl said, "It's me! It's…"

Ascent

Haven gained consciousness in a dark, grungy alley. The haze of the streetlights blinded her as she tried, to no avail, to ascertain her whereabouts. Shaking and lightheaded, Haven was unable to utter any recognizable words, just grunts of discomfort. The cold, harsh concrete reminded her of the pain in her joints as she tried to move. She could barely make out the faint voices that rang in her ears. Even worse were the foggy images of the people surrounding her. She couldn't tell who any of the people were.

"Hurry, let's get her inside. Be mindful of her wounds," said an elderly woman.

"And bring the staff."

The staff, Haven thought. *The staff saved me.*

As she was lifted from the ground, Haven closed her eyes. The breeze that lightly lifted her hair seemed very familiar. With eyes still closed, Haven took a deep breath in. I'm home, she thought to herself. I'm finally home.

Mom?

"There, love. You're going to be just fine."

Haven then drifted off into a deep sleep.

The late afternoon sun shining through the raised blinds forced Haven to open her eyes. She took a look around the cozy, inviting room dressed in country décor and she thought to herself, *No. This is not home.*

As she moved to raise herself up, she was quickly reminded that the pain was still there. Her bones still ached; her muscles were tight enough to snap and her head still throbbed. Even so, she pushed herself up to a seated position and rubbed her temples in an effort to push away the pulsating pain.

The door creaked open.

"Good afternoon, love," said the elderly woman. "I hope I'm not disturbing you."

Haven gasped and pulled up her covers.

"Forgive me if I frightened you, love. May I come in?" she asked.

"Sure," Haven answered. Haven could smell the warm soup and fresh-baked bread her caretaker brought with her.

"I brought you some warm potato soup," the woman said as she entered the room and placed the soup on the table next to Haven. "You've been asleep almost the entire day and you need some nourishment."

Haven relaxed her arms and shoulders. "Thank you," she said.

"No worries, love. How are you feeling?" the woman asked.

"A headache. Backache. My arms are burning too."

"Feel free to rest as much as you can. This is your room," the woman said as she pulled a bandage wrap out of a drawer. Rose then sat down next to Haven and began to wrap her arms. "Here, love. Hopefully, this will stop the burning."

"Where am I?" Haven asked.

"My name is Rose, and I run the shelter here. You're in the Desert Rose Shelter for Women."

"But I am back in Charity Vane, right?" Haven asked.

"Yes, you are. We are in the lower south district."

"'The Mire,'" said Haven. "I have a friend who lives here. I need to try and contact her."

After she finished wrapping Haven's arms Rose placed her hand on her shoulder. Not fully trusting her, Haven instinctively pulled back. "Easy there," Rose added. "You've been through a great deal and there is much to discuss."

Haven sat on the edge of the bed. Rose gently handed her the soup. Haven grabbed the soup and took her first spoonful. "This is really good," she said. And then she ate some more. "Easy now," Rose said. "Don't gorge yourself."

After a couple of spoonfuls, Haven paused. "Who are you? Really? And what do you know?"

"I come from the line of Maro, a family line of watchers that came forth from an ancient sect known as the Virgilian Order," Rose explained.

"What does this order do and what does it have to do with me?" Haven asked.

Rose sat down on the bed next to Haven. "Centuries ago, your ancestor; a man by the name of Dante Alighieri lost someone very dear to his heart. He was devastated by this loss and searched desperately to find some kind of solace for his soul. On the road to healing he travelled through the nine circles of hell and endured the wrath of every vice known to man. It was after this terrible ordeal that he finally found the peace he craved." Rose got up from the bed and looked out the window pensively as if reliving a painful memory. "However, he did not travel alone, His friend and guide, a man named Virgil, went with him. I am from his line."

"So the two families have been joined at the hip, I take it."

"Not exactly," Rose replied. "Those who established the order thought it best to watch and guide from a distance in order to not interfere with the natural development of those they watched. Non-interference became their mantra. The Order protects the Dante family line from harm by the great evil, but otherwise stays out of their way. The only interference the Order is permitted is for the safety of a Dante, especially upon their exit from the trials."

"The trials. The terraces I just travelled through?"

"Yes," said Rose.

"And here I was, just thinking that it was all a dream," Haven said.

"It was not a dream, love. You were really there. It is the duty of the Order to ensure the safety of the one called from the Dante line once they successfully travel through the terraces."

"There was someone that I met right before my last trial," said Haven. "Benjamin Dante, mentioned this 'great evil' you're talking about. The Aristocracy."

Rose turned around. "Yes, the Aristocracy. When the first Dante left their world unscathed, it was a slap in the face to the guardians of the Nine Circles of Hell. They banded together, and after years of infighting for leadership, they formed what is today called The Aristocracy."

Rose walked over to the corner where the staff had been left. As she examined it, she brought it over to Haven and handed it to her. Haven ran her fingers over the markings. "I didn't have a chance to really sit and examine it before. It's beautiful."

"It's a wonderful gift you've been given--Haven. The staff adapts to the person who wields it and melds with its holder. You and the staff become one."

Haven put the staff down and walked around the room, remembering what it was like to sleep in her own bed and wake up to the place that warmed her heart . . . home. And then she remembered what had happened just before the trials.

"My dad," she snapped. "While I was there, I saw him in his jail cell. I need to let him know that I'm OK." Haven jerked her head towards Rose, as if she had just snapped back to reality. "Does he know about any of this? This family line and everything you've just told me?"

"Yes," answered Rose. "But there's more. And you might want to sit down."

On the outer edge of The Mire close to the old, abandoned Olem Mineshaft, indigents who had found no place for themselves within the confines of the city camped. These were the homeless exiles of Charity Vane. The rats near the mineshaft were as large as small dogs, but that, and the horrid stench of filth and excrement, didn't seem to bother the indigents who lived away from the rush of life.

They huddled together under the mining tower to keep each other safe from authorities who periodically inspected the campsites, and from other homeless souls and from the unknown.

A mother dressed in rags clutched her young son who wore hand-me-downs as they huddled in front of the fire. The boy, who was about seven years old, had obviously not bathed in at least a week. The boy's mother took a drink from an old metal coffee cup.

"Mommy? Can I get it?" he asked his mother.

"Get what son?"

"You 'member? That red car-wagon thingy?"

"Oh. Right. I hope so, son."

"OK, Mommy."

The boy's mom put the cup down in front of the fire when another nomad approached.

"Hey, you stole that can opener, didn't you!" accused the man.

"No," answered the mom. "We talked about this. Maybe Mary forgot to put it back in the huddle. She had it last, Billy. Now leave us alone."

"Look woman, I think you did take it."

"I said leave us alone," the mom repeated.

Suddenly, the earth shook. The tremor was so great that it knocked some of the tents down. The indigents ran screaming as the earth opened up beneath them. The crackling of old, dead tree limbs filled the air followed by an ear-splitting rumble as a sink hole formed beneath them, sucking in loose dirt and rock. The woman snatched up her son and ran behind a rusty old truck. Then she saw it. A massive, yellow-eyed creature standing about nine feet tall with brown fur and fangs. His sharp, white horns pointed straight up to the sky as did the razor-edged tusks protruding from his chin. He had a yellow, armor-like skin covering his shoulders and chest. He struck at the defenseless. Some he threw, while others he snapped in half. One man screamed in horror as the creature gouged him with his horn. His long tail had a dagger at the end of it. Roaring, he skewered the body of one of the nomads with his tail and swung him off, causing him to slam into another junk car just behind the frightened mother of the boy. The child yelped and his mom quickly covered his mouth, hoping the beast would not be alerted to their presence.

The beast finished its killing spree in a matter of minutes, annihilating eight families. After letting out a thunderous roar, the beast leaped into the air and out of sight, no doubt searching for its next prey. It would search without mercy and discrimination and it would not stop until it found what it was looking for. The woman and her young son emerged from behind the rusty truck and stood in the devastation of what was once her home. She held her son tight, knowing that her true treasure had not been lost nor damaged.

And she was grateful.

"Two years?" Haven shouted. Her breathing got so heavy and course that it felt like a weight had drowned her soul in sudden flood of anxiety. "It was like a week for me. I remember resting at night and waking up in the mornings. At least I thought I did."

"You existed in a place that stands outside of time, love," Rose explained. "A day there is a week here and vice versa." Haven grabbed her elbows and sat back down on the bed. "So that means that Dad has been in jail for this long?"

"Yes," Rose answered, her brows knit in concern. "He's on death row now, but his execution has been stayed pending a psychological evaluation."

Haven's face blanched. "I think I'm going to be sick." She ran to the bathroom and threw up. Haven could feel her gut contract into a tight knot every time she heaved. When she was done, she rinsed her mouth out in the sink. "I want to see him. I also need to call Sol and let her know I'm all right."

"I understand," Rose soothed. Taking a deep breath, she added, "But there is something we need you to do first."

Even the razor-edged stalactites protruding from the ceiling of the Aristocracy's vast central council chamber exuded a vile steam filling the soulless void that surrounded them with a putrid fog. In the immense chamber sat members of the Aristocracy on equally sharp, towering stalagmites, which surrounded the center of the room. Each stone chair was like a throne that stood high off the ground. Each seat was accompanied by a lower stalagmite to its right that served as a pod for the host each member inhabited until it became time for the demon to form the 'hybrid': the convergence of man and monster. Nothing good or noble dwelled here: no hope, no future and no love. All had been consumed by the fires. Each seat had the symbol of its respective Circle: limbo, lust, gluttony, avarice, wrath, heresy, violence, sorcery and betrayal.

One lone chair rose high above the rest, its occupant attentively listening to all. His small face remained in the shadows; a chilling presence yet to be unveiled.

Lord Hordran, the giant dragon of the Circle of Hoarders spoke first. His host, Dominic Reins, was encased in muck in a catatonic state in the pod next to him. "We welcome, with great satisfaction, our newest member, who will be known as Solstice, yes. She has proven to be quite resourceful in our quest and I am so very delighted to have her here in our midst, oh yes I am," he said as his massive tail swayed in the air. "She will wonderfully represent the Second Circle of the Aristocracy."

Sol sat in the seat of the Second Circle. Still joined with her beast, her eyes glowed yellow and her smile was now wry as one who had embraced that which lived within her. As she spoke, her voice was raspy and gargled. "Lord Hordran has kindly educated me on the importance of what we are trying to achieve, and I am honored to be a part of it. Given the threat to the plan posed by the Dante line, I feel it is imperative that I assist in bringing that plan about given my history with the Dante family. In fact, I have already been in contact with the one who now holds the mantle."

The giant red beast with giant horns and yellow eyes spoke next as his host, Harry Reeve, sat catatonic in the pod next to his seat. "As Lord Traiton of Circle Nine, I would know treason when I see it and I am not so sure that your loyalties are with us. What are you willing to do to prove your loyalty to us?"

The pod next to Lord Vengus was empty since Anorexic Man could not leave his prison cell. Lord Vengus had the head and body of a lion with the giant wings of a bat and spoke in thunderous roars. "You may know treason, Lord Traiton, but as the lord of wrath, I know wrath and you speak as one with great malice towards our new cohort. Let us hear her reason without prejudice!"

"Thank you, Lord Vengus," added Solstice. "I am aware of the location of the chosen one and have already dispatched this information to Lord Hordran. Wisely, Ravage has been sent by Lord Hordran to take the shelter down and kill everyone in it unless the chosen one is prepared to surrender the plans for the weapon to us."

"Yes, yes," interjected Traiton. "Lord Voratum has been sent to take down the weaponer known as Gardener but was unsuccessful."

Lord Voratum, who sat in the seat of Circle Three, with the boy Chuck Flegman in his pod, did not like the sound of that. "His weapon separated me from my host, yes it did," he grunted. "I had no choice."

Lord Limbus of Circle One then spoke up. Limbus was known as the paver of the road to the abyss and as such did not need a host. His task was simply to serve as the bringer of captured humans to the Nine Circles. "We have a unique opportunity to bring the chosen one here using the memory of her dear-departed mother to lure her here. But what of the ones who aid and shelter her?"

Lord Retic of the Sixth Circle moved forward in his chair to address the concern. His pod was empty since the host was forbidden to leave the monastery. For some time, the other Circle leaders questioned the purpose behind joining with someone from within the Virgilian Order, but recently it had become more and more evident that without him their plans would not succeed. As he moved forward, his appearance came into view and he spoke directly and matter-of-factly. The beast known as Lord Retic had the most human appearance of all the demons of the Nine Circles. He was completely bald and imposing and sat with an elegance that would deceive anyone into believing he was righteous, if not for his double iris' that glared side by side. Like his eyebrows, his eyes slanted upwards and had a hypnotizing effect on anyone who dared stare into them. Tall and muscular, he wore a robe of fire that fluttered in the darkness of the cavern.

"Lord Retic," Traiton added. "Speak."

Lord Retic began, "Consuls Rose and Gardener have been assigned to The Mire and tasked to shepherd a refuge for the refuse of society in an effort to keep them . . . shall we say . . . out of the way? Although they have been expulsed from the Order, we remain well-versed of every aspect of their operations. This information has already proven quite useful." Retic rubbed his hands together and frowned. "There is one slight problem, however."

Luminos sat quietly waiting for Retic to elaborate.

"One of the sovereigns grows suspicious," Retic continued. "Most of the sovereigns are complacent in their positions as watchers, but this one is not. There is great risk with Sovereign Valerio."

"He should be eliminated," Traiton suggested. "We've come too far to be stopped by some religious fool."

"It will be done," answered Retic.

A minion demon removed Harry's watch from his wrist as Traiton continued. "Solstice, you will place this device in a secure location at the shelter. Once activated, it will draw the mindless Ravage to his destination. As the newest ranking member of the Aristocracy, you will carry out this task."

"This will be done, Lord Traiton," Solstice acknowledged proudly as she accepted the watch and put it on.

Lord Limbus interrupted. "Splendid. Not knowing the gifts that the chosen one has been given I feel it wise to accompany Ravage on his mission and bring the chosen one here."

Lord Lock of the Eighth Circle interposed. As the hybrid known as Mist, the Lord of Sorcery wore a fashionable long black leather jacket with three nebulous demons chained to the inside of his jacket. He wore his white hair long and he too had yellow, glowing eyes.

"What of the adoptive heir to the Aristocracy, the eminent Luminos? What does he have to say about our plan?"

Up until now the occupier of the lead chair had sat quietly, intently listening in on all that was being said and planned. He sat forward in the chair that seemed just a little too big for his small stature. He was very young, about ten years old. His brown hair was long on top and shaved on the sides, and he wore spiked leather braces around his wrists and a leather-spiked collar around his neck. His eyes glowed yellow, but not from any one of the Lords of the Circles inhabiting him but from his continued presence in this dreadful place. He had clearly been here all of his life and had come to know the Aristocracy as his family. When he spoke, he spoke authoritatively, but with the voice of a young boy.

"I find this plan to be a grand one indeed," he said. "Finally, we will establish our kingdom in solidarity on the surface and we will reign in freedom! No longer will we be subject to the chastening of inequality with mankind. We will show the humans what real justice is and take back what has been taken from us with the advent of man!" With those words, those present in the chamber were joined by the monsters and demons of the dark, as they chanted their war cry.

"Power! Dominion! Sovereignty!"

Phantasms

"I don't know if I can handle going over there," Haven declared in frustration as she and Rose walked the halls of the shelter headed towards the courtyard. "During my trials, there were some feelings that I had to let go of about my father, but there was always something about that building that I guess I'm just not over. I just hate going there and I always have. That company was his life."

"The company was his dream. Unfortunately, you and your mother were left behind as he pursued his dream. and that you did not ask for. That place represents his abandonment of you and your mother, so it is perfectly natural that you feel that way."

"I've forgiven him for that. I just don't get why you want me to go back there," Haven said.

"The information that your father's former assistant has was retrieved by your mother on the night she died. Your mother saw what was happening to your father. She saw his obsession and his drive to save the world from the Aristocracy with only his intellect as a weapon. She saw how he lost sight of what was good and right in those efforts and how it blinded him to what was going on in his own company. We tried to talk her out of going after the information herself, but in the end, she was too determined to know the truth. In order to keep her safe, we aided her. We failed miserably, and she was lost. Beatrice was about to download the data she so desperately sought when she was caught. In order to throw off her pursuers, she transferred the data to a secure file that only Jinx knew of. Whatever she found within the confines of that building is with her. She will not release it, save to a member of the family . . . you."

"You were there the night that my mother died?" Haven asked angrily. All activity in the courtyard came to a halt when they overheard Haven shouting at Rose.

"We wanted her safe," Rose answered.

Haven's blood began to boil. "And look where your help got her. Look where we are today. Where I am today. Tell me something Rose. Do you have that same obsession and drive that pulled my father away from us?" Haven jabbed her finger at Rose for emphasis as she added, "Is this just a mission to you or do you really care about the people?"

Rose turned towards the courtyard where children played and mothers shared their war stories.

"I . . . most certainly hope so," she whispered.

"I'll get what you need, but after that I'm out of here," Haven said angrily. "All of this fighting and we end up right back where we started: nowhere to go but down. I'm done with it!" Haven marched towards the garage.

"Haven, wait," Rose said.

Haven turned. "What?" she asked sharply.

"There's more," Rose said. "It's about Sol."

Haven front-kicked the doors to the garage open and walked inside to look for the first available vehicle she could grab. Then she saw it. A bright shiny new black Harley-Davidson Crossbones, just like the one her dad had given her before. She knew that this had come from him. Haven sighed deeply.

"Thanks, Dad."

With her staff shortened and tied to her back, she jumped on. The key was still in it, which reaffirmed to her that this machine was meant for her and her alone. She took a breath and turned the key. She revved the accelerator, making the modern machine hum and ready for what lay ahead. Popping the clutch, Haven spun out of the garage and headed for Dante Tower.

Moments later, the doorbell to the shelter rang and one of the residents ran to answer it. The young mother of two shooed her children away from the door and opened it. Standing at the doorstep was Soledad Alden.

"Hi. I'm here to see Haven? She called me last night and I haven't seen her in a long time, so I rushed over here as soon as I could."

"Come on in," the resident said. "I'll get Rose for you. She heads up the home here and likes to know who comes and goes."

"Sure, no problem," Sol answered.

Rose was already on her way in. "You must be Sol," Rose said.

As they made eye contact, the seed of suspicion took root behind the eyes of each.

"Yes, ma'am. I got a call from Haven and came as fast as I could." She walked towards a large wall mirror and stared at herself. "She and I grew up together, so I was pretty floored when she called out of the blue. Any idea where she's been?"

Rose took a step away from Sol. "I'm sure she'll explain it all to you when she returns."

Sol turned back to Rose. "Where did she go?"

"Oh, she just had to run a quick errand. She'll be back very soon," Rose answered.

"Doesn't make sense that she would call and then leave."

"Haven said she needed to tend to an urgent personal matter. I'm sure it's nothing. Now come. Let me get you some tea. What is your favorite?"

"Darjeeling, Ma'am . . . and very hot. That is, if you have it." Sol turned back to the mirror. She could feel the presence of the person on the other side and stood for a moment staring.

Rose began to walk towards the kitchen. "As a matter of fact, I do have Darjeeling. Come, love. We'll wait for her at the table."

Sol winked at the mirror and walked with Rose.

Gardener stood and watched her walk away from the other side of the mirror.

Haven walked through the grand entryway to Dante Tower. Passing the marble sculptures and the terraces, she took a second look at the painting of a small boat powered by paddles that ferried passengers to the Valley of Rulers.

"Not entirely accurate," she muttered under her breath.

She came to the two guards who regularly screened visitors. Although it was late in the day, Jinx Jenkins had become accustomed to working late, given her level of dedication to the Dante family.

The two stopped her at the gate.

"Can I help you?" Eddie asked.

"I'm Haven. I'm here to see Jinx.

Eddie gave Frank a perplexed look. "Should I know you?" Eddie asked.

"My last name is Dante. Rob and Beatrice are my parents."

"I'm sorry, but I'm going to have to call this in. Mr. Reeve's orders."

Eddie picked up his com and dialed. Haven watched his expression as he read his readout.

He and Eddie exchanged sad looks. Haven figured they felt sorry for the poor orphan girl.

"I'm sorry," Eddie said. "Go on up. Jinx will meet you up top."

As the elevator floor indicator passed the 200-mark, Haven gritted her teeth nervously. It had been years since she rode up this elevator and the last time she did, it related to a not-so-pleasant experience. Mom had planned a party for Haven's ninth birthday and Rob had forgotten to show up. She had been able to read the hurt in Haven's eyes. Her mom brought her to see her dad so she could see for herself how excited her dad would be to see her. After all, it was her birthday. When they arrived, they found Rob leaving his office to board a plane to Hong Kong for a business deal that couldn't wait. Rob and Beatrice got into a heated quarrel about it, which made matters worse for Haven. After that, she never came back to Dante Tower. She cringed as the doors to the elevator opened on the 220th floor, her dad's floor. Jinx was there to meet her.

"Haven!" Jinx shouted as she rushed to hug Haven. "Oh, I was so worried about you. It's so good to see you."

Although Haven refused to return to the tower, Jinx always made a point of aiding Beatrice by reminding Rob of his family commitments. Haven's heart had opened up towards Jinx when she found out that it was actually Jinx who sent flowers and gifts on her dad's behalf. It made matters worse for Haven and Rob's relationship though.

"First of all, how are you doing?" Jinx asked as she picked up one of Haven's arms and examined the wrap.

"I'll be OK. I understand that you've met my new 'friends'?" Haven asked, with a twinge of misgiving.

Jinx motioned Haven to come into her office and Haven followed her.

"I have," Jinx responded as she closed the door. "Gardener had been working here for some months before he disclosed who he really was. Some of this . . . well, quite frankly, I find all of this still a bit outlandish. They've told me about a group called the Aristocracy that wants to destroy your family and that they are responsible for everything that has happened to your mom and dad -- and now you. If all of that is true, then I would guess that it has something to do with the technology created here, in addition to the information that Beatrice died retrieving."

"Have you been able to look at it?" Haven asked.

"No, I can't decipher it. It's encrypted."

"Gardener thinks he should be able to crack it open and see what's inside," Haven said.

"OK," Jinx added. "And how do you feel about Rose and Gardener? Do you trust them?"

"I'm not there yet. In fact, I'm thinking of leaving them once this is over. I just found out that the night my mom died these people were with them," Haven added.

"I'm sorry to hear that," Jinx said. "I was actually suspicious of them myself when I first met them. Gardener lied to me about the real reason why he wanted a job here, but I suppose I couldn't blame him. He needed answers.

So he offered me his resignation. I hated accepting it. He was so good at his job and always kind. I'm just glad that they're keeping you safe. Surely that means something."

Jinx leaned over her desk and pressed a button. A vat with fluid that was a light blue hue came up and she dipped the compad into the vat. The light emitted from the vat showing the upload reflected on Jinx's concerned eyes. "By the way, I have some insurance papers, I need you to sign. We're going to resurrect you. You were, after all, declared dead." Jinx pulled the papers out and laid them out in front of Haven who picked up a pen.

"So, I guess it is true what they told me. About where you've been," Jinx said.

"Yes. Yes, it's true," Haven answered as she signed the documents.

"Do you have a place to stay?" Jinx asked.

Suddenly, the office door swung open.

"Haven?" Harry asked. "Haven, is that you?"

Jinx immediately turned to block the upload from Harry's field of view and shoved the papers back into her drawer.

"Yes, Mr. Reeve. It's me," Haven said. The compad was still uploading.

"Well, Jinx why didn't you tell me that she was coming?" Harry asked.

"She just came by to sign some insurance papers," Jinx said begrudgingly.

Harry reached out his hand to Haven to shake it.

It took a couple of seconds for Haven to muster up the strength to shake his hand, given how her mom felt about Harry and the fact that it was he who kept her father away from home for so many years. Since she was taught to be polite, she hesitantly raised her hand to shake his. And then she saw it.

On the middle finger of his right hand was a gold band with the letter 'A' on it.

Holy crap, Haven thought to herself. He's one of them. *I don't believe this. He is one of them and that means that if Jinx knew where I was then he's got to know. I've got to get out of here. I've got to warn them.*

Jinx finished what she was doing and slid the compad right into Haven's pant pocket without Harry noticing. Haven then started moving towards the door.

"Are you in a hurry?" Harry asked.

"I just came by to say hi to Jinx.. That's all. I've got to be heading out to catch up with an old friend," Haven said nervously.

"Ah, very good," Harry said calmly. "Friends in time of tragedy can be like a mending brace. They make us stronger, help us to weather the storms of life, wouldn't you agree?"

"Yes. I would," Haven answered reservedly.

"Your commitment to your friends is admirable," Harry added.

Haven stood motionless and in shock for a millisecond. *Friends?* she thought to herself. *I said friend, not friends. Does he know about the shelter?* She glanced at Jinx and said a quick "Bye," and breezed out of the office. She walked briskly to her motorcycle and took to the streets of Charity Vane.

Haven raced through the city dodging cars and running red lights, striving to make it through the outskirts into The Mire. She could see the shelter in the distance. Haven revved the gas and popped the clutch to pump as much as she could out of the already strained engine.

Come on. Come on, she thought to herself. Almost there.

She dodged a child crossing the street, barely missing her. Thank God. She could see the name of the shelter out in front of the building. Desert Rose.

All right, she thought. Made it. Haven pulled to the driveway of the shelter. Yes!

The blinding light of the explosion was followed by a shockwave that knocked Haven clearly off of her motorcycle, sending her tumbling. Her motorcycle shattered into a million pieces and flaming debris came falling down on Haven, burying her in rubble.

The blast had knocked Rose to the ground, and she was caught between the smoldering fallen frames of the building that had collapsed around her. Still dazed, she looked up and could see Gardener was out cold, lying face down on the ground. Sol was nowhere in sight. Rose could barely move her head to look around and gauge the devastation when through the steamy haze she saw it. A nine-foot-tall creature with glowing, yellow eyes and armor plating frantically searched the debris. Easily casting aside heavy timber, the beast growled as he feverishly hunted his prey. He turned and saw Rose watching him and marched towards her, shaking the ground with each step. As he got closer, Rose could make out the horror that he was with flat horns growing from both the top of his head and his chin. He quickly picked up the burning lumber that had trapped Rose and easily cast it aside. Rose could barely muster a word under her breath.

"Whwhat . . . do you want?" she stammered.

"Wwwwhere is the Dante? Wwwhere is the staff?" the creature growled.

"I . . . I don't know," Rose answered.

The creature raised his arms in an angry rage. "Liar!" he growled. "Give her to me!"

"Who are you?" Rose asked.

The creature moved towards Rose and bellowed from the deepest part of him.

"I am Ravage!" the creature roared.

Rose could not help but scream in panic. Gardner might be dead. Haven was gone and there was no one left. Who knew how many people died in that explosion: people they had been trying to help. People they had been trying to keep safe.

Oh no, Haven thought to herself. She was trapped beneath the falling embers and splintered chards that had buried her. Rose.

They've killed Rose now. This can't be happening again. They've taken another away from me. When will it stop?

As a pot of rage began to boil inside her soul, Haven could begin to feel herself get heavier and weighted. As her rage turned into frenzy, the markings on her arms began to glow through the wraps and she could feel her body tensing up even more. Parts of the wraps fell to the ground. *When will it stop?* Then without thought, Haven Irena Dante punched an explosive hole through the pile of debris that once held her down.

Haven spotted the beast moving towards Rose. "Get away from her!"

Haven, daughter of the Dante line and holder of the mantle, rose from the rubble to take her place against the dark. The markings on her arms glowed in the dark like beacons in the night. Her eyes glowed like white fire and left a trail of light with every movement. She pulled her staff from behind, and as she held it, the staff grew in length and in brilliance. It too, shared the markings of the one who had travelled through the trials and conquered them all.

The beast sprinted towards his new enemy. Every step shook the ground more and more as his thunderous sprint turned into a savage run for his prey. Holding her staff steady, Haven stood her ground and braced for impact as the growling beast hurled himself towards her. She felt her body become dense and even more weighted… like stone. The resulting clash sent them flying into nearby debris with a loud crash. The monster rose from the debris first and lifted Haven by the hair and flung her wide, sending her smashing into a wall. Haven had solidified as she made impact, but not soon enough. Blood trickled from her lip and brow as a result. The beast lifted a portion of fallen shelter wall, and as Haven was picking herself up, he thrust the large piece of brick and mortar towards her.

Once I thought I'd be just fine with . . . moving on from this life, she quickly thought to herself as the wall came towards her. Just so I could be rid of all of this: from life. And be with Mom again. I'm so scared.

As Haven braced for impact, the wall phased completely through her.

And for some reason that means something. Being scared means something.

The wall met the debris behind Haven, smashing it into smaller fragments. Haven ran towards the beast.

My turn.

She thrust her staff into the belly of the giant and then spun around for a second strike to the head. Before she could get another strike in, the beast grabbed her by the neck.

"RRRrrrrr. You smell fresh and tasty." The wretched beast licked Haven's face. Haven grabbed his tongue and pulled it towards her with her right hand and slammed her left fist into his face, between the horns.

"You smell like hell!" she shouted.

The creature jerked its tongue free and spun around, elbowing Haven in the temple. While Haven was dazed by the blow to the head, the thing had time to wind up for an upper cut to her chin, sending her flying upwards. Her staff slipped from her hands, falling to the ground.

No! No! No! Too high! Too high! Her eyes glowed brighter. *I'm falling. I'm . . .*

. . . flying!

Haven floated stationary in the air above the city skyline.

I'm flying!

Nervously, Haven propelled herself even higher, just to make sure that she was not dreaming. That this was really happening. "You'll be different," the child had said to her just after the trials. *I didn't think she meant this,* Haven thought.

Haven peered down at the ravaging beast.

Haven could swear the beast looked frightened. And surprised. Probably wasn't used to feeling fear.

Haven descended like a two-ton missile and slammed into him, burying him in the street. She quickly ascended from the hole she had just created and hovered. Her mouth gaped open. I did that! Seeing her staff nearby, she flew to it and landed softly on solid ground. Then the street directly in front of her began to give way. The beast rose up from the ashes of dirt and asphalt and hurled himself at Haven, who moved away just in time. He landed on the street, but before he could raise a fist, Haven swung her staff and slammed it into his dense body. This time, instead of sending him hurling through the air, the staff took on a life all its own and wrapped itself around him. The creature's eyes widened as the staff became tighter and tighter. When the end of the staff reached the top, it quickly formed into the head of a snake. The ravaging beast turned away in fear as the snake hissed and showed its fangs to its victim.

Stunned, Haven held on to the other end of the staff holding the beast in place while the tip of his tail flung wildly. Haven stood her ground until a voice from behind her sent chills up her spine.

"Release him," said the slithering, eerie voice. Haven turned to see another beast standing in the flames. The monster wore tattered rags with which it hid its leathery, red skin. His yellow, slanted eyes glowed much like the first beast except this one had a skull-shaped head with spiraling horns pointed straight up and protruding teeth with no lips to cover them.

"I said, release him," ordered the monster. "That we may speak of things of great importance."

"What the hell are you talking about?" Haven shouted.

"Why the hell don't you find out?" said the imprisoned beast.

"Who are you? What do you want?" Haven demanded.

The monster waved his long, almost-skeletal fingers in front of Haven's face. With each wave of a finger, a trail of yellow energy followed in its wake. "I am Lord Lock of the Eighth Circle. The brother that you hold in captivity is Lord Ravage of the Seventh Circle and we are of The Aristocracy."

Ravage growled in agreement as Lock continued. "You will unbind my brother, now."

Haven held her ground, holding the staff in place, if not tighter. "I will not. And I will not surrender the staff, since that is obviously what you came here for."

Lock moved closer. "You are correct in your assumption. But you also have information that you've retrieved from your father's company, and since we are obviously in stalemate, I will tell you that we come to make an offer."

"I doubt that you have anything that I could possibly want," Haven answered sharply.

Another foul voice emerged from the darkness. "Oh, but we do child, we surely do," added Lord Limbus. This monster also had red skin and yellow glaring eyes but was in fact hidden inside of a cloak. Hovering over the ground he moved towards Haven. "We do indeed."

Suddenly, a voice that Haven had not heard in two years met her ears with a sweet comfort that gripped her soul and jarred her heart.

"Sweetheart? Little Star?"

It was Beatrice.

Beatrice's likeness phased in as a shower of fine mist. At first it was hard for Haven to make out the true identity of the apparition, but the longer she hovered, the clearer she became. Her face, her hair, her voice all brought Haven back to when she was a child again, safe in the arms of her mother. Haven's staff retracted to its former state and she gently placed it on her back again as she carefully walked towards the specter that had taken Beatrice's appearance. When Haven approached her, she trembled to the very core of her being, like paper in a brisk wind.

It took all the strength that Haven had to say the words. "Mom? Momma?"

"I'm here Sweetheart." The voice was hers. It was trailing in and out, but it was hers.

Haven's voice cracked. "But Mom. How?"

"What matters is that I'm here, now. And I've missed you so much," Beatrice said sadly.

"Did they take you?" Haven asked.

"No, sweetheart. I came willingly." Beatrice said.

Haven stood motionless for a moment. Willingly?

"Momma. They hurt me." Haven added.

"Enough!" Lock bellowed as he waved his finger.

Beatrice quickly dissipated and was gone in a flash.

"No!" Haven cried as she dropped to her knees.

Limbus moved towards Haven as Ravage and Lock took a position behind him.

"Come see for yourself. We have treated her kindly and she stays of her own accord," he said as he hovered above Haven. "You grant us our wish and we will return to you what you have lost."

"The staff," Haven said plainly.

"No! Don't do it Haven!" shouted Rose from the darkness. Holding her injured arm Rose emerged limping from the wreckage. "The staff wields a power unmatched on this earth and should the Aristocracy take control of it their power will be limitless!"

Haven slowly walked to Rose and hugged her. Holding her tight, she whispered in her ear. "The staff and I are one." As she said those words, Haven slipped the data retrieved from Dante Tech into Rose's pocket and moved away. "I have to," she added.

Rose grabbed Haven's arm tightly and slipped something underneath her one bandage as she spoke words of caution.

"Come home," Rose whispered.

"I will."

With those words Haven turned and walked towards Limbus, Lock and Ravage.

Limbus, the traveler as he was sometimes called, waved his hand over the four of them and as the dust from his hand fell, the group of four disappeared into the night. Before their departure, Haven's voice trailed through the night.

"Promise."

Abandon All Hope

As Limbus and Haven descended on a floating platform of cavern rock, Haven could feel the fumes of despair and lost dreams within the very walls. Every insult, anguish and tear ever shed reached out to ensnare her and make her share its torment. *I remember,* she thought. *Mom mentioned hell and how memories only serve to remind those who are here of what they can never hold close again.*

As they approached the level of the Dark Wood, Haven cautiously walked to the edge of the platform to get a closer look at the dense forest. Suddenly, an enormous growling she-wolf lunged at her from the edge of the forest. Thankfully, the beast was beyond her reach and could only snarl in frustration. Haven gasped and moved back towards the center as the she-wolf howled in the night. As they descended deeper into the abyss, she noticed a spotted leopard watching them intently from a tree branch, as if about to pounce on its dinner. Its haunting yellow eyes pierced the dark and brought a chill to Haven's spine as it rumbled a low growl through piercing white teeth.

Haven was relieved to some degree when they passed the Dark Wood. As they descended even deeper, the walls of the cavern became dark red and seemed to close in on them to where she could almost touch them. They finally arrived at a large opening and landed in a vast open area where cavern walls, seething with the vapors of human vice and weary souls, filled the darkness and generated their own brand of light.

"We are at the Great Gate," Limbus stated.

The Great Gate had evolved over the centuries. It was located just before the river Acheron where Charon piloted his hopeless passengers into the deepest parts of Hades. With the formation of the Aristocracy, and the common goals of the Nine Circles, it became necessary to establish a Central Chamber where the plans for the annihilation of humanity could be concocted. Other rooms and areas within the gate served different purposes.

Limbus pointed to an alcove with a rock that was separated from the wall, much like a door with markings of stick figures of a boy and a girl on the front, as if drawn by children.

"Our prince awaits us in the central chamber." He turned towards Haven and motioned her to follow. She reluctantly did. Inconspicuously, she reached into her arm bandage to make sure that whatever it was that Rose had hidden was still there. She could feel a small bump in her bandage. A beacon? she thought to herself. As they walked away from the platform and towards the door, Haven looked up and noticed the inscription on the upper side of the entry way to the gate.

Lasciate ogne speranza, voi ch'intrate

"Abandon All Hope, Ye Who Enter Here," Haven said to herself as she passed the entryway. Her studies had aided her at least partly.

"Through there he awaits," Limbus announced.

Haven stood by as the door slowly moved open. Limbus went in first. She hesitated for a moment, but then she heard something rather peculiar. She heard children playing. Haven rushed in to confirm what she thought she had heard. *Children,* she thought. *These monsters have stolen innocence.* She studied the children, who were no older than twelve or thirteen, playing on monkey bars and swings and upon closer inspection she noticed that some of the clothes the children wore were dated. A boy, who was around ten years old, had on a pair of trousers held up by suspenders. He also had on black and white shoes, white knee socks and a white dress shirt with a newsboy hat. A young girl around the age of eight years old had on a bright yellow pair of polyester pants with flowers on the bottom and a blue and yellow, checkered shirt. One young boy, who was around 12, had a long slick comb over and wore jeans with bright red suspenders and a white t-shirt. The alcove itself was a vast playing area for the children, who had obviously been there for years, and some for decades. Although it was still deep within the cavern, the walls sheltered this area from the outside conditions of the outer gate. The stone terrain was stable and smooth with gravel paths leading to the play area.

The children went about their play and seemed to not notice the arrival of Limbus and Haven. As they proceeded further into the alcove, Limbus pointed Haven into the direction of the monkey bars. A boy of about ten with a spiked collar around his neck, a netted tank top, hard-knuckled half-gloves, boots and torn jeans sat watching the children play from on top of the bars. Underneath his pierced eyebrows, his saddened eyes glowed yellow and he intently watched the children playing. He followed every movement as if he was in careful study of every detail, not wanting to miss a thing. His concentration was broken by the arrival of Limbus and Haven. The prince turned to greet his guests.

"Greetings. I am Luminos. Welcome to my kingdom."

Dumbfounded, Haven cautiously took a step closer. "You're just a boy. How did you get here?" Luminos was annoyed at the question. "I have always been here. I will always be here and very soon I will be up there," he said as he gazed upwards.

"You mean you were taken. I'm guessing all of these other kids were taken too."

Luminos jumped down from the monkey bars and faced the children. "They have everything they will ever need here. They want for nothing and that is how it should be. Look at them," he said as he pointed towards them while facing Haven. "Do they seem miserable to you?"

"It's all they know," answered Haven.

"You are the smug one, aren't you?" snapped Luminos as he marched from side to side and then approached her. "Why don't you lie to me and tell me that you're not miserable. Your parents are gone and here you are living in a homeless shelter. You've lost all of your riches and so called 'security'. From what part of that can you derive any joy?"

Haven ignored the question. "Why are they here? Why are you here?"

Luminos crossed his hands behind his back. "As generous as the Aristocracy has been to me and as much as they have cared for me since I was but a baby, they do not understand humanity. I am here to bridge that gap. To help them understand how humans think."

"And yet you've not been among humans for most of your life," Haven added.

Luminos looked away. "Humans are far too arrogant. They make poor choices. Their lives are in complete disarray and as a result they cannot govern themselves."

Luminos excitedly pointed his finger at the children. "They can't even watch over their own children! They need someone to guide them and to lead them from chaos to order. We will usher in a new era for change and bring about this new order. We will take our place as the rightful heir of the surface world and bring about a new freedom for all. One that is better and where all are equals and not one is discarded."

"Humans learn from their mistakes," Haven snapped back.

"Like your father?" Luminos asked. "Has he learned from his mistakes?"

"He will have to answer for that. Now where is my mother?"

Luminos narrowed his eyes at Haven. "You will renounce the claim to your inheritance. Namely, Dante Technologies."

"Where is she?" Haven demanded.

This time, it was Luminos who ignored the question. "You will surrender the staff of Moshe and the plans stolen by your mother or you will never leave this place!"

"You're looking for something and it's not the plans or the staff. You're looking for something more meaningful than that and trust me, I would know."

"You know nothing," Luminos snapped back.

"Really? Tell me something. What is your mother's name?" Haven asked.

"How dare you," growled Luminos.

"What is her name?" asked Haven.

"Surrender the plans!" shouted Luminos.

Haven pulled out her staff and it slowly stretched to combat length and its markings began to emit a soft glow. "If you had my mother, you would know where the plans are!" Haven roared. Her staff lit up the dark of the cavern as she spun it around her back and over her head.

"She is here!" shouted Luminos.

"Liar!" Haven growled.

Luminos breathed heavily as his eyes glowed brighter. "Very well," he said angrily. "Kill the brat," he ordered.

And with that order, winged and grounded demons alike surrounded Haven as she stood poised for attack. She could feel herself getting boxed in. The feeling of being trapped began to boil her blood as reflected in her glowing markings. As a martial artist, Haven was taught that whoever attacks first in a fight is bound to win. The closest demon caught the first blow. Haven used her feet and hands with spins and kicks that confounded the enemy.

"Leave it to the little guy to do your dirty work, eh?" Haven asked sarcastically.

Blow after blow Haven took it to the very demons of Hell while unbeknownst to her the merry-go-round that some of the children were playing on began to spin faster and faster. After several revolutions, the machine came to life and planted its arms into the ground. Haven caught this out of the corner of her eye. What is that?

Luminos glared at Haven as he stood in front of the transforming device smiling proudly.

No time to figure out what that is. Need to get out of here. Haven reached into her bandage and pulled out the device that Rose had snuck into her wrap. She had never seen the device before and didn't know what would happen if she pressed the white button on top.

Do I trust them? she asked herself. Do I?

Haven pressed the button which began a countdown of five seconds. Four. Three. She slammed it down on the ground and prepared for an escape. . . . one.

A massive static discharge shot out from the device, striking every corner of the cave. One discharge struck Luminos head on, sending him into convulsions. A glob of snakes slithered out of his mouth as if he were throwing them up. As quickly as they came out, they converged together on the ground. Morphing and growing, the snakes merged into a giant beast that filled the cavern. With the massive wings of a bat, the prince of the underworld made his appearance. His screeches were ear-splitting and resonated throughout the cavern. The monster hovered wildly within the cavern, filling it with evil incarnate.

"The Arm of Hades will be your undoing!" he cried as gusts of wind emanated from the flapping of his giant wings. As the monster hovered, the boy-host lay limp on his side watching everything. Unable to move, he blinked once as he watched Haven. He blinked again and his lip began to quiver as he shed one tear that rolled down his sorrowful face.

The demons surrounded Haven once more and backed her into a cavern wall. Panic set in. Haven trembled. She took slow steps backwards, hoping that the wall would somehow disappear. But instead . . .

. . . she phased through the wall of the cavern.

"Find her!" the beast howled. He then turned to once again merge with the lifeless boy. Demons scurried upwards into the cavern.

As Luminos ceased shaking, Solstice came out of the shadows and helped him to his feet.

"There, brother," she said wryly. Luminos stood and straightened his shoulders. "Are we ready to begin deployment?"

"We are, Prince Luminos," she replied.

"And our guest?" he added.

"Safely secure," Solstice answered. "But you are weary from the confrontation with Haven. I strongly suggest you rest and let us continue the work."

"She is right," said a voice from the shadows. "The children will see to your needs, Lord Luminos," the hybrid Mist said as he emerged from the shadows. As the host of Lord Lock, Vadik Lenka proved to be essential in the trade of children on the black market and was responsible for the operation that brought them to that place.

High Sovereign Paolo agreed as he too, stepped out of the shadows.

"Very well," replied Luminos, exasperated. Solstice then walked Luminos to his resting pod, much like the ones that housed the hosts of the Aristocracy in the Central Chamber.

"Don't worry," Solstice affirmed. "Very soon we will regain what we have both lost, a family." The pod closed and Luminos fell asleep. "Rest, my prince." As Solstice locked the pod, Luminos' eyes became heavy, and just as he was about to fall asleep, he looked outward from the pod and whispered, "Haven? Are you there?"

Geryon the shade slithered through the halls of the dark, wet cavern where the humans were kept, and with a whip of its scorpion's tail, unlocked a prison cell. With eyes widened in shock, Rob Dante moved to the back of the cell. The giant shade wrapped its tail around Roberto and proceeded to remove him from his cell with no finesse whatsoever. With its hairy paws, the shade escorted Rob passed the cell of a grungy, long-haired prisoner who had been there since before Rob had arrived. As the shade slithered and crawled by the cell, it hissed and shook its tail at the prisoner as if it were mocking him. The captive looked up, and with dry, parched lips said, "One day, my friend you will bow to me. And on that day, you will call me master."

After Haven passed through the wall, she hid in a small recess within it as the demons rushed upwards. She waited a moment and then reluctantly launched herself into the tunnels shooting upwards. *I think I might actually be getting better at this,* she thought to herself.

Haven shot out of the pit into the night sky not fully realizing where in the world she could be. She stopped a moment, looking for monsters of the air, and finding none, she fixed her eyes upon the point of exit.

Olem Mines. I'm not far from the city, she deduced. Haven flew upwards, so as not to be detected. She knew the monsters would be looking for her close to the ground, so she had to stay above the clouds. Despite the hellish experience she had just been through, she found some solace in flying just above the clouds. As the winds lifted her high above the city, her long hair waved like a flowing gown in a calm breeze.

Her heart sank for the boy inside of the monster that was Luminos. She wondered what life would have had in store for him had he lived among humans. Strangely enough, it felt better to feel burdened for someone other than herself. Haven had spent so long inside a dark cold cave of anger and pain that, like Luminos, she had forgotten what it was like to live above the ground. *He did have a point,* she thought to herself. *Was I ever really happy?* She had everything that life could offer, and it never seemed like quite enough. There was always something nagging and clawing inside of her; a question for which she could never seem to find the answer. At some point, she was going to have to grow out of this. Maybe now is that time. *There had to have been something he deeply wanted or needed, she thought. After all, he's not that much different. And neither is Sol.*

Sol!

Haven shot over the skyline and headed back to the shelter.

Masks

The fire department, with its high-powered water hoses, had doused all evidence of the life that once existed in Desert Rose. As soon as Haven landed in the charred remains, she scoured the area looking for survivors. She moved debris from side to side hoping to find something, someone . . . anything that could be traced to a survivor. After finding no one, she stood staring at the debris in a pool of hopelessness and disbelief. With smoke and cinders floating up into the night sky, she wondered where Rose, Gardener and the residents had gone.

All those families, she thought. *Gone. Just like that. There were children here. We were supposed to keep them safe.*

Then, out of the corner of her eye, she saw a lonely figure standing in the midst of the smoldering piles of wreckage that now adorned the former place of refuge. Much like Haven, the shadow appeared to be in mourning, absorbing the impact of what had just happened.

It was Rose. She's alive, Haven thought to herself. Haven ran to her and embraced her like a relative she had not seen since childhood. Rose met her with equal excitement and tears in her eyes.

"Are you all right, love?" Rose asked as she brushed away Haven's hair from her forehead.

"Yes, I'm OK," Haven said through pants with downcast eyes.

Rose lifted Haven's chin with her gentle hand and met her sad eyes with eyes of hope.

"It's good to see you, dear. I feared the worst."

"I'm OK, for the most part," Haven affirmed. "I was afraid for you when I left. I'm sorry, Rose."

"It's quite all right, love. I'm glad you made it out of there in one piece." Rose said.

Haven's heart sank as they walked together in the midst of the wreckage. Everything that they had worked towards was laid waste.

"You were taken into their domain, I take it," Rose queried.

"Yes. Yes, I was." Haven replied.

"It must have been horrible."

"It's like being inside of hopelessness," Haven said. "A complete void of anything good."

"How did you escape?" Rose asked.

"Through an old-abandoned mineshaft just outside the city."

"Come with me, love. I want to show you something." Rose wrapped her arm around Haven's and guided her through the wreckage to a seemingly ordinary door.

"Wait! My friend Sol. She was supposed to come by here. Please tell me she wasn't here when it happened."

"No one died in the attack, love. Most were sheltered below and those who were injured were taken to the hospital. I'm sure she's fine."

"But I should go see if she's OK," Haven said frantically.

"Soon, love."

Rose placed her hand on a section of the door, which instantly turned into a fluidic sensor wrapping itself around her hand.

"Rose! Watch out!" Haven exclaimed, as she tried to pull Rose's hand away from the fluid which enveloped it. Rose pulled Haven's hand away. "It's all right, love."

The fluid then retracted and rejoined the door, which opened for Rose. Haven hesitated. "Come, love," Rose said assuredly. "It's OK." They both stepped into what appeared to be a chamber and the door closed behind them, leaving them in the dark. With a loud swoosh they began their alarming descent at alarming speed. Haven anxiously grabbed the sides of the elevator and Rose responded by placing her comforting hand on Haven's shoulder. Soon, lights flickered from floor to ceiling as they passed floor after floor. Haven then knew that wherever they were going. It was buried deep. They descended to the sub-levels where Haven could then see all of the activity through the transparent elevator wall.

Sub-level 6: Education and Training.

The children of the shelter were engrossed in study within individual classrooms equipped with the latest in fluidic technology.

This level was followed by...

Sub-Level 7: Biochemical Technology

Sub-Level 6: Organic Technology and so forth. The level of sophistication in these lower levels astounded Haven.

"This is incredible," she said with a gasp. "We're almost there, love," Rose said proudly. The elevator came to a halt and Haven could see Gardener working on the other side of its door. Noticing their arrival, Gardener turned and came to the elevator to greet them. When Haven saw the technology on display in the meeting room, both practical and experimental, she was astonished. Fluidic technology with fluidic screens and sensors lined the walls and augmented every worktable. The readout panels and the main sensor, which hovered above the center conference table, provided most of the room's illumination. Gardener stepped forward and held out his hand.

"Welcome to the Garden," he said in a deep, calming voice. Haven noticed the bump on Gardener's head from the blast. "Are you OK?" she asked.

"Yeah, I'm all right," he replied. "Don't you worry about me. I'll be just fine."

"This is amazing!" Haven said as she took Gardener's hand and stepped off the elevator. "How did you do all of this?"

"Well, Gardener designed it," said Rose. "And as such, it is aptly named. As for the funding and all of the equipment, we have your father to thank."

To some degree, Haven was almost disappointed to hear those words. But they had everything they would ever need there, and for that, and for once, she was grateful.

"This does seem like something he would have a hand in," Haven answered.

"More than a hand," Rose added. "He not only provided the funding for it, but the technology that we employ here came from his research."

Haven suddenly turned to Rose. "My mother was never there," she confirmed.

"I know, love," Rose consoled. "Let's talk." They walked over to the conference table and sat down.

Haven sat forward in her chair and began to report what she saw. "There was a young boy, about nine or ten. It's someone they've had for a very long time, so he's been there since birth or close to it. He's their leader, and he claims to be the gap in understanding between the Aristocracy and us. His name is Luminos."

Gardener and Rose looked at each other. "Interesting," Rose replied.

Haven continued. "There is also a device of some kind. It was strange, because it started out as a merry-go-round in a playground."

"A playground?" asked Gardener.

"Yes, a playground. They've been raising children there for a very long time, generations even. I'm guessing they raised them and used them for hosts and who knows what else," Haven explained. "These kids had to have been taken from their families and homes or wherever they're from."

"That explains the slave trade," Gardener added. He slid his hand into a vat of liquid which instantly brought up the Virgilian Order Database which he had access to during his time with the Order. A readout of a man with long, white hair and a black, knee-length leather jacket popped up. "This is Mist," he explained. "He's been running a slave trade organization for years now. He's a dirt-bag of the lowest kind. The way he takes a kid," Gardener said, as he pointed to the gaseous demons in Mist's inside jacket, "is that he uses those demons. You see those? He uses them to entice the children to do what he wants, and they disappear. Sometimes he asks for a ransom. I'd been digging into where I came from, and it led back to him. That was all I could find until we got kicked out of the Order."

"This is truly disturbing," Rose commented.

"We have to get them out of there," Haven demanded.

"And do what with them?" Gardener interjected. "They've been down there all of their lives. We're talkin' kids that are gonna have some issues."

"We all have issues," Haven replied.

"And speaking of issues, Harry Reeve is one of them," Haven added. "When I went to Dad's office, I noticed he was wearing the ring of the Aristocracy."

"Figures," Gardener commented.

"This news escalates matters," Rose stated. "With Reeve in control of the company, the technology developed by it will be made available to the Aristocracy."

Haven almost glared at Rose. "Not if Jinx can help it. She's been a loyal friend to the family since before I was born. There's no way she'll help them."

"Hope not," Gardener added.

"What about the device?" Haven asked. "When I threw the static bomb down . . ."

Gardener interrupted. "Did it work?" he asked.

"Oh yeah. It worked," Haven answered. "Anyway, the beast inside Luminos left the boy and said something like the 'Arm of Hades will be your doom.'"

"Yea, about that," Gardener said. "I checked out the information that Jinx downloaded into your compad. It talks about a project called Armades. I'm guessing that's short for 'Arm of Hades'."

"That must be it," Rose added.

Gardener continued. "It's not just one device we're talking about, but many. It's like an EMP net. Normally, an electromagnetic pulse shuts down all electricity, but the pulse in this thing has a dual purpose. It shuts down everything in its 20-mile radius, but then the EMP sensor on the other devices are triggered and those devices send out a pulse to the others in its range. I mapped each one and found that there are a ton of these bad boys planted throughout the city on top of something that's important to the city, like a fault line, a water main, an electricity hub, stuff like that."

Rose sat up in her chair. "What happens if we destroy one of these within the city limits?"

"You can't," Gardener said. "The shutdown sequence can trigger a pulse. You shut one down, they all go off."

"So how do we stop it?" Rose asked.

"We go to the source that created this tech. My father," Haven said reluctantly. "I haven't seen him since I've been back. Guess I was going to have to sooner or later."

"Are you sure you want to do that, love?" Rose asked.

Haven looked her straight in the eye. "Yes. Yes, I'm sure."

"I'll go with you," Gardener added.

"No. I need to do this alone. I'll ask him to write the instructions on a compad that I'll take with me."

"All right then, but tonight you rest," said Rose. "This can wait until tomorrow, and you've been through enough for today I would think. There are upper-level quarters that you can sleep in tonight."

"You're right." Haven stood up.

Gardener reached behind his chair and pulled out a satchel. "Take this," he said. "It'll come in handy for your trip." He and Rose stood up and watched her walk towards the elevator. Haven entered the elevator, but to the surprise of Rose and Gardener, she did not remain in it. Instead, Haven shot up through the elevator ceiling and the shaft faster than the elevator ever could.

Rose and Gardener remained pensive after watching her fly up towards the surface.

"I did not want to speak of this while she was here," said Rose, "but with Soledad showing up just before the blast, things could get even more complicated than they already are."

"I saw her from behind the wall," Gardener added. "Whatever she used must have been very small and untraceable. The police didn't find anything and neither did I."

"I left her for only a moment in the kitchen," Rose said as she sighed. "This is all very taxing. Very taxing indeed," lamented Rose.

Gardener knew what she meant.

"We're finding out the hard way who wears masks, she added. "They've been hatching this plan for quite a long time."

"Yup," Gardener agreed. "They've planted someone in all the right places which means there's one place left that we haven't checked."

"The Virgilian Order," Rose stated.

Gardener nodded. "You got it."

Rose moved towards Gardener with a perplexed look on her face.

"I think it's time we pay a visit to an old friend."

Haven flew through the afternoon sky in a state of dread, not just because she was soaring through the clouds, but because of the inner turmoil that came as a result of seeing her father again. She had practically grown up believing one thing about him, and then, all of a sudden, what she thought was true wasn't necessarily so. *He believed he had to confront this great evil, but at what cost?* She thought to herself. *Should a man leave his family to go save the world? I don't know that I could ever answer that question. I gave up on him so long ago. Gave up trying. But things are different now. The way he looked at me from his prison cell when he was first arrested. He uprooted everything I had ever believed about him and turned into something else.* Haven's eyes glowed and left a streak through the sky as she raced across the night to see the man who had caused her so much pain. *I don't know what to believe anymore.*

Being late and after visiting hours, Haven chose to sneak into the prison where her father was being held. She landed on the old rooftop and ran towards one of the access doors, looking side-to-side for guards. She held her breath and phased through the door to the Charity Vane Maximum Security Prison, also known as Judas' Cradle, right behind one of the negligent prison guards. Being loyal to Dominic Reins had its rewards, so the guards tended to succumb to slothfulness when it came to being watchful. This allowed Mr. Reins to continue with his secret activities among the prison population. An occasional scream heard throughout the halls went unnoticed. Languid corruption was a way of life and everyone accepted it. Covertly, she came to the outer door of the prison block and phased through it. She was in. She could smell the stench of lives lost and long-dead dreams in the musty halls of the cellblock. She dodged some rats feasting on something red and fluidic, with a pungent odor almost like rotten potatoes. "Uhh," she let out as she covered her nose and proceeded on.

After a few steps, she thought she could hear voices through the trickle of water in the corridor. As she walked further, she could clearly tell that one was male and the other female. The female's voice sounded oddly familiar and they were clearly close to where Haven intended to go. The closer she got, the fewer cells there were, and she thought that whoever was carrying on a conversation, her father had to be a part of it. Wanting to hear what the nature of the conversation was, she slowed down and looked up. An exposed, large air duct, which ran down the ceiling of the corridor, would provide a perfect cover. She clenched her fists and closed her eyes once again. A soft glow began to shine through her eyelids and with one hop she floated up to the conduit and phased through it.

Made it, she thought to herself, relieved.

On her hands and knees, she slowly crawled through the large air duct, so as not to be heard. She could see the small trickle of light that came through the vent and could hear the conversation much more clearly. She stopped for a moment. *Can't be,* she thought. She moved closer to the vent and peeked through. From that vantage point, she could see and hear everything.

"Lord Vengus," Sol began. "The shelter is destroyed, but the plans could not be located." A very skinny man sat calmly in his prison cell behind a wall of glass on a steel cold bed. "Oh come now, my dear, there's no need to get your pretty little hair in knots. The plan will come together. It always does. You are one with Lord Hedonis now, and as such you are stronger, so there should be no doubt in your mind that this plan of ours will work!"

Haven cringed. She could not believe what she was hearing. What have you done, Sol? She bit her lip and tried her best to stay quiet in order to learn more.

Sol frowned and crossed her arms across her chest. "The plan will come together? You saw what she did in the abyss when she figured out that you didn't have her mommy. These new friends of hers may have hidden the plans."

The man interrupted, "Which you didn't recover, correct?"

"My orders were to destroy the shelter and I did just that," snapped Sol.

"And quite nicely from what I hear," he added.

Sol continued. "I must admit that joining with Hedonis has taken some getting used to. As a hybrid, I feel stronger, but at the same time, apprehensive."

"Now that's your human side talking. You'll learn in time that the Solstice that stands before me is more powerful than the Lord of the Second Circle and Soledad could ever be on their own."

"I understand," Solstice agreed. "What is the next step?"

"The next step for you is to relax," he answered. "Everything is falling into place. You should be proud of what you've accomplished. Truly, you are of us!"

Solstice bowed her head. "Thank you, Lord Vengus."

"We should transport to the Central Chamber for any further discussion," Vengus added.

She hesitated for a moment. "As I have yet to learn to transport myself between dominions, I have only you to rely on."

"Agreed then," he stated, as he moved back in his cell. He removed the ring of the Aristocracy from his finger and placed it in his pocket. The man's eyes began to glow, and soon after, a glob of snakes slithered out of his mouth and dropped to the floor in one big pile. The black, slimy echoes of the dark merged and morphed until they formed the giant, bat-winged monster known as Vengus. With fangs drooling in the head of a lion, Lord Vengus flapped his wings mercilessly within the cell. He had steel bracers with chains dangling from them and in one swing he shattered the glass between himself and Solstice.

"Your chariot awaits, my dear," growled Lord Vengus. Solstice approached Vengus and turned around as he embraced her from behind. He wrapped his wings around her, hiding her from Haven's view, and in a blast of black smoke, both Vengus and Solstice disappeared.

Haven phased through the duct and landed on the musty floor in a state of shock. She ran over to the cell next to the man, who was lying catatonic on his prison bed.

This is insane! Haven thought to herself. *What have you done, Sol? You! You stupid, dumb piece of . . . what were you thinking?* Haven put her head down between her hands as tears flowed down her face.

I can't. I can't take this anymore. It's too much. No, no, no, no. Her heart was pounding. She grabbed her chest as it tightened.

"No," she whimpered. Her breathing became shallow and hard.

The prison alarm sounded loudly and echoed through the chasm that was the corridor. Haven heard the rush of the guards' footsteps. She turned to phase back into the duct when a whisper came from the shadows.

"Oh, poor little daddy's girl."

Haven turned around. "Harry!"

Harry walked out of the shadows and approached Haven. "Well, well, well. Poor little daddy's girl with no daddy to save her."

The guards surrounded Harry as a show of support.

Haven looked around at the number of guards and then turned her gaze upon Harry.

"I don't need him to save me, you jackass!" Haven replied.

"Such language from such a pure soul," Harry responded sarcastically. "I wonder what your daddy would say if he heard you now."

"I could say the same thing about you, Harry. You've had all of this planned all along," Haven shot back.

"Figure this out, did you? Smart little daddy's girl," Harry replied. "How long have you known? Well, about me, that is."

"You were always a cause of division for my family. Always coming up with emergencies that only Dad could handle, always coming up with excuses to take him away from us," Haven replied angrily. "That, and your stupid ring gave you away!"

"Your father needed no excuses. He was a man on a mission. Serves him right for not paying attention to what's right under his nose." Harry walked around and looked inside the cell that once held Rob Dante. "As for the ring, I tried to explain to them that it would be our undoing, but since the ring enables the host to remain joined, it was necessary. Without the ring we are weak. With the ring, the two become one. Much like your staff from which you derive great power."

Haven pulled out her staff, which began to extend. "You monster! You've taken my parents, my friend. What more can you take from me?" she cried.

Harry removed his ring and placed it in his pocket.

"What more indeed," he growled.

Harry shook violently. His eyes glowed and snakes slithered out of his mouth and fell to the floor. Harry's limp body fell to the floor with his eyes and mouth wide open. What stood before Haven now was the monstrous Traiton, Lord of the Ninth Circle. The red beast with massive horns, the head of a bull and scales on his shoulders and forearms stood before Haven, huffing and puffing in the damp corridor. Traiton grabbed Haven by the throat and held her tight.

"For years I've watched you grovel at his feet like a vagrant eager to taste a scrap of attention no matter how small. You humans are so pitiful. Tormenting you is a treat to the senses." Traiton lifted Haven up with one hand and wound up the other to strike. "And I shall enjoy watching you die!" Traiton punched Haven in the face sending her flying into the wall behind her in a loud crash. Haven despondence over Sol's treachery warring against the sweet memories of her childhood friend now paralyzed her. Traiton raced towards her and rammed her with his horns, pushing her further into the wall.

Thankfully, her molecular density had increased substantially to the point of withstanding a crippling puncture.

Traiton backed up to ram her again.

When he did, Haven managed to grab him by the horns and pulled him in and pushed him into the wall. The entire wall came crashing down on Traiton, sending a pile of dust into the air.

Then from the darkness, more demons arrived to aid the Lord of the Ninth Circle. A scaly beast wrapped its tail around Haven's neck. Haven thrust her staff into the stomach of the beast, sending it squealing. Another beast jumped from the ceiling, hoping to overtake her from above. Haven spun around and slammed the edge of her staff against his face, flinging him into another demon. The monsters howled in the night as, one-by-one, they attacked a weakened soul. More demons came out of the darkness to wage war against the daughter of Dante. The more she fought, the more came to join the fight. Monster after monster came and piled on top of her until the mound of beasts rose to the ceiling. Haven began to droop from exhaustion. Her spirit waned as she leaned one hand against a nearby wall. She pushed herself off and tried to rage on but only for a moment. Haven tripped and fell on her knees.

"Enough!" ordered Traiton. The beast motioned some of the monsters to move away from Haven. A demon held each arm while the staff of Moshe lay next to her on the floor. Traiton walked closer to ascertain the level of Haven's exhaustion, who was sweating profusely and breathing in quick short breaths.

"Tired?" Traiton asked.

Haven could barely get a word out. "Not too tired to kick your big fat red ugly . . . ."

The demons roared.

"Silence!" ordered Traiton.

Haven glared at him with all the hate she could muster. He stood in silence, glaring back.

"Throw her down the shaft," Traiton ordered with a growl. The demons roared a howling cheer. Two demons raced in with chains and bound her hands and feet. Another demon picked up the staff and handed it to Traiton.

"Aaah, the staff of Moshe," Traiton said proudly. "We'll see what this staff can do in the hands of real power."

The monsters roared and cheered once again as they lifted Haven from the floor and placed her in a caged gurney used for experiments by the warden. They ran the chains through the cage and tied her down. Now absolutely despondent, Haven could fight no more. The demons chanted and cheered as they carried Haven into the mine shaft elevator. One of the demons scurried on top of the elevator and jumped up and down in excited anticipation. Traiton made his way over to the elevator door to gloat.

"Don't be afraid, daddy's girl. Soon this will all be over. You don't have to worry about having to deal with your father's legacy. Soon it will be in good hands and you will finally find rest."

The demons cheered one last roar in unison.

"Drop her," Traiton ordered.

The demon on top bit the line of the elevator, sending it jetting down the shaft. Haven could hear the echo of the demon's cheer as the elevator shook and rumbled on its way down. Haven's breathing slowed as she became aware of where she was and what was happening. The faster the car went the louder it shook. Haven tried to loosen the chains to no avail. Haven looked around once more, and then closed her eyes and reopened them.

Her eyes turned white hot.

The car slammed into the bottom of the shaft in a fiery explosion, sending pipes and parts flying in loud clanks and fireballs outward and upwards. The cage was incinerated in a fiery explosion, and in one loud unified shout, the demons screeched and howled in victory.

One of the demons approached the car to gloat over their victory. But it was empty. And the howl of victory quickly turned to a roar of despair and defeat.

The Pot is Stirred

The next day, Rose's gray robe flapped in the strong sea winds as she stood on the rocky coast of Charity Vane just beneath the Sons of Virgilius monastery in a heated discussion with a life-long friend.

"You know I'm right about this," Rose argued.

"You should not have come here," asserted Valerio. The sovereign stood in his traditional garb trying to convince Rose of the error in her argument. "It's too dangerous."

"You know very well that there is no other time when the sovereigns are together," Rose added. "You know it's him."

Valerio looked away at the open sea. "It's true I did suspect that there was something wrong when you were disfellowshipped, my sister. But I have not yet arrived at your conclusion that it was the high sovereign himself!"

Her voice rose in agitation. "I am telling you that this is the truth, and you are simply choosing to bury your head in the sand. You are risking the peril of mankind by choosing to ignore it!" Rose turned away and gazed upon the open sea. "As the brave Dietrich Bonhoeffer once said, 'Silence in the face of evil is evil itself. Not to speak is to speak. Not to act is to act.'"

Those words clearly shook Valerio. "It just seems unbelievable to me that they would go through this much effort to destroy us. It would take years of planning and positioning to accomplish such a task. He may have acted rashly but he's done so many great things."

"My brother, that is what makes them evil. They are patient in their planning, and they will go as far as cloaking themselves in good deeds to accomplish a greater evil," Rose explained. "It is not good enough to simply watch any longer."

Valerio cast a final gaze upon his friend of many years and sighed. "The dinner bell is about to ring. And I must take my leave of you now, so once again, goodbye, my sister."

Valerio carefully walked over the rocks and headed towards the monastery. He quickly climbed the steep stairs of the citadel and went into the monastery undetected. Valerio then quietly went into his quarters to change into the dinner cloak as tradition dictated, but when he went into his closet, he found something . . . or someone that did not belong. His eyes widened. He peered up at the menacing, shadowy figure and gasped. "Oh my. Hello."

On the outskirts of Charity Vane, inside the old abandoned Olem Mines, Lord Ravage summoned monsters and demons from below to his side in a loud roar that was carried to the very center of the Earth. Within moments, winged demons shot out of the mineshaft in a flash of wind. A demonic minotaur joined by a shade burst through the mines to heed the call. In a loud explosion, a giant blazing chariot pulled by harpies emerged from the earth to ferry the land-based demons on a mission. The minotaur and the shade both boarded the red-blazing chariot while the harpies screeched, anxious to get underway. In a thunderous boom, the chariot raced towards the sky and the harpies screeched and pierced the night with the flapping of their wings to begin their quest; to destroy the Sons of Virgil.

It was customary for the sovereigns of the Virgilian Order to dine together, albeit in the light of a single candle at the center of the vast dining hall, and in complete silence. There was always a procession in which ended with the High Sovereign, as a sign of humility, he entered with the chalice that contained the juice that would be consumed as communion by the sovereigns that evening. Also, as a sign of humility, their places at the table were different every night, so as to not to give the illusion of a higher rank for whomever sat closer to the High Sovereign. Each sovereign wore a cloak to hide their identity and maintain a sense of equality among them and washed their hands as they entered. On this evening, all washed except one.

The evening dinner bell always rang at 7:30 sharp and lasted 30 minutes – no more, no less.

The sovereigns, followed by the High Sovereign, took a seat at the supper table in silence with heads bowed in humility. One by one each plate was blessed and passed from hand to hand. Each sovereign had a cup of their own that they would drink the communion from.

High Sovereign noticed that one of the sovereign's head was lowered even further as the plates were passed around. It must be Valerio, he thought to himself *It is unfortunate that he has chosen to align himself with the disfellowshipped*. The High Sovereign placed his hand over the chalice and discreetly opened a ring that unleashed a liquid into the cup. Then he passed it on to the next sovereign. Each sovereign poured a portion into their communion cup and passed it on. The chalice made its way over to the sovereign whose head was bowed low, who placed it on the table before him. When the last chalice returned to the High Sovereign, everything stopped, and the sovereigns sat in silence.

Although he did not utter a word, the High Sovereign then broke the bread and passed it around. Each took a portion to save for communion. After this, the High

Sovereign raised his chalice. The sovereigns raised their chalices in unison. The sovereign in question raised his last. High Sovereign noticed his hands were rugged and worn like that of a gardener.

"Consul Annucci, you grace us with your presence," Paolo said angrily.

"Actually, it's Gardener now." And with those words, Gardener threw open his cloak and threw it down. "Now let's get down to business!" He pulled out a small device that had been hidden in his cloak and pushed the button. In a flash of brilliant light, Paolo was thrown from his chair and landed right beside Gardener in a fetal position. His eyes rolled to the back of his head as he mumbled, "Returnnnn. Returnnnn." The other sovereigns were thrown back against their chairs and scrambled for safety inside the vast hall.

"Stay that way," Gardener shot back. As he turned, the light faded revealing the Lord of the Sixth Circle, Retic.

The demon heretic stood tall in his coat of fire and stared down Gardener with terrifying eyes that had double irises. "Weaponer. You dare call me out of my host?" Retic protested. "Soon the sun will set on your kind and the filth that is the human race will reign no more!"

Gardener reached into his cloak, but before he could grab a hold, Retic reached out to him and grabbed him violently by the arm and threw him against the wall. Gardener slammed against the hard stone and landed in a loud thud that almost knocked him out. Retic went in for the kill once more. Being much larger and taller than Gardener, Retic was able to lift Gardener with great ease and tossed him once more against another wall. Gardener groaned in pain, but once again tried to get up. Then a voice came from behind.

"Stay your hand on him beast!" cried Valerio, who burst through the door with a set of bolas in his hand. Retic made a run for Valerio, but before he could make it to him, Valerio swung the bolas in one motion and flung them at Retic. The chain between the bolas wrapped itself around Retic's neck and when the bolas on each end met, they exploded unleashing the holy water that was contained within them. Retic screamed in agony and moved away from Valerio. He stumbled towards the massive table and came down crashing on it, laying it to waste. Valerio ran to Gardener to ascertain his old friend's condition.

Valerio helped Gardener up. "Are you well, my old friend?"

"Just peachy," Gardener replied sarcastically. Suddenly, the entire wall behind where the dinner table once stood, collapsed in a rain of fire. Ravage burst through along with the demon minotaur and shade. The harpies flew into the monastery in a mad dash. Ravage then disembarked from his chariot, landing on the ground in a loud thud, shaking the floor beneath him.

"Aaah, it is the legendary Weaponer! What a delight it will be to crush your flesh into oblivion and send your soul into the pit!" Ravage growled.

Gardener sighed. "Come on, baby! Come to papa!"

"You are standing on holy ground, monster. You will leave this place at once!" ordered Valerio.

Retic moved forward. "What chance have you against us? You humans are weak and flawed and you will soon fall to the kingship of the Aristocracy!"

Sovereign McKenzy whispered from behind, "Flawed yes, but not weak!"

The other members of the Order rushed in behind Sovereign McKenzy and stood ready for battle.

"Especially after a quick trip to the armory," Sovereign Choudron added. Sovereign McKenzy raised her sword and lunged at the minotaur, who blocked it with its mace. Sovereign Justus raised his bolas, lunged and launched them at a harpy flying overhead, sending it crashing down. Sovereign Choudron pulled his kamas out of his cloak and lunged at the centaur.

Gardener reached inside his cloak once again and pulled out a circular, flat device, but just before he activated it, Ravage raced towards him and knocked it out of his hand.

Ravage then threw a back fist at Valerio, which sent him crashing into the wall. The device landed at the feet of an unsuspecting sovereign still hiding in the shadows. Before Gardener could get to safety, Ravage lifted him up. Ravage sniffed him and licked Gardener's bald head like a lollipop. "You taste bitter, but you'll do!" The savage beast Ravage roared and then moved to strike a deadly blow when the voice of an elderly woman came from the door.

"You are no lord, beast!" declared Rose. She pushed a button on the device she held but nothing happened. Rose looked at the device quizzically, and then at Gardener.

"Wait for it," he said. "But I'd get down if I were you." All at once the sovereigns dropped and lay flat on the floor. Rose tossed the device on the table before she hit the floor.

A deafening sonic wave shot out from the device and cut through every piece of furniture in the room. When the wave hit the minotaur and the shade, they instantly dissolved into snakes and fell to the floor in a flutter of thumps and bumps. The harpies that were hit also dissolved into snakes while some managed to frantically fly away through the hole they had created in the wall.

All Retic could do was watch the wave come directly at him. As it sliced him in half, snakes flew everywhere, finally falling. Ravage tried to scurry to his chariot as he saw the wave coming, but he too was too late. As he jumped for the chariot, he was caught in mid-air as were the harpies that were pulling it. They all instantly dissolved into snakes and fell to the rocky shores below the monastery.

As the snakes fell, the sovereigns tried to avoid them and shrugged them off of their backs. Once the wave completed its journey, Gardener sprung to his feet. He noticed a medieval war hammer that was as long as he was hanging on a wall and quickly retrieved it.

"It's go time," he screamed as he began to smash the heads of the remaining serpents. Gardener whooped and hollered as he swung his hammer and crashed it down on the snakes that scurried for their lives. The serpents that were not killed raced towards the opening of the wall and slithered out to the rocks below. Gasping for breath and with a smile on his face, Gardener looked over at Valerio. "Can I keep this?" he asked.

"It's yours, friend," Valerio answered.

"You're having too much fun, it seems," Rose stated.

Gardener nodded, "Heh, heh."

Sovereign McKenzy sheathed her sword. "Watching got boring anyway," she stated. All of the sovereigns then turned to look for Paolo, who was still catatonic on the ground.

Valerio knelt down and patted him on the back. "You're not alone, brother. We'll help you get better." Gardener and Rose walked over to Valerio. "What will you do with him?" asked Gardener.

Valerio stood up. "He's still one of us. We won't rest until he is well, but he will have to be placed in protective custody in the infirmary until he recovers."

Rose placed her hand gently on his shoulder. "We have a greater concern. The armies of the Aristocracy are assembling, and they have a powerful weapon at their disposal."

Still groggy, Paolo came around. Barely able to lift his head, he uttered, "The weapon has been activated. It is too late."

Sovereign McKenzy, Sovereign Chaudron and Sovereign Justus all gathered around. Sovereign McKenzy was the first to speak. As the youngest of the sovereigns and only in her twenties, she was also the most forward-thinking. "Sovereign Valerio, we can't continue in the mandate of non-interference. The danger now is too great."

Valerio turned and began to lead them out of the now-destroyed dining hall. "Walk with me," he asked them.

"Where are we going?" Gardener asked.

"You'll see, answered Valerio.

Resting beneath the sunset of the city of Charity Vane, Haven Irena Dante dropped to her knees and held her face in her hands on the rooftop of St. David of Chaudron Cathedral. She had escaped just before the elevator car reached the bottom, but was tired and weak after the revelation of Sol's betrayal. Her best friend, her sister had succumbed to a great anger. She reached towards her side and touched her staff. She closed her eyes and sighed.

Haven asked herself how Sol could have allowed herself to get to such a point where she would sell out humanity for a sense of belonging. She thought of Sol's first crush on an older boy named Billy Stein, who was in the ninth grade. They were in the eighth grade then. It was her first real crush, and she was devastated when Billy called her a kid and told her to quit pestering him. Haven thought of the time that she got her first motorcycle and crashed it into a pile of trash cans in Sol's neighborhood. Haven's dad had told her that she wasn't allowed to take the bike out until she took riding lessons, but she was so eager to show Sol her new bike.

Receiving big gifts from her dad was always hard on Sol and Haven wondered if she could have done a better job of maybe not showing her stuff off. *I just wanted to share my life with my best friend*, she thought. Sol did seem to learn to live with the fact that Haven's family had a lot of money . . . or did she? Haven remembered that she had tried her best to encourage Sol to not let stuff like boys and bikes bother her and to focus on the simple things, but in the end, it seemed, the bitterness was too overpowering.

Wanting to be alone, she removed her satchel, stretched out and laid her head down on it. And once again she anguished in the sting of loss while seething in the heat of betrayal. She fell asleep with a single tear rolling down her cheek.

Gardener turned to Valerio. "Sovereign McKenzy is right. We need all the help we can get."

"I know," Valerio said as he stopped in front of a control panel. "This is exactly why I will take action and alert the others."

Rose stepped beside Valerio as he raised the screen. "The other sovereigns scattered throughout the world should hear of what is transpiring."

Valerio brought up a map of the entire planet. On a clear pad, he typed in an automated message that radiated out to all recipients. "Yes, I will alert them as well."

Rose and Gardener exchanged bewildered looks.

Valerio smiled and said to Rose, "You've saved us from ourselves and we are forever grateful. As you can see, we are without a High Sovereign. As you have led us through this attack and into a new era of more than mere observation, I propose that it be you. Consul Rose, you shall lead us to the next phase of the war against the Aristocracy."

"I am most honored by your request, Sovereign," began Rose, "but I already have a place of my own now. I cannot operate within the confines of the rules of the order. There is much work to do in rebuilding what has been devastated, so I must return immediately. And we still need to come up with a way to nullify the weapon. Someday perhaps, but not today."

Gardener turned to Valerio. "I'll do it."

Valerio turned to Gardener and chuckled.

Gardener looked at both Rose and Valerio and threw up his shoulders. "What?"

"From where did Haven say she escaped the Aristocracy?" Gardener asked Rose as they exited down the long stairs of the monastery.

"She said it was an old-abandoned mineshaft just outside the city limits. Any ideas?" Rose asked.

"Olem Mines," he replied. "That mine was abandoned years ago when it was closed down. All of those people lost their jobs and now they're all homeless."

"That must be it. The Arm of Hades must be in the depths of the mine. It only makes sense. We've got to find the signal frequency and jam it," Rose added. "If we isolate the frequency, we can stop the trigger of the devices throughout the city."

"What about Haven?" Gardener asked.

One Girl Army

Haven woke up with a massive headache on the rooftop of the St. Chaudron Cathedral. She slowly tried to get up and slipped. She sat up as she rubbed her neck. "Uh. Hurts," she mumbled. Rubbing her back, which was sore from falling asleep on a hard roof, she slowly stood. Still reeling from what she had witnessed the day before, she walked over to the ledge of the cathedral. The cathedral itself was named after the 14th century artisan David Chaudron, who gave of his talent to raise necessities for the poor who were affected during the scourge of the Black Plague. Since Rob was an admirer of his work, his artistry and architecture were responsible for the look of about seventy percent of the buildings in Charity Vane. She activated the com in her ear.

"Gardener, do you read me?" she asked.

"Yeah, Haven. What's the story?"

"Dad wasn't in his cell," she said.

"Sounds like they need him," Gardener said.

"I know," Haven answered.

"Kid…No. Don't do what I think you're about to do. We need a plan B."

"We have one," Haven answered.

"Kid, don't…"

Haven cut off her com and walked over to the ledge.

As she tied her hair into a ponytail, she thought of Sol. Her eyes narrowed and she gritted her teeth.

She sided with the one who violated me and tried to kill me.

She sided with the ones who killed my mother.

Mom, I wish you were here now to help me straighten all of this out in my mind. You always knew just what to say even when I was too angry to listen. You told me once that we choose what we do when we're angry. I'm listening now, Mom.

Haven closed her eyes. "God, I don't know what to do," she said. "I'm listening." She opened her eyes and looked up at the sky. "I'm listening."

Over a gust of wind, she heard a voice.

"Go!"

Haven stepped away from the ledge and began to walk towards the middle of the rooftop. She turned and prepped for her run.

Here goes chaos.

With all the strength of sorrow and fear, Haven ran towards the ledge, and with one great leap, she pushed herself into the cold night air of Charity Vane, leaving a wake of light and sound behind her. She shot across the sky and over rooftops, knocking down communication rods and sending any loose debris scattering into the air.

Solstice stood at the gate just outside the alcove while Luminos was kept safe in a secured pod. Somehow, some way, she knew what was about to happen and she had been preparing. Lords Retic and Ravage had been severely weakened from their defeat at the hands of the weaponer. The hybrid known as 'Mist' had gone to ensure that his operations on the surface were secure before the attack. After their victory, he would continue to gather the children as hosts should there be a rebellion within the ranks of the survivors. Those would, in turn, aid them in their quest to reclaim the rest of the surface world; a task that would take years. As a hybrid, Dominic Reins would maintain his post as warden of the Judas Cradle. Lord Limbus prepared for the coming assault while the hybrid Chuck Flegman, who was inhabited by Lord Voratum, anxiously stood by waiting to devour any human who stood in his way. The whereabouts of Harry Reeve and Anorexic Man were unknown. This fact was trivial though, compared to the impending confrontation. The demons scurried in a nervous frenzy, knowing what was about to happen.

The air was disturbed by the scent of the bold.

"She's coming," Solstice said with a shrill to her voice.

Haven began her descent when she reached the out-skirts of the city. As she came closer to the ground, the wake from her gravity wave plowed through the ground, creating an instant burrow, shooting dirt and rock upwards. Her long ponytail cut the air like a bullwhip as she raced across the landscape. She could see the mine tower up ahead and the entrance right next to it. Despite Lord Ravage's attack on the settlement of homeless people, tent dwellers and scavengers remained nearby. A little girl with her dusty teddy bear was awakened by the sound of a sonic boom. As she lifted her head, she saw a projectile coming at them at breakneck speed.

"Mommy! Look!" she cried. "Mommy wake up!"

Just as her mom opened her eyes, Haven shot past them and into the mine.

"Honey, what is it?"

"Mommy, Mommy, a girl fell out of the sky!"

"Honey, go back to sleep," ordered her mom.

Haven shot into the cavern like a bullet dodging curves and loose rock. She clenched her fists to push harder. The faster she flew the brighter the glow from her eyes became. Deeper and deeper she shot down like a missile approaching its target, until she could see the minions of Hell on fast approach.

"Bring it," she said to herself.

One of the harpies latched on to Haven's ponytail and swung Haven into the wall. Haven flipped in mid-air and landed on the rocky surface feet first. Pushing herself off, she jetted towards the harpy. Grabbing it by the neck, she kept her forward momentum and landed on the opposite wall, harpy in hand. She phased the monster's head into the wall along with her hand. She snatched her hand back and shot downward, leaving the harpy's head stuck in the cavern wall frantically trying to dislodge itself. Two more harpies came at her. Flying past them, she grabbed each by the neck and flew past a narrow stretch of cavern, leaving both stuck in the rock. As Haven shot down past the Dark Wood, the she-wolf howled, and the leopard roared in protest of the trespasser. As more harpies shot towards their prey, Haven's thoughts shifted to a fear of becoming a victim of cruelty again. In response, her molecular density became even lighter and she phased right through the onslaught and left unscathed. She pressed on towards the gate with a sinking feeling in her stomach that she was about to face her worst nightmare. Before she landed at the gate, she clenched her fists in angst, making herself denser than the hard rock she had just flown by. Haven Irena Dante landed at the gate of the Nine Circles like a sledgehammer. Crumbled rock shot away from where she now stood. She slowly raised her head and paused.

As the yellow-eyed Solstice stood in front of the alcove, demon minions slithered and scattered around her as if to protect her.

"Been waiting for you . . . sis," she said in a gruff voice.

Haven clenched her fist. "Which one of the monsters are you?"

Solstice slowly walked forward, closer to Haven. "Any monster you want me to be, darlin'."

Haven cringed as she recognized the inflection as Willy's the night that she was violated. And now the monster had made its home in the heart of her childhood friend. "Do you have any idea what you've done to me?"

Solstice looked away. "Don't you want to know why?"

"Does it matter?" Haven asked.

"You said . . . No, wait, you promised you would always be there for me, remember that?" Solstice answered. "Want to know what happened after you disappeared?"

"You made a choice," Haven answered.

"And so did you," Solstice snapped back. "And others suffered because of it. You had everything on earth you will ever need, and you still left it and me, and you didn't even care what happened to me."

"I was attacked and taken. I didn't have a choice," Haven said. "But you've sold out the entire human race. And for what? Do you really think these monsters will let you live after they've used you up?"

"They already have. I've lived freer than I ever thought possible!" Solstice shot back.

"No. Your freedom is a lie. They've watched you for as long as we've been friends which for us is all of our lives."

"You're just jealous," Sol answered.

"They killed your mother, Sol," Haven added. "Yes, that's right. They killed your mom!"

"You don't know what you're talking about," Sol said.

"But I still care about you . . . the real you. You . . . you were always like a sister to me. So whoever you are, let her go!"

"Shut up, Haven," Sol said.

"We were sisters," Haven said.

"I said, shut up!" Sol shouted. She darted towards Haven. But before Sol could strike, Haven jumped into the air and came down with a fist slam towards Sol's face, which Solstice quickly dodged.

"You weren't the only one who took home a trophy, sis."

Haven roared as she spun around to deliver a hook kick to Sol's mid-section. Solstice immediately took two steps back, and flipping back towards Haven, she delivered an axe kick to Haven's shoulder, which Haven did not expect. Hunched down, Haven grabbed her ankle and lifted her off the ground throwing her backwards. Solstice landed on the sharp rock that protruded from the walls. Her eyes glowed brighter. As if by command, the demon minions surrounding them made a mad dash towards Haven. Instinctively, Haven pulled out her staff and extended it. Each blow Haven delivered put a demon out of commission. A wingless monster with yellow eyes and claws for hands and feet raced towards Haven. She went for the blow, but instead was surprised as the staff took matters into its own hands and extended around the creature's neck. The end of the staff stretched out until it morphed into a giant serpent with its body wrapped around its prey. As Haven held the other end, the serpent opened up its mouth and swallowed the head of the beast whole and proceeded to do the same for the rest of its body. The harpies watched in horror as the monster was gulped down. Haven secured her staff and turned to face Solstice. "This ends now!" Haven said.

Haven's hand began to glow. She rushed towards Sol and plunged her fist into her chest and pulled out a handful of snakes. Sol hunched over and dropped to the floor. Haven dropped the snakes and as they fell, they gathered together to merge and morph.

The massive satyr that once violently assaulted Haven and threw her out of a 20-story window stood before her once more.

"I've missed you, darlin'," Hedonis said. "As I am sure you've missed me."

"Release the children," Haven ordered.

"You beloved never give up, do you? So smug. So arrogant," Hedonis said.

"Jealous much?" Haven asked.

"You have a more pressing matter at hand," Hedonis answered.

"The weapon is set to go off," Haven shot back.

"A more pressing matter than that, I'm afraid."

Haven thought for a moment, and then her eyes widened in shock. "He's here. My dad is here."

"Smart girl," Hedonis answered. "But you are also a late girl. The countdown has begun and there is nothing you can do to stop it. The Arms of Hades will stretch its reach out into the outskirts of the city and detonate the seismic bombs planted along the fault lines and our kingdom will be restored. So you see, my dear, the choice is yours. Save your father. Save your friend."

Haven backed up towards Sol, but she was stopped in her tracks. The harpies screeched in unison, and out of the darkness more of the same wingless demons came out of the shadows and quickly rushed Haven, pushing her towards a ledge and then over. As they fell, Haven pulled them off one-by-one, even ripping one of them in half as they descended. Haven pulled the last demon off just before she landed on a lower level below the gate in a loud crash. Dazed, she looked up, and there in front of her, was a massive device with tentacles buried deep within the earth's crust. The mammoth machine hummed with life. Haven carefully and slowly walked up to a compartment inside the device large enough to house a human. Her eyes widened and her jaw dropped when she looked inside its one small window.

"Dad?"

"Dad, what are you doing here?" Haven asked. Rob had turned around to see his only daughter, the one who had paid so dearly for his ambitions and lost so much.

"Haven! What are you doing here? You've got to get out of here!" Rob said.

Haven threw up her hands. "Dad, why are you in there?"

"Honey, they used me as bait for you. Just before you showed up, I managed to get free and reverse the polarity of the magnetic shielding surrounding the device, so that no one else can get in it. I've managed to disable the network, but I'm having trouble disarming the bomb itself."

"Dad," Haven interrupted. "Get out of there! Let's go home!"

"I can't leave yet," Rob said. "This is all my doing. I created this thing and now they're using it to destroy us. I have to stop it!"

Haven reached out her hand. "Dad, don't talk like that," she started as she tried to phase her hand through the room. The resonance waves blocked even her light-density molecular structure. She stepped back. "I can't pass through the wall!" Haven cried.

"Honey, it's the resonance shielding that is not letting you in. We could both die if you come in here."

Saddened, Haven moved closer and ran her hand gently over the glass. "Dad, there are children here."

"I've heard them, Sweetheart. You've got to get them out of here," Rob said. "I know you can, Sweetheart," he added.

"You know . . . about everything?" Haven asked.

"Yes, I do. It runs in our family. Now get going! Hurry!" Rob demanded.

Haven took two steps back. "I'll be back for you. I promise." Haven readied herself and shot straight into the cavern above, wondering if she could get the children out in enough time to come back for him.

Haven landed in a loud crash at the entrance of the alcove. Even though time was short, she felt that caution was still warranted, so she proceeded slowly. She approached the door to the alcove with its handwritten stick figures and children's drawings.

The children that filled the alcove were as full of life then as they were the first time Haven saw them. Some were playing catch, while others were swinging back and forth, daring each to see how high they could go. Something had been done to these children to make them unaware of their surroundings. Something had been done to make them forget who their captors were and what they had left behind. Despite their predicament, the giggles and laughter of a game well played ruled the air. Cares still went unnoticed until the time came for them to become a host for the purposes of the Aristocracy. When this happened, all choice was destroyed.

A young girl who was about five years old slowly approached Haven. Much like Haven, she had big brown eyes and brown hair. She held a sock puppet in her arms. Wide-eyed, she looked up at Haven, who froze in her tracks.

Haven's heart sank as she accepted that the awkward and lonely friend that she had met in the third grade in Mrs. Blackburn's class and bonded with at the annual field trip to the Blackburn Farm was gone. They had sat together in front of a campfire and comforted each other as they listened to stories about empty and forgotten buildings that housed whispers of the past. It was a field trip they never forgot and carried with them always. From there, they shared their hopes and dreams, as well as their tearful nights caused by the storms of life. As all of these thoughts rushed through Haven's mind she gulped and held back the tears. Then, sadness turned to rage as her thoughts turned to the children in the alcove. With a swift motion, she removed the staff from her back strap and raised it high. As she began to spin the staff of Moshe above her head, every fury of defeats and victories past was channeled into the staff, and with the force of the fire in her soul, she declared in one strong voice, "This . . . ends . . . here!"

Haven brought the tip of the staff down on the ground, erupting the earth beneath her feet. The dirt and soot flew into the air like an erupting volcano and was followed by a rippling of the rock below. The light that emanated from the staff was blinding as it impacted the rock. What immediately followed shook the children as they scurried for safety. In the ripple effect, rock began to rise from the ashes and form a massive staircase, swiftly shooting upward and outward to make a clear avenue of escape for all who wished to leave this place and rejoin the living. Haven thought of stories she had heard about this staff and how it saved a nation, but it was quite different to see it for herself. After the stairs completed their journey upwards, Haven spun around to the children.

"Let's go!" she cried. "We need to get you out of here now!"

A young boy who seemed lost pulled on Haven's shirt from behind. "But where are we going?" he asked.

"You're going to be safe now. I promise," she answered. The boy walked out of the confines of the alcove and was instantly transformed into an adult, in garb consistent with his era. He wore a pink t-shirt with slacks and shoes that once were referred to as penny-loafers.

He panned his gaze on Haven from head to toe. "How long have I been here?" he asked.

"A long time, I'm afraid," Haven responded.

"I remember my mom dropping me off at an arcade to meet some friends and a man with long white hair and yellow eyes passing out change. He had long chains hanging from the inside of his long, leather jacket and he stunk really bad. The kids called him 'Mist'. They always made fun of his long white hair saying that he looked like a white witch. He offered me a special coin that would work all of the machines. That's the last thing I remember."

"I'm sorry but we'll have to figure all of this out later," Haven said. "You have to go now. Please." One by one the children left the alcove. As they did, some who had been there for some time were instantly brought into adulthood, while others aged only some. Imprisoned outside of time for so long, a few of the prisoners' skin and muscles flaked off their bones and turned to dust. Their skeletons fell to the ground in a cloud of dust. The rest sprinted up the stairs to higher ground and to a new world, or so Haven hoped. When she saw that they were well on their way, Haven placed her staff into her strap once again and swiftly took to the air.

Elsewhere in the caverns, the chains and steel rods that kept prisoners in check began to rattle with the rippling of the rock. Something had happened nearby to cause the prison bars to come undone. One prisoner in particular had grungy hair filled with soot and a long beard that was equally foul. The grimy prisoner slipped the cuffs that had held him securely to the rock, over the loosened hook and unraveled the chains. He rose to his feet and shuffled towards the rusty bars of his cell. He lifted his chains and wrapped them around the top of the bar and pulled with all of his might. It was not enough to simply pull, so he lifted his feet and planted them against the surrounding wall and pulled with all that was in him until the gate finally snapped open dropping him to the ground. He got up and poked his head through the opening. After looking both ways, the prisoner, now an escapee, squeezed the rest of the way through to emerge on the other side.

As he walked by another prison cell, a harpy laid injured. In pain, she cried out to him, "Please, don't leave me here! Take me with you!"

The prisoner took pity on the harpy and loosened the chains that bound her. Immediately, the beast morphed into a fragile female and he lifted her to her feet. He grabbed her hand and looked into her eyes and tried to comfort her.

"I am a Dante. I leave no one behind," he assured.

The woman looked at him and smiled. "Argelius, let us go and make our own way."

Argelius Dante lifted the harpy to her feet and escaped imprisonment by the Aristocracy.

A Peg or Two

Haven landed in a loud thud with soot and rock flying into the air around her. In a mad dash, she ran over to the Arm of Hades device where Rob was still caged and slammed her fists against the glass.

"Dad! It's time to go. Now shut it off and let's get out of here!"

Rob looked up into Haven's eyes, and with tears in his own, uttered, "I can't leave."

Angrily, Haven slammed her fist against the outer wall of the device. "No! Not again!" She pulled back and clenched her fists to where her eyes glowed brightly, and with a starting run, she slammed her shoulder up against the wall's device. She bounced off the shielding and into the wall directly behind her in a painful crash. She shook off the loose rock that fell on her and stood up. Haven marched up to the machine and took an offensive posture as she clenched her fists even harder. She could feel the scorching heat of the luminescence filling the markings on her arms, burning off whatever parts of the arm wraps were left. The glow of her eyes now filled the room as she shook. With a growl and gnarl Haven dashed for the wall of the device as fast as she could. This time she bounced off the shield with greater intensity and speed and flew headfirst, deeper into the wall behind her, bringing the larger pieces of rock down all around them.

Rob cried out from inside. "Haven, stop it!"

Haven came out from the hole in the wall that she had buried herself in and ran towards the cell. Rob put his hand on the glass.

"It's no use," he said sadly.

"Oh, Daddy," Haven replied.

"This machine needs to be destroyed and I need to make sure nothing like it will ever be used again so it is OK. This was the prototype, so with it gone there's no hope of building another one."

Haven looked up into her father's eyes as the glow within dissipated and her eyes filled with tears. She gently placed one hand on the glass.

"Haven," Rob began. "My little star. If I could go back and start over with you, I would be a better father than I was. I am so, so sorry. I was so driven to find some kind of significance."

Haven choked with tears when she heard those words. "Maybe I could have been a better daughter, Dad. Maybe if I hadn't been such a pain to you all the time . . . ."

"No, listen," Rob interrupted. "Whatever you do, don't you ever, ever blame yourself. Our relationship is not your burden. I'm the dad here and it was my job to see to it that you and I have a good relationship, and I failed you. Don't you carry that weight."

"OK, Daddy," Haven answered with a whimper.

"Honey, I just need you to do one thing for me."

"What Daddy? Anything!"

"Just tell me that you forgive me," Rob answered.

"Oh, Daddy."

"Honey, I just need to hear you say it. Please?"

As Rob and Haven shared their last moments, the countdown on the device lit up.

1:30, 1:29, 1:28 . . .

"I forgive you, Daddy."

"Thank you, my little star. I love you."

. . . 59, 58, 57 . . .

"Don't let them win, honey. Don't ever let anger consume you and don't let your responsibilities keep you from living your life. I believe in you. You have to go now, Sweetheart. "

50, 49, 48 . . .

"Go!"

They shared one last look and then she backed away from the glass.

"Bye, Daddy."

Haven shot up into the air like a rocket leaving her father with the device, looking up as a proud father of a hero.

Haven shot upwards through the cavern like a missile, dodging every piece of falling rock that came down around her. Ducking and weaving, she came across the falling staircase that she had just built as an escape route for the children of the alcove and found that the last of them had thankfully made it to safety.

She shot past the Dark Wood at such a high speed that even the beasts of that realm were shaken by the thunderous roar of the sonic boom she created and her wake that swept through the foliage.

She clenched her fists once again and increased her velocity. A sonic boom trailed in her wake.

. . . 5, 4 . . .

Rob looked down and breathed in a heavy sigh.

"I'm coming, B."

. . . 0

The fiery destruction of the Arm of Hades blew Haven out of the mineshaft and into the night sky. As quickly as she had ascended, she came down hard onto the ground. The earth bubbled up as a result of the explosion and came down, taking the mine tower with it into the abyss below. As the indigents who made this place their home scattered in a frenzy, new crevices formed in the earth beneath their feet. Fearing loss of life, Haven quickly recovered to her feet and leaped to keep the helpless from falling to their deaths. A small child had just fallen over a ledge when Haven caught her in mid-air and returned her to her panic-stricken mother. An old man was rescued from falling embers when Haven stood between them and the frail soul. Most of the homeless were able to make it to safety away from the camp. As the campsite was swallowed by the earth, harpies began to shoot out of the newly formed fissure. One harpy landed directly in front of Haven and challenged her with an eerie, loud screech that echoed through the night. Haven removed her staff from her holder and took a defensive posture.

"You got something to say to me?" she challenged in return.

Suddenly, from the smoke and shadows behind the harpy, the sound of large hooves thumped closer and closer.

"I have something to say, cretin!" Hedonis declared as he ripped the harpy in half and ran towards Haven. "You and I have unfinished business!" Hedonis marched towards Haven and knocked the staff out of her hand. She quickly turned towards Hedonis, and with the fierceness of a resolute warrior, Haven took a step back and grabbed Hedonis by the wrist and pulled him into an arm-lock. She then came around him and held him there.

"No, monster! We are done!" she affirmed as she snapped his arm from behind. The demon let out a painful cry that shook the night. "And I have had enough of you!" Haven added. She then pulled the monster towards her and flipped him over her back sending him crashing to some debris nearby. As soon as Hedonis landed, Haven took to the sky, and altering her molecular density to increase her weight exponentially, she came crashing down on Hedonis' chest. His head and torso hunched up, reacting to the heavy blow. Haven then pulled him up by his gaudy necklace and lifted her fist to strike. She cried, "You killed my parents!" as she dealt a blow. "My friend…my sister is gone!" she shouted as she dealt him another. "You destroyed my life!" Haven said as she imparted a double upper cut.

Hedonis started to push himself back away from Haven as if he was afraid. Given that demons were the agents of fear, it was somewhat unnerving, but satisfying, to see Hedonis feeding on the dish that he had handed out to others so many times before. Haven retrieved her staff. As she did, the staff came alive with power as if it knew what it was about to do. She pointed the staff at Hedonis in an offensive posture.

"Feeling beaten down? Crushed?" she asked Hedonis. "I've been there. To the pits of hell and back, after losing everything I ever loved. Not that you know what love is or ever will, but all that is to say that I've been there."

Hedonis' countenance turned from afraid to quizzical.

Haven slowly walked towards Hedonis. "I can help. Really. But you have to listen carefully and do what I say." She walked closer.

Hedonis slowed from pushing himself away from her and let his guard down.

Haven took two more steps. "I'm only going to say this once. Now, are you ready?"

Hedonis stopped where he was.

Haven lifted her staff. "Go to hell!"

She slammed the staff down with all of her might. The staff lit up the sky while simultaneously opening a rift into the abyss, which immediately sucked Hedonis down. She watched as Hedonis fell deep into the darkness with a sense of bittersweet satisfaction.

"And stay there," she added.

Suddenly, a harpy landed behind her and pushed her to the ground. Haven landed face down. She quickly turned to face her attacker when. . . .

Zzzzip!

A weapon discharge found its way to the harpy, immediately disintegrating it into a fast-moving pile of snakes that slithered into any crack it could find. A deep, boisterous voice came from the smoke and cinder.

"Yea baby! Now that's what I'm talkin' about!" Gardener came out from the shadows with what appeared to be a modified Gatling gun that fired pulses of static electricity that harmed demons from below. As more harpies flew in for an attack, Gardener began his volley of torment upon the creatures that filled the air. For a moment, it seemed that Gardener could not keep up with the onslaught, until to Haven's surprise, an army made up of the children of the alcove, along with the few sovereigns who had joined their ranks, engaged in battle against the demons of the Aristocracy. It was on that night that the children of the alcove became the Army of Haven.

The firefight lit up the night as this new army sent the monsters back to where they came from, until there were few left behind. Haven joined the fight by slamming demons into the ground with the weight of a truck behind her small fist, or into the air to pierce them with her ethereal hand, only to solidify it while still inside, sometimes ripping them open from inside. She fought alongside those who stood for freedom from tyranny. She fought with all of her might for all who were weary, worn, and brave.

Haven rushed over to her staff and lifted it once more becoming the beacon that warned everyone to find shelter. She slammed the tip of the staff down into the ground and the earth opened up once more in a loud, raucous rumble, only to collapse, sealing the cracks and crevices that had formed along with the mine entrance itself. Tired and spent, Haven dropped to her knees. She folded her hands and stayed pensive for a moment as her newfound family slowly walked up behind her in comforting support. "Goodbye, Daddy."

Unbeknownst to all who fought, a lone shadowy figure emerged on another part of the ash and smoke, rising from the haze of war. The Anorexic Man carefully lifted Soledad from the wreckage of the mine tower and held her in his arms for a moment.

He then carried her into the night, away from the ravages of war.

Gardener began to make his way towards Haven and shouted, "Kid…you ok?" Haven barely had the strength to lift her head. "Yeah, I'm good," she said as she panted. Suddenly, a bright light pierced the night sky. Gardener and Haven looked up as it descended. As it landed, debris spread out from its touchdown point. Haven stood up and held her hand over her brow and tried to get a better glimpse of what was happening. The large transport vehicle's engines stopped and its lights dimmed. That was when Haven could make out the lettering on the vehicle.

ArGen.

A shadowy figure disembarked. As he walked towards Haven, she could make out the sharp suit he was wearing along with the scarf that covered his mouth and nose. The shadowy figure walked into the light and removed his scarf.

It was Argelius.

"Miss me?" he asked. Haven gasped.

"How?" she asked.

"The black. The conduits can take you to any place at any time."

Haven pointed towards the transport vehicle. "And what is all this?" she asked.

"I found 1848 to be a good year. It was a year of new beginnings. New goals. As is the game of life some were reached while others, not so much. But I have no regrets," Argelius said.

"You killed Benjamin," Haven said.

"From where you stand, he's been dead for hundreds of years. But I will say I did enjoy watching him die one last time. Which brings us to the present. I wonder if Beatrice stayed alive the entire way down? But I digress," he said. Argelius then pulled out his fire sword and ignited it. Haven pulled out her staff and extended it.

"But before I kill you, I want you to know that I really do have a deep admiration for you. Your tenacity, your spirit. No matter how justified you feel in your anger, you are still capable of a great love. A love you didn't even recognize yourself."

Haven readied her staff. Her arms began to glow brighter.

"This isn't love that I'm feeling for you right now, Argelius. It's wrath. And I'll make sure you taste it when the fire of hell reaches you," Haven said. Her staff morphed into a scythe. Haven leaped towards Argelius and sliced off his hand. But just as quick, it grew back. Argelius smiled.

"The gifts are irrevocable," he said. Argelius then swung his sword at Haven. With her staff, she blocked his deathblow, spun around and kicked him in the stomach. Argelius was sent flying across the street and landed on a car. Haven shot up into the air and came crashing down on Argelius and culminating in a fiery explosion. Haven flipped backwards and landed on the street. Argelius then stood revealing his charred body which immediately began to heal.

"A wonderful gift of healing this is along with longevity," he bragged.

"I can go piece by piece," Haven said. She slammed the tip of her staff down on the ground. The ground opened up but Argelius dodged the crevice opening up beneath him. He pointed his sword at Haven and it spewed fire. Her body hardened, she was unscathed. She rushed towards him and they locked in battle. Her staff met his sword in a vicious flurry of attacks and counters.

"The only way mankind will learn is through suffering," he said. Haven's staff morphed into a giant dagger. She plunged it through him and on the other side, the point then morphed into a three-headed snake that bit into his flesh. Argelius screamed.

"How's that for suffering?" she asked. She then pulled the staff out. Argelius screamed again but after the staff was removed, he began to heal again. He touched the poison left behind from the bite with his finger and licked it. "Poison. You know, with the power to heal comes the power to create," he said arrogantly. He rushed towards Haven and placed his hand on her forehead while holding her against the wall. Haven began to sweat profusely.

"At first, I thought the Black Death was my masterpiece. Then came cancer. That is until COVID came along. But I'll have a vaccine in no time. Don't you worry." She struggled as her skin turned pale and then began to shake. "What's wrong? Blood sugar low?" Haven shook even more.

"You know," Argelius began. "You may have been the catalyst in my journey through time. The whole speech on Mount Judgement was riveting. What was it that you said? Oh yes, something about a delusion that

I would save mankind and be lifted up on a pedestal. Well, I'm sure I'm paraphrasing to some extent but look at me now! I can cure any sickness! And as it turned out, I didn't need the staff after all!"

Haven grabbed his arm, twisted it and threw him over her should into the wall of an adjacent building. "Yeah," she said. "Look at you now." She leaped into the air and landed on Argelius. Haven raised her staff and plunged it into him once again. This time, a slew of snake heads emerged, bit into him and sunk their teeth in. Argelius screamed in agony. Haven then yanked him up with the staff and slammed him into the ground. She then closed her eyes. Her markings and staff began to glow so bright that night became day. Straining, she tightened her grip on the staff and kneeled down.

The ground beneath them began to shake and crack. The cars surrounding them rattled and shifted away from where she knelt. And in a sudden gravity shock, the ground beneath them swallowed them whole. The ground beneath had given way to the devastating weight of Haven's dense molecular structure. As they sank, she turned to face downward and in one thrust, shot down through the earth while pushing Argelius with her staff. Layer after layer, they seemed to go on forever, but their journey came to a halt when she came upon a vast opening inside of a cavern and came crashing down onto a floating rock platform.

Weary, Haven stood to her feet. She looked around and amidst the hues of dimming red and rising vapor and fire from the darkness of the pit where she stood, came the foul stench of things wicked and vile. This was hell itself.

Haven reached for Argelius and lifted him with both hands. She held him with her left and formed a glowing fist with her right. "This time, stay down." Haven struck Argelius in the face and thrust him over the side of the platform. She walked over to the side and saw him fall into a lake of fire.

"Heal from that," she said.

Then she felt a chill down her spine. As if someone was watching her from behind, she looked up fully sensing the presence of the incarnation of evil that was behind her. She turned around. Two massive yellow eyes glared at her through the fire in the cavern. She knew who it was.

And in a display of triumph and defiance, she raised her hand and showed him her middle finger.

Haven then shot up into the cavern above her and through the path that she had carved herself. As she shot out from the surface, Gardener looked on to notice a streak of light shooting through the air.

"Go, kid."

The next morning, Rose watched the news as the sounds of construction went on all around her. CVN reported that Harry Reeve, CEO of Dante Technologies, was about to hold a press conference.

"Tobias Shaft here, and I'm in downtown Charity Vane where the CEO of Dante Technologies is about to speak on rumors of Rob Dante's passing. Dante had created technology for seismic research that may have been responsible for the mine explosion that destroyed several city blocks last night. The company had also created other technologies with consumer applications such as the Fluidic Interface, which allows water to be used essentially as a computer interface, enabling the user to access and retrieve visual data through a liquid substance. Since his trial and immediate sentencing in the death of Willy Holman, he's suffered a series of mental breakdowns while in prison. Let's listen in."

Harry stepped up to the lectern and addressed the reporters.

"First of all, our thoughts are with those affected by the mine explosion last night. With the significant and tragic loss of life and the damage caused to nearby structures, it is certainly a dark time for our great city. For many years, Mr. Dante suffered greatly with mental illness from over-work and exhaustion, not to mention the death of his son, and eventually his wife. This series of emotional stresses took their toll on Mr. Dante as they did with their daughter resulting in her disappearance. After the trial and sentencing, Mr. Dante suffered many emotional trials that, at times, caused him to question his very existence. Early this morning at around three o'clock, Mr. Dante overdosed on medications not prescribed for him by the prison. As an investigation is underway, I'm sure the truth will be found. We will relay the results of that investigation when the facts are made clear. As far as Dante Technologies, I want to assure everyone that we will continue with the Dante vision, which I for one, believe in. No questions please."

With that, news anchor, Tobias Shaft returned to the screen.

"There you have it, folks. It's interesting to point out that the mine explosion that we reported on last night happened at the exact same time as Mr. Dante reportedly took his own life. Back to you . . . ."

Rose turned to Gardener, who stood behind her with a look of grave concern.

"We've got our work cut out for us, don't we?" Gardener commented.

"That we do, love," Rose answered. "That we do. By the way, is Haven up yet?"

"Oh yeah, she's up alright," Gardener answered. "I'd love to be a fly on that wall."

Rose smiled. "She'll do splendid."

Harry Reeve walked into his dimly lit office. Behind his desk, Jinx was standing by a shadowy figure sitting in the chair of the CEO.

"What is this?" Harry asked.

"Those weren't insurance papers she signed," Jinx said. "They were a transfer of ownership." Harry looked closer at the shadowy figure in his chair. Suddenly, Haven's eyes lit up in the dark.

In the countryside of Grozny City, Chechnya stood an orphanage that housed displaced children who had been forced to walk the streets. The mansion suffered from years of neglect, it was cracked and withered, its lawns full of weeds. A knock on the massive door awoke its elderly Chechen caretaker.

"Oh you're here, thank goodness! We've needed help for so long," said the caretaker in her native tongue.

"I'm glad to help. Thank you," Soledad answered in her language as she walked into her new home.

The Letter

As the bright morning sun rose in the east, casting its warmth on the city of Charity Vane, Haven stood on the roof of Dante Tech, taking in the view. She reached into her pocket and pulled out an envelope that Jinx had given her. It was addressed to "My Little Star." She rubbed her eyes and breathed in a heavy sigh.

Dear Haven,

The very second that I first laid eyes on you I became a totally different person than who I was before. I looked at you and instantly knew that I would give my life for you. Seeing you for the first time left me powerless. More than anything, I want you to remember that this will always be how I look at you. I know that along the path, I lost my way but know that I love you and that I always will. This great charge that is carried by our family to shed light on evil is not a light one. It is not a charge that we alone bare.

Powers or not, Dante or not, it is a mission that we should all be a part of. But that mission cannot be carried out without love. That is the lesson that I wish I had learned. This should be the mission of all of us, wherever that takes us and whatever truth about us it uncovers. So I leave you with this. Love well. Love yourself because you can't love others until you know what love is. Seek the truth no matter how uncomfortable it is. Fight the dark.

Oh and there's one more thing. You are not alone. There are others. Now go find them.

Love Always,
Dad

She folded the letter and placed it back in her pocket. She then secured her staff holster on her belt. Haven then looked up into the bright shining sun, closed her eyes and let the rays dance on her face.

"I'm listening," she said.

Go!

Haven's eyes glowed white hot as she shot into the sky on a new quest, a new mission, a new reason to fly. . .

. . . to find the others.

Epilogue: Fun in the Sun

Outside of time, on the green grassy shores of a crystalline lake, a butterfly flew up the hill to a large oak tree and landed on a branch. The tree branch swayed in the cool breeze like a finely-honed brush on a canvas. Just below the branch and beside the swing that hung from it, a little girl was just finishing up a jigsaw puzzle that she had feverishly worked on for quite some time. Her bright, brown eyes widened as she laid the last piece of the puzzle into place.

"There. All done," she happily said. She leaned back to take in her handiwork. The image was of Haven Irena Dante, as she is, or perhaps as she will be: whole and full of life.

"That's my girl," the child added. She then pushed aside the opened gift box with the tag that read, *For Beatrice. Welcome home.*

From the other side of the hill behind her came the voice of another child, breaking her focus from her masterpiece. The voice was that of a young boy about six years old who was eager for play. He had been waiting on her for a short time but would wait no longer.

The boy shouted, "Hurry up, B!"

The young girl turned to the boy. "Be nice!" she shouted. She turned for one last glance at her puzzle before skipping down the hill to meet her playmate.

About the Author

Leonardo Ramirez is an American science fiction and fantasy author of Puerto Rican descent. He is also a screenwriter, singer and a martial artist with a 4th degree black belt in Karate and a brown belt in American Bushido Kenjutsu which is the study of the katana (samurai sword).

As a husband and father, his family is his first joy. As a child, he's lived through the hardships of extreme poverty and homelessness in a single-parent home. But these have only brought him to recognize the strength of family and the faith in God that keeps them bound together in love.

Leonardo Ramirez lives with his wife Kristen, their daughter Mackenzy and their two dogs, Duchess and Tinkerbell in a suburb of Nashville, Tennessee.

You can learn more about the author by visiting his website at http://Leonardoverse.com

Other Books by the Author

The Jupiter Chronicles is a children's steampunk series. Steampunk is a genre of science fiction that has a historical, 19th century setting and typically features steam-powered machinery such as steam-powered robots, rockets and more. In book one, it is the year 1892 and Ian and Callie Castillo have had to suffer the hardships of a single parent family since their father went missing five years ago. Since then Ian has refused to use the last gift that his father left the wounded boy; a telescope that sits collecting dust in the attic. When Callie decides to peer through its murky lens it activates the device and sends the Castillos to the steam-powered floating cities of Jupiter where they discover the secret behind their father's disappearance.

There are three books in the series:

The Secret of the Great Red Spot
The Ice Orphan of Ganymede
The Orb of Terra

Haven of Dante: The Graphic Novel depicts Haven's story in graphic novel form. With beautiful art by Davy Fisher, the epic graphic novel depicts the ancient war between the family line and the nine circles of hell through the ages.

www.ingramcontent.com/pod-product-compliance
Lightning Source LLC
LaVergne TN
LVHW091529060526
838200LV00036B/535